LEAVE WHILE YOU STILL CAN

LEAVE WHILE YOU STILL CAN

JULIA COWAN

www.blkdogpublishing.com

For Alex and his paper ghosts

DAY 26

The fan oscillated back and forth but it did nothing more than circulate the muggy, night air. The midsummer heat made it difficult to sleep – close, sticky and almost suffocating. Over the last few weeks, the storm clouds had been threatening but never fully unleashing their power, just a few sporadic shower bursts every now and again. Another storm was on the horizon. The fan was merely an attempt to cool the room down in any way possible but really all it was doing was a good job of moving the already warm air about.

Valerie's bedsheets were already tangled, as though she had been trying to fashion some kind of rope ladder with her covers. The open sash window provided little comfort, the air so still that the net curtains remained motionless. Thank goodness that she was able to leave the window open – it was quiet most of the time due to the dwindling number of residents in the area. Many of her neighbours were elderly, like her, determined to live in their own houses for as long as possible until being ferried off to assisted living in town.

She tossed and turned in bed before settling on a cool spot facing the wall. The fact that she managed to stay in this position for longer than five minutes gave her the faint hope that she would soon fall asleep. She could feel her tension slowly easing. Her mind felt heavy. Her limbs slowly melted into the mattress. All that was left was the sound of traffic in the distance and the neighbour's cat jumping onto the nearby dustbins. These were familiar, comforting sounds, informing her that all was normal in her world.

Then, just like clockwork, everything slowly started to wind back up. The traffic wasn't passing through as it normally did. It was approaching the street. The sound of engines grew louder and closer until they crescendoed and settled outside her bedroom window. She grumbled loudly to signal her annoyance and refused to open her eyes to acknowledge their presence or her worry. This was something she had been anticipating for a while now as the events on this usually mundane street were catching up with everyone who lived there. However, after a few moments, the temptation was too great, and she slowly began to focus on the wall. The blue and red lights danced around her bedroom rhythmically. Valerie resigned herself to the fact that she was now further from sleep than ever, in fact, wider awake with every passing second. The lights informed her that everything was far from being all right. She fumbled for her glasses on the bedside cabinet.

She had discreetly positioned a chair by the window a while ago, so she was able to observe the comings and goings of her neighbours without being spotted. The stories she could tell! She was an upstanding member of the community with a keen eye and a stern demeanour. She had founded the Neighbourhood Watch Committee a long time ago, not that this made any difference to the residents, but it gave her peace of mind and maybe justified her need to look out of her window now and again. It gave her a kind of power and sense of importance to hold the knowledge of some of the things she knew – some things that could provide a lot of bother for some of her neighbours.

She spotted two emergency vehicles – an ambulance and a police car – which momentarily made her blood run cold. This was serious, everything pointing to this being more than a standard attempted break-in or a callout for a domestic disturbance. The lights continued to blink in sequence, punctuated by the opening and closing of doors. They were headed for the house directly opposite her own. That was when she grasped the cushion she had been holding closer to her and held her breath. After all these years, everything that had happened – could it be that it was finally ending tonight? Number 30 had a story to tell. There had been no permanent tenant in there for a while. Her memory was still relatively sharp. There had been a steady stream of tenants over the years but no buyers interested in the property. This did not come as any surprise to her. For one reason or another, a series of short-term leases seemed to be a common trend for this particular house. A new family had moved in less than a month ago and Valerie found herself mentally ticking the days off to see how long they would last. For no one seemed to stay longer than a month, no one seemed to *last* longer than a month…

She had already rehearsed several times how she would describe them to the police:

Well, Officer, from what I've seen, a single mother with a young girl were staying there. The girl couldn't have been more than about five? Unruly, curly hair - a kind of blonde colour. like straw. Very pretty little thing; knee-length pink dress and white socks with ruffles on. The mother, well, she looked like you'd expect any single mum to look – bedraggled. Longish brown hair. Eye colour, well let me think … sadly I never did get close enough to see. They kept themselves to themselves you see. She walked with her head down a lot of the time. No, maybe that's not the right way to describe it. She walked as though she didn't want to be seen. She was always quite guarded and a bit jumpy if I'm being honest when I saw them out and about. Barely said two words to me. I didn't really have much to do with them at all. But then she had reason to be on edge living in that house. The things that have happened in that house and the one next door over the years…

Valerie steadied her nerves and got to her feet. She knew it was probably worth her giving up on trying to get back to sleep now. She now had a purpose for the rest of what remained of the night. It was time to get dressed now as surely someone would be knocking on her door before too long. They would be questioning surrounding residents about what they knew about Number 30 and indeed the neighbouring property, Number 28. And they would definitely, without any doubt in her mind, want to hear what she had to say.

DAY 1

It started the day they buried Stevie. Or in fact, just after. Birdy had scrunched her face up and reached for her mother in support. They both stared at the disturbed earth for some time, almost in a joint silent prayer. After a few moments of quiet, Carrie cleared her throat a few times to signal that was the end of the ceremony.

'Mummy, I'm sad,' a small voice piped up in the best mournful voice possible.

Carrie patted her daughter on the head and then turned this into a comforting rub. 'It's just a goldfish, Birdy. You can get another ...' Her voice hung suspended heavily in the air. She looked down and saw that Birdy's bloodshot eyes were brimming with tears. Her bottom lip quivered in an overt display of grief.

'He wasn't just a goldfish, he was my friend,' she whined, in the way a five-year-old does.

'Come on, let's go back inside. I'll make you your favourite pancakes.' She watched as her daughter's face morphed into a smile. 'That's better!' she declared as Birdy skipped off towards the open door. Carrie paused to cast her eyes up and down their house, a standard two up two down. The garden they stood in wasn't much better than the house itself and they were surrounded by the beginnings of an extension that had never taken off. Deep trenches for foundations had been dug long ago but nothing much had progressed since. Carrie rather suspected that this was due to their dwindling savings but in all honesty, she didn't know. They could in fact have used the existing hole for Stevie but Birdy had insisted they dig a new one for his grave. Their house was a post-war build, crumbling on the outside and equally as grim on the inside. However, she had heard the phrase many times that a family makes a home. Sadly, if their family was anything to go by, then the house would surely be condemned.

Birdy sat swinging her legs on the chair as she made short work of the pancakes. Carrie sat opposite her, a cup of coffee poised thoughtfully in one hand, as was often her position these days. She spent most of her day plotting their escape – she and Birdy fleeing their awful house in the early hours of the morning. Anywhere, direction unknown but anywhere would be markedly different from this setup. Anything to escape *him* and the veil of misery that cloaked their existence.

'Can I go and watch TV now Mummy?' Birdy cocked her head to one side, awaiting her mother's response although she had already begun backing out of the kitchen.

'Oh, sure, pumpkin,' Carrie was snapped out of her thoughts as she focused on her daughter's expectant face. The puffiness around her eyes resulting from excessive crying was receding but the bruising would take several days to heal. Stevie's burial was now a fading memory from Birdy's mind, a distraction from the other nightmares they had to endure on a daily basis. Carrie watched as she scampered off to the lounge and heard the distant sounds of cartoons.

Carrie rubbed her head, almost too vigorously at first, forgetting herself. Her fingers made contact with the swelling, still prominent. Her bruises would take a little longer to heal and her long, mousey hair could only hide so much. Normally, she wore it tied back for practicality but now sported it free from a ponytail in an attempt to cover her face. She sighed and busied herself clearing up the dishes, looking out onto the muddy mess and the patch of land to the side which now supported a makeshift cross for Stevie. It wasn't as though she could take care of the garden in any way – she wasn't allowed. In her darker moments, Carrie had sickening thoughts that he hadn't filled the foundation holes in on purpose. It was often one of his sick jokes that he would threaten to do away with her and bury her in there. He would always brush this off afterwards that he'd been winding her up and she was too sensitive. Carrie reached for the cloth and absentmindedly wiped down the tops, around the kettle and toaster, around the vase of freshly bought flowers next to the window. Of course he was sorry, he always was. And he always bought the same flowers to accompany this apology. However, the sentiment was gradually losing its value along with his words. He would never get cross and shout at her so loudly again, he didn't know what had come over him, he was so, so sorry. It was work, he was stressed about work and the pay cut he'd been forced to take. This was why they couldn't go ahead with their planned home improvements. The bank wouldn't lend them any more money. The excuses were endless, and these words were now a vacuum. However, this was the first time he had struck Birdy, who had inadvertently got caught in the crossfire. Jon had raised his hand to Carrie and their child had been in the wrong place. All it meant to Carrie was a few days of walking on eggshells around him, not daring to do anything to provoke him again whilst they were still in the reflective period. It was some comfort that Birdy was home schooled otherwise this would have resulted in a few days off school whilst her bruise faded.

Carrie checked the clock and quickened her pace as she realised there was still time. She threw a glance around the door and saw Birdy now settled comfortably on the sofa, entranced by the cartoons on the television. Carrie retrieved the laptop from the cupboard as she did every chance that she could. Every day that Jon was not in the house, she could continue her research, plot their escape. It was an old laptop that he had discarded after upgrading to a newer model. Yes, it was as slow as anything, but it had internet access, a window of escape. Carrie did the same thing every day – she looked for their exit out of there, just a small and safe house away from here whilst she planned their next move. Far away from the outskirts of London, a move into the countryside.

She scrolled down the list of available properties. She

immediately discarded those with a waiting list, those requiring a sizeable deposit. She couldn't risk choosing anything that required a direct debit to be set up for payments. Having just managed to scrape together all the money that she could, her options were limited. They would probably have to resort to staying somewhere that would require all of the money up front. She decided to navigate away from the rentals pages and move to the *Snooze and Stay* website. This was popular with travellers needing short term lodgings without a notice period. Carrie knew that people could stay for anything from one night to weeks and even months if they needed to and in all honesty, she wasn't sure how long they would need to plan their next move. It would be markedly more expensive if the rent had to be paid in advance but it may be their only option at the moment.

Glancing at the clock again to check how much time she had left, it caught her eye. At the bottom of her filtered search, there it was: a glowing beacon of hope. Surely this was too good to be true. It was vacant and the rent was affordable. The house was available now. This was ideal as it meant that maybe in a month's time, they would have to move again but this was the next step in assuring their safety.

She found herself clicking on the advert for more details. Okay, it wasn't brilliant. The area looked a bit run down but the house was furnished. This would do. Carrie made a note of the number and frantically thought about how she would be able to get out of the house later to find a working phone box to make the call. He would never let her go out and would be far too suspicious. She couldn't use her mobile as he made it his business to carry out surprise checks. To hell with it, she'd call from their landline. It was a while before the next bill was due and he wouldn't be able to check the calls made from the house until then. Carrie cast a final look at the webpage before reaching for the phone. Number 30 Dunberry Crescent. She'd call them now.

The house was perfect. It looked better on the inside than outside. From the photographs on the webpage, Carrie could see there was a separate lounge area, a moderately sized kitchen with a large table in the middle and a small utility room situated just off this. Upstairs looked to be a converted bedroom. It was open plan which made Carrie think that this had once been a lounge area too. It seemed too exposed to have been a bedroom originally. There was no bedroom door and the room began at the top of the staircase. Regardless, Birdy would love this to be her room as she'd be able to see out into the floor below. There was also a small toilet and shower room next to it. On first glance, the layout appeared jumbled and poorly designed but they would know more once they arrived there.

Beyond the ground floor was a converted cellar. There were two further bedrooms and a large bathroom with a marble tub underneath the window. The floor also housed the boiler in its own separate room and a small courtyard. There were floor plans on the website and Carrie could see that the basement area appeared smaller than the other two floors. Never mind, as long as it didn't have a drug den underneath the house, it would be perfect for the two of them.

She called the owner. A raspy, older sounding woman answered. She was somewhat doddery with her words which made Carrie feel even more anxious. As she was still clock-watching, every word was precious, and she did not appreciate this woman's mentality of 'why use two words when ten would suffice?' Regardless, in a moment of bravado, Carrie arranged for their arrival at the house to be the following Monday, just the other side of the looming weekend. All she had to do now was discreetly pack enough clothes for Birdy and herself and think how and when to leave their house without causing too much suspicion.

By the time Jon arrived home from work, Carrie had safely stored the old laptop back in place and had even managed to secretly put some clothes to one side.

'What have you been up to today?' His question was more of an interrogation than one of interest.

'Birdy's goldfish died, we buried him out back …' She instantly regretted giving too much information. It looked as though she was deliberately trying to make herself seem busy as opposed to *I've actually been planning how to leave this prison you have forced me to live in …*

However, he didn't pick up on this. Instead, he frowned at her and put down his coffee cup. He clasped his hands in front of him and spoke with measured words as though he were addressing a small child.

'Who? Say her name properly, Carrie.'

Carrie moved her mouth but for a few seconds, no sound came out. 'B-B-Bridgette,' she managed to stutter finally.

'Now Carrie, you know I don't like that nickname. Her name is Bridgette … That's the name that she was registered under.'

Carrie sighed. 'You know I didn't choose that.'

His tone became more serious as he acknowledged her disapproval and the fact that she had answered him back. He moved a few steps closer to her, his tone remained condescending. 'Bridgette was my late mother's name. Are you saying there is something wrong with it?' It was almost as though he had increased in height as he stared down at her, his eyes seeming not to blink at all.

'No, no. That's fine.' She whispered in response. Her eyes fell to study the floor tiles, anywhere was better than looking him square in the eye.

He changed tack now. 'No more pets,' he announced, his tone was softer but still heavy with authority. 'No dogs, no cats or hamsters. I'm not having it. She'll soon get bored with them and it will be up to us to look after it. Barely managed a goldfish as it is.' That was it. No negotiation or anything. His word was final, always.

'No, I wasn't saying that we should get another pet,' Carrie stuttered nervously. 'Just that she's been a bit down today.'

He looked back at her, his mouth set in a thin line. It seemed to placate him that she had not continued to provoke him for an argument and he wandered through to the lounge to take root in front of the football for the evening. That was their cue to keep the noise down as it was forbidden to disrupt him during his time in front of the television. With everything that he had to endure at work, he informed her, he deserved this time by himself in the evening. Carrie heaved a sigh of relief that there would be no further conversation for a while and started clearing the dinner plates. As she took her familiar place in front of the sink gazing out into the garden, she felt her spirits lift slightly when she realised she had a purpose now. She would get Birdy and herself far away from this house.

Friday rolled into Saturday and then to the end of the weekend. She had less than twenty-four hours before she and Birdy would set off to their safe haven. Carrie resigned herself to the fact that she could not wait until Monday morning to leave. Jon called her at regular points throughout the day whilst he was at work and would immediately become suspicious if she did not answer. This would cause him to rush home to enquire why she hadn't picked up the phone and then complain to her for wasting his time. It was just one of his many controlling techniques. Nothing was caring about it; it was purely to control where she was during the day, that she was where he wanted her to be. One time, she had been out at the shop when he had called and didn't she pay for that when he got home!

So it would have to be in the middle of night when she was certain he would be asleep. That would give them a good few hours head start and put some distance between them. Carrie sat at the edge of the bath whilst Birdy played with some bath toys.

'Listen, Birdy ...' she moved nearer to the edge of the tub and lowered her voice. Before continuing, she glanced towards the door and despite hearing him clattering around downstairs, she kept her voice low and pushed the door so it was only slightly ajar. 'I've got something to tell you,' she whispered to her daughter. 'It's like a surprise, you like surprises, don't you?' Carrie wore the most convincing smile she could muster.

'I love surprises!' Birdy replied and each syllable of her words bounced joyfully.

'Good,' she edged closer still until her face was a few inches from her daughter's in the bath. 'We're going on an adventure ...' Carrie waited for a response from her daughter and saw as her eyes grew wide. 'Without Daddy, just you and me.'

A wide smile accompanied Birdy's curious eyes.

'But listen carefully,' Carrie whispered. 'You can't say a word to Daddy, not even a tiny bit. Can you do that?'

Birdy nodded enthusiastically back at her. Carrie wondered if she felt the same relief that she did that they would soon be free. 'Not a whisper, baby. But the special thing is we need to leave after bedtime. I'll have to wake you up and we'll have to go when it's dark.' She waited with trepidation for the endless questions which she would surely be barraged with next. However, Carrie had spent the whole weekend anticipating every possible question – we'll take a taxi, then we will get a train for the rest of the way. Yes, I have packed your clothes, yes there will be snacks to eat on the way, yes you can go back to sleep if you get tired …

Birdy looked thoughtful for a moment before asking, 'Can Mr Bear come too?'

Carrie's face broke into a relieved smile. 'Of course Mr Bear can come!' She paused, waiting for further interrogation that was important to a five-year-old. Surprisingly, there were none. 'Remember what I said baby, not a word to Daddy,' she reaffirmed as she towel-dried her daughter's hair.

'Is the surprise for him too?'

Carrie faltered. 'Kind of. You know how busy Daddy is and he'll need to stay here and work. The surprise for him will be that we are giving him all the space to work and peace and quiet.'

It was easier than she thought to slip a sleeping pill into his dinner. She still had a few left over from an old prescription when she had visited the doctor with stress before the abuse had accelerated. After she was sure he was deeply asleep, she crept over-cautiously around the house, freezing every time she made a noise louder than a whisper. Every chair leg scraping caused a flash of adrenaline to course through her. He was out for the count but there was still a slim chance he could stir.

Waking Birdy was easier than she'd thought. Luckily, she'd left enough time in her plan to do this slowly but also, more importantly, not have her awake too soon before they were ready to leave. There was no way she could risk having her bouncing around the house asking questions about their impending trip. She knew Birdy would be tired later, but they would be a safe distance away by then and this would be much easier to deal with. Carrie gathered their bags which she had placed near the front door after she had woken up. Truthfully, she doubted whether she had had any decent sleep anyway. Carrie cast a last look back into their house as they stood on the threshold. She wished she had felt some kind of longing nostalgia but there was nothing. She just harboured the feeling that this was long overdue and she should have done it much sooner.

DAY 2

On arrival at number 30 Dunberry Crescent, Carrie squinted at the padlock which permitted their entry to the house. The journey that they started late last night had taken them into the morning. The journey had progressed relatively smoothly, she had just clammed up when the overly chatty taxi driver had enquired where they were setting off to at such a late hour. Carrie had smiled awkwardly and made her answer as succinct as she could. She found it quite easy to lie and say they had been called to a family emergency and had to leave there and then. Their train had been delayed by a few minutes which caused repeated checking of her watch as she mentally calculated how long it had been since they left the house.

She looked up and down the street and was surprised that it looked exactly the same as the photographs, albeit a little more run-down than she had anticipated. She wondered how old the pictures were on the website. However, it seemed quiet which was perfect for both of them. Some of the surrounding houses were tightly packed together yet others were detached. It looked as though the various house designs had been thrown together. Some of the front doors led directly onto the street, like the one they were to stay in. However, the house next door had a few steps leading up to the front door. There was a small area in front of the house with just enough room for the bins to be stored in front.

In the past, Carrie was sure the owner of the

property would have been standing outside the house waiting, jangling a set of keys to the house. Things had changed and now there was just a numbered padlock with rolling dials securing the property. Carrie had been emailed the code and been informed there would be a set of keys inside as well as instruction manuals on how to operate the various appliances. Carrie checked the piece of paper she'd been constantly and reassuringly touching in her pocket. This had the security code on it.

Birdy stood quietly by her side, the excitement of their trip dissipating. She was now succumbing to her tired state and yawned several times.

'Just a few more minutes, baby. I just need to check the code again,' Carrie reassured her, although she needn't have worried as her daughter's patience was surprising her.

'Need any help?' a curt voice sounded behind her and made Carrie jump. This caused her to nudge Birdy out of an almost upright sleeping position.

'Sorry, you startled me!' Carrie laughed nervously, not wanting to appear hostile to someone who appeared to be one of her neighbours.

The woman nodded at her and switched on a formal smile which disappeared from her face in the same fashion. Her appearance reminded Carrie of an old school mistress from decades ago. Carrie noticed she wore her greying hair in a tight bun and his colour seemed to be the theme as she cast her eyes over her coat. She peered at them over the glasses which balanced on her nose.

'Belongs to the Fishers, this house,' she nodded towards her. 'The lock is a bit stiff, so I'm told. I've some oil if you need it.'

'Uh, no, I think it should be fine.' For some reason, Carrie just wanted to get inside. She wasn't afraid of this woman by any means, but they had been outside for too long and she felt as though she needed the sanctuary of four walls again. The woman stood behind her still, watching the struggle. Birdy hugged her leg tighter, obviously a bit unsettled at this unfamiliar woman looming behind them.

Carrie muttered some obscenities under her breath

out of frustration at the lock. Her hands were also becoming sweaty, which wasn't helping. This caused her daughter to chastise her, 'Mummy, you said a rude word, I heard you.'

'Please, Birdy, just give me a minute,' Carrie placed the lock between her palms to warm it up as though that was the problem. She felt the old woman's presence becoming more claustrophobic by the second, her eyes seemed to bore into her. This coupled with the thought that Jon could by now have woken up from a deep sleep, still feeling groggy but discover they were missing. At last, the lock sprang open and Carrie closed her eyes and smiled triumphantly to herself. 'Thank you for your offer,' she turned to face the woman. She quickly pushed Birdy inside.

'How long you folks here for, anyway?'

'Oh, just a month or so, we're renting and will be looking to move on …' By now, Carrie had placed her bags in the darkened room and was keen to get in herself, but it seemed rude to cut this old woman off whilst she was mid-conversation.

'I'm just there if you need anything. The name's Valerie by the way.' Her tone was still clipped and somewhat unfriendly. She pointed to a house behind her but kept her gaze fixed on Carrie.

'Oh, thank you, but we'll be fine, I think. Besides, like I say, we're only here for a month.' She smiled an exhausted smile before edging the door closed. However, before it was fully shut, she could've sworn she heard the reply, 'My bet is that you are out within a month …' before she strode off. Too tired to mull over this thought, she breathed a sigh of relief at the safety of inside.

It had been straight to bed for both of them, without even using the time to have a proper look around the house. As the top bedroom was exposed, it had been the first bed Carrie had spotted. As she had been on the go for what seemed like an eternity, she flopped straight on the bed. Birdy joined her and they decided to rest fully dressed on top of the covers to make up for their lack of sleep that night. Too exhausted to even dream, Carrie felt her eyes close the minute her head hit the pillow.

Carrie woke before her daughter. She squinted in the semi-darkness. A curtain had been drawn to cover a window somewhere downstairs, but it didn't help that the sun hit the side of the house they were facing. For a moment, she allowed herself the stillness of being free. The emotional relief was immense. She was able to finally feel some sense of accomplishment that she had succeeded in what she'd set out to do – they were finally safe. However, just because she was awake, it didn't mean she was able to get up, seeing as Birdy had her limbs wrapped around her. She gently placed a hand on Birdy's head, flattening her wayward curls somewhat. Carrie tested her ability to free herself from her grasp. Laying in one position now that she was fully awake was proving more uncomfortable by the second. For a fleeting moment, this reminded Carrie of the times she had remained frozen in her marital bed, afraid that any movement would disturb Jon. The longer he had remained asleep had been a blessing.

She needn't have worried as Birdy began to shift gradually. She slowly raised her sleepy head and met her mother's eyes.

'Morning, baby,' Carrie smiled warmly down at her before pausing to look at her watch which she had placed on the bedside cabinet. 'Or make that afternoon, we've been asleep for a while.' She flicked the switch on the bedside light.

'A one and then a thirteen,' Birdy confirmed.

'Or how do we say that as a time?'

Birdy paused for a moment, eyes cast to the ceiling as she tried to recall her knowledge of telling the time. Carrie was by no means the best teacher but tried her hardest. 'One thirteen?'

'Or thirteen minutes past one. Or past lunch time?' They both sat up on the bed together. Carrie wondered what to make them for lunch considering how much food they had bought with them.

'Do you have any sandwiches left over from earlier?' It seemed like ages ago that they had left home.

'I've still got all of mine,' she smiled. Carrie knew this meant she had snacked on chocolate and crisps on their journey. 'Will this be where you will sleep, Mummy?' Birdy bounced on the bed a few times in her seated position to test the springs.

'I thought you might like this bedroom.'

'But where will you sleep?' Birdy looked around and her expression was relatively easy to read. Her mother would be too far away for her liking.

'There are two more bedrooms downstairs. Want to have an explore?' Carrie asked with a smile and jumped to her feet. The staircase leading up to the bedroom was a fashionable winding one, which made Carrie wonder how they had ever got the furniture up there in the first place. It occurred to her that a great deal of negotiation would have been required to winch everything from the floor below and over the banister. Carrie had second thoughts about Birdy sleeping in this area. Not that she had ever shown any signs of sleepwalking but all it would take would be a midnight trip to get a drink of water and she would tumble down the stairs. No thank you, they hadn't escaped the clutches of a violent man to break a leg here.

Birdy wandered from room to room on the ground floor, cooing occasionally and rubbing the sofa, patting various surfaces in every room. She was a very sensory child and often needed to touch different materials. She scrunched up her nose. 'Where are the bedrooms, then?'

Carrie laughed. They were standing in the lounge area and it was obvious no further rooms were leading off. 'There's a secret basement, want to see it?'

Opposite the front door was a wooden set of stairs curving down below. They just hadn't seen it upon entry as they had been too tired, that coupled with the curtains still drawn over the window to the left of the door made the room still relatively dim. Carrie wasn't sure what to expect downstairs, but the bedrooms appeared fresh, albeit one was a bit gloomy due to a lack of window. This showed definite signs of being a conversion where space had been used to its full potential. A larger bedroom would have benefited from the window as in the second bedroom, there was a floor to ceiling glass which had a view of a small courtyard.

'Do you want this room baby? You might be able to

see some birds if you're lucky.' Carrie peered out of the window and was able to see into the neighbouring house if she stood at the right angle. This meant that hers and Birdy's privacy would be slightly too compromised for Carrie's liking, since they would be able to see into this bedroom too. The bathroom window also shared this view; as it was the room next to this one. Carrie made a mental note to ensure the bathroom blind was always pulled down.

The area downstairs also had a room that housed the boiler. An old metal shelving unit was pushed against the wall and what looked like paint cans that had not been disturbed for a while judging by their rusted lids and faded colours. The unit itself looked unstable to the point of collapsing if the slightest pressure was applied. Carrie spied a wooden panelled door at the end of this room. She tried the handle and found it to be locked. Carrie rattled the door a few more times and wondered if she'd seen a large key on the set which had been left. She recalled the floor plans which had been on the website and remembered that they had appeared smaller on the basement floor. Therefore, there was a further area beyond this door – perhaps a covered veranda or something similar. All in all, it appeared that the house had been extended and converted several times as many rooms did not seem to fit or appeared haphazardly placed.

'We need to find a shop for some food and think about what to have for dinner,' Carrie suggested as they sat at the kitchen table finishing their lunch. 'You up for a bit of a walk?'

Birdy nodded her head enthusiastically, mouth still full. Carrie put their rubbish in the bin whilst Birdy busied herself looking for her shoes. Having not being able to bring a phone with them to use the maps, she hoped that they would find a shop on their travels. It was one of the sacrifices she had made to leave their house. The idea of taking her phone with her had been out of the question.

Carrie checked her pocket several times for the keys before she allowed herself to close the front door. It would be the ultimate nightmare if she were to lock them both out on their first day. They both stood, backs to the house as Carrie looked up and down the street as she figured the best direction to take. She wished it had been proper daylight when they had arrived, or that she hadn't been so tired so she would have a rough idea of the area.

'Looking for something, dear?'

The voice made Carrie jump more than she'd liked. She reckoned her nerves were still on edge and would be for a while to come. In front of her stood an elderly lady wearing an oversized flowery, waterproof coat. Her hair was neatly confined in a transparent plastic hood. Carrie couldn't see much else of her apart from the bright pink lipstick which had been applied too liberally. 'Uh, I, we …' Carrie stuttered and proceeded to clear her throat. 'We were just looking for the nearest shop.'

'You'll find it back that way.' The woman pointed in the direction she had just come from. Sure enough, Carrie could see what appeared to be a busier road than the one they were currently on. Several cars passed by, but they were far enough away to preserve the relative quietness of the street.

'We're a dead end here, that's why we don't get the traffic. Though sometimes people don't see the signs until it's too late. You'll see lots of U-turns down that end.' She waved a gloved hand towards the road. Carrie wondered if it was a standard issue for elderly ladies to be dressed like her. The weather promised to be warm today yet here she was, dressed as though she was expecting a monsoon.

'Oh, thank you,' Carrie breathed. 'We just moved in …'

'Then we're neighbours. I think we spoke on the phone.' The old lady beamed back at her. 'I'm in number 28 just there. I'm Agnes, by the way.'

'Carrie,' she nodded back. 'And this is my daughter, Birdy. Well, that's a nickname for her. She's actually called …'

However, Carrie could tell Agnes wasn't actually listening to her and was still looking in the direction of her house, as though she needed time to process the conversation and was still on the introducing her to her neighbouring house part.

'I think we can see your house from one of the bedrooms and the bathroom,' Carrie said.

'Oh, it's a very small area between the houses. Don't worry, though. We don't often go in the back bedrooms. Ours is at the front, see?' She pointed to the curtained upstairs window. Carrie craned her neck upwards and could indeed see a window obscured from daylight.

'Our house has a bedroom upstairs but doesn't take up the whole space" Carrie mused and wondered why she was explaining this to the landlady. 'Maybe the house designs are all different.'

'Well, I'll let you and your little one get off, dear.' Agnes smiled at them.

Carrie returned her smile and watched as she shuffled off and after a while, reached her house and let herself in. The old lady appeared slow on her feet, so it was several minutes of pretending she was looking for something in her bag as Carrie didn't move until the door closed behind her. Carrie smiled to herself, amused. Poor old Agnes was either deaf or losing her marbles a bit. It was almost as though she'd not heard half of what Carrie had said. She concluded that Agnes had probably had an idea of what to say in her head and hadn't really been paying attention to any of Carrie's responses.

They walked down the street, hand in hand, to the busier road. Carrie baulked at the idea of being addressed as 'dear'. It was a term of endearment reserved for old ladies, but she objected at this somewhat as it was clear she was at least half of Agnes's age. However, she resigned herself to the fact that if old Agnes was indeed hard of hearing, the expression of 'dear' would mean that one size would fit all. 'Dear' would have to do then. Perhaps it was for the best that the less Agnes knew about them, the better.

Birdy chose the largest pepperoni pizza she could find in the shop as they milled around the aisles at their leisure. Just the idea of not having to shop to a timetable was enough for her. Carrie tried to select the biggest amount of shopping that they'd be able to carry but didn't worry at the thought of having to repeat this trip in a few days. However, she noticed that it was often a feature of the *Snooze and Stay* properties that people would often leave toiletries and such behind so other tenants would have less to pack and take with them. This would cut down on the heavy items to carry back.

Carrie sat opposite her daughter at the dinner table, they exchanged silly conversations and she found herself laughing at Birdy's childish humour. It felt as though a weight had been lifted off her shoulders. Even her posture felt different – no longer was she sitting stiff as a board in her chair, waiting for the next instruction or command. Now, they could take their time with their dinner, taking all the time in the world to dip the pizza crusts in the sauce, whilst Birdy sported a tomato ring around her mouth, resembling some kind of circus clown.

'Maybe, little one, we should think about getting you in the bath.'

'But I had one the other day.' It was an attempt at a complaint but executed poorly.

'Your skin won't wear away,' Carrie grinned at her. They went downstairs to the bathroom and a pull-cord light illuminated the somewhat dated furnishings.

'You could get in, too, Mummy. The bath is big enough for us both,' Birdy announced as they watched the bubbles rising.

'I guess so,' Carrie laughed and watched her daughter hop in after she had checked the temperature. She studied her child for a few moments and even though she was only five, it already seemed that Birdy was much more relaxed too.

'Come on slowcoach!' Birdy admonished her. 'I'll scooch up to the end and you'll fit behind me!' she patted the water to emphasise this.

Carrie nodded but waited until Birdy was preoccupied with the bath toys again before removing her clothes. It had always felt uncomfortable undressing, half due to the pain from any injuries and also from the uneasy feeling of scrutinising eyes on her. Too fat, too old, past your best, let yourself go, could do with some sessions at the gym … these were all unwelcome phrases in her memory. Carrie caught her reflection in the mirror of the medicine cabinet as she lowered herself in. She was quite a slim build and by no means fat as she had been told so often. Pausing to look at herself, the bruise on her shoulder still looked quite angry.

Carrie absentmindedly shampooed her daughter's hair, giggling as they made beards out of the bubbles and she made a spiky shape on her head before rinsing. Birdy's infectious laugh was a tonic to her, kept her going and reassured her that there was joy to be found in the simplest of things.

From the corner of her eye, Carrie spotted a light being switched on from the window opposite. She looked up as her smile froze on her face and dropped.

'What's wrong, Mummy?' Birdy's voice piped up as she was as aware of her mother's faltering touch.

'Just the light, baby ...' she offered and blinked a few times to focus. The window opposite had its curtains wide open, even though it was now dark outside. Had they been drawn earlier when they had looked around? Carrie struggled to remember. 'Oh my God!' she shot up with so much vigour so that some of the water splashed over the side. The bottom panel of their window had frosted glass but the top half was clear. This meant that at the right angle, the person opposite could have a clear view into their bathroom. Carrie realised how exposed they were, in more ways than one. With one leg out of the bath to stabilise her, she frantically reached for the cord for the window blind which she had forgotten to draw before getting in the bath.

'Come on!' she urged as the cord failed to drop the blind down. Carrie didn't even think of what she must look like, naked and soapy. She just had to block out the view from the figure that stood in front of the window. The figure was indeed taking full advantage of the clear glass. The faint light shrouded it with a ghostly glow. Motionless and dominating, it faced them, watching.

'Mummy!' the whines were growing louder from the bath, Carrie was unsure whether it was due to the speed in which she had stood up or the choppy water that Birdy now sat in.

'For the love of God, come on!' Carrie cursed at the blind as it finally released and crashed down. The figure, stock still, had not moved but now it was out of sight. She felt unsure of what was more worrying, the fact that this person was brazenly watching them or realised they had been spotted but hadn't scurried out of sight, embarrassed at being seen. She breathed deeply as she retreated back into the bath. This seemed to pacify Birdy but Carrie sat uneasily, staring at the blind. She could just about make out the light being turned off. Despite the warmth of the water, she suddenly felt chilled.

Carrie was surprised how well Birdy had settled into the window room downstairs. She must have still been tired from their journey and overwhelmed at the excitement of new surroundings. Making sure all of the curtains were drawn with no gaps exposed, Carrie pulled the door so that it was ajar before settling herself in the room next door. She had allowed Birdy to stay up a bit later, still on the pretence that they were on some kind of holiday.

She sat reading a book with the covers pulled up around her. Although it had been a few hours since their bath and they had watched some television, she still felt unnerved at being watched in the bathroom. No, that was too timid, sickened was more accurate. Had Agnes mentioned she lived there alone or did she say 'we'? Even though it had been dark, the figure hadn't looked like a woman. Agnes had appeared to be short and plump when they had met in the street. Yes, her raincoat had added extra padding and made it difficult to judge her true size but the figure in the window had looked taller and slimmer.

Carrie sighed and closed her book. She knew she wouldn't settle until she had gone back to the bathroom to check the blind was definitely down and also check Birdy's curtains were drawn.

The door creaked ever so slightly as she pushed it open to check her sleeping daughter. She had turned over, Mr Bear still clutched tightly to her chest. Happy that the curtains were closed and overlapping, she retreated out of the room. Thankfully, the curtains were also made of heavy fabric and there was no possibility of seeing through the material.

The bathroom was exactly as they had left it. The tap in the sink dripped sporadically and the drops patted gently on the ceramic. Carrie used the toilet before standing next to the blind. Gingerly, she used one finger to lift it. It was now pitch-black outside and only a small part of the wall was illuminated by the moonlight. Carrie squinted to adjust her eyes to the darkness outside. Tall enough to see over the frosted glass, she had a full view of the area. After a few moments when her eyes had adjusted to the moonlight, she was able to make out the grubby patio tiles and neglected flowerpots. The area could not have been larger than a garage. The exposed window next door had now been concealed with a curtain and remained dark. She had no idea what or who was behind this and didn't want to know. Agnes had pointed out her front bedroom, therefore, this window was part of a different room. A chill ran through Carrie at the possibilities and she dropped the blind before scurrying back to her room. Childlike, she felt comfort once she was safely in the bed again.

DAY 3

She slept surprising well but woke with no real idea of what time it was due to the lack of natural light from having no window. However, the chink of light coming through the gap in her door told her it was daytime. Carrie was surprised she'd had no midnight visits from Birdy. But then again, this had never happened at home either; there was no way Jon would tolerate her in their bed as well.

Carrie crept out of her bedroom in case Birdy was still asleep. She stopped at her door as she heard a voice from her daughter's room. Frowning, she edged her way closer, fully expecting to see a full-blown conversation between Birdy and Mr Bear, obviously with the voices both coming from her. However, when she walked in, Birdy was at the window, having pulled the heavy curtains open to reveal a large gap in between.

'Baby, who are you talking to?' For one horrifying moment, she imagined that the figure in the window was back and Birdy was addressing him, or her, whoever it was.

'Look Mummy!' she exclaimed excitedly. 'Real birds and they came to see me!'

Carrie moved to the window, giving Birdy the impression she was looking at the patio when really, she was doing her best to arch her neck around to get a good view of the neighbouring window. Thankfully, their curtains were still drawn. Therefore, she cast her eyes down to where Birdy pointed and sure enough, a small number of birds were hopping around on the paving slabs.

'They came to see me!' she repeated. 'Oh, Mummy, can one of them be my pet? I promise I'll look after it …'

'Oh, sweetheart,' she cut her off. 'I know you'd look after a bird. But these are wild birds. They belong outside.'

Seemingly ignoring her, Birdy continued, 'I'll call my bird, Birdy. Just like me!'

Carrie smiled down at her daughter. 'How about some breakfast for my little Birdy? And sweetie,' she added, making her voice sound as airy as possible. 'It's very important that if you are ever getting dressed or undressed, to keep these curtains closed. Do you understand?' She didn't want to say too much more, to worry Birdy with thoughts about a potential pervert spying in on them. However, Birdy was still young and such thoughts would never enter her head. 'And when we're in the bathroom too, remind me to check that the blind is always down.'

'What about the toilet?'

Carrie pondered. 'I guess that too.'

Birdy shrugged and began to make her way up the stairs. She muttered as she went up, 'For my breakfast, I would like pancakes, no … waffles. With chocolate sauce. And juice. No milk …'

'We'll see,' Carrie replied. She was well aware of what Birdy had put in the basket whilst they were shopping yesterday. They had bought treat foods, which had been limited whilst at home, but Carrie was aware that they wouldn't be able to sustain that kind of spending for too much longer.

Birdy munched on her waffles as Carrie moved to check her bag. She had managed to withdraw as much cash as she could from a savings account Jon was not aware of but would be unable to withdraw any from their joint account in case he had some way of tracking her movements. She could picture him going into the bank to demand an itemised statement as he scrutinised the transactions. She was half tempted to turn on the news and see if there were any reports of a missing person. Shaking her head, she dismissed this. There was no way the news would bother about a person who'd been missing for only a day, let alone put this on the national news, local maybe … or perhaps he would go to the police and make an extravagant sob story about his beloved wife and child going missing. Then the police would be forced to act and he would make a massive show of welcoming her back once they'd tracked her down. And she'd pay for it once he got her home.

Carrie checked her bag. As she'd suspected, there wasn't a great deal of cash left. The house had taken a sizeable amount in rental fees from what funds she had managed to scrape together. There was no way she could get a job, what with Birdy to look after. Besides, that would definitely make locating her easier. As withdrawing any more money was out of the question, there was only one more option she could think of.

'Baby, when you're done, get dressed. We need to go out.'

Carrie managed to find an internet café and amused Birdy with a drink and a snack whilst she logged on.

> <u>New Message</u>
> To: Maggie Fuller
> From: Carrie Waterson
> Subject:

Carrie paused over the email and turned to face Birdy. She smiled to herself, her baby was worth saving. She continued the email.

> Subject: I've left Jon
> *Mum, I can't type too much but am letting you know that I've walked out. I've got Birdy with me.*

Carrie felt the tears welling up in her eyes and blinked them back.

> *Is there any way you would be able to transfer me some money? I'll pay you back as soon as I can, I promise. I have the card to my old savings account, the one that you send money to for*

*Birdy's birthdays. I can only check my emails now and again
as we don't have internet access in our new home. Hoping you
read this before you go away. Sorry, I can't tell you where I am
but promise you we are both safe.
I love you.*

Carrie x

Carrie sniffed and reached for a tissue. Her mother had been
telling her for years she needed to leave him. She had
tolerated Jon for a while now, always wearing a painted smile
around him. Carrie was sure if her mum knew the full extent
of the abuse, she would have personally come round to
forcefully remove her herself. Carrie often felt shame when
thinking of what she had suffered in the past. It was too
embarrassing to reveal the full extent, even with family. Her
finger hovered over the send button and pressed it before she
had the chance to change her mind.

'How are you doing there, sweetie?'

'Good Mummy, who are you writing to?'

Carrie moved her hand to stroke her hair. 'Just
Nanny. Just to tell her we aren't at home.' She cast her eyes
down at the list of emails in her inbox. Sure enough, there
were several from the same sender: Jon Waterson. The period
between the times sent was small. She looked around
anxiously, fearing a stranger's eyes over her shoulder. They
would see the emails and would know. Carrie felt her skin
prickle as she faced up to the reality. The sent emails were
what she had been dreading. This confirmed to her that her
plan had obviously been unsuccessful. He had woken up that
morning. She daren't open them as he would see from his
end that she had, and then what would happen if he could
trace where she was when she'd read them? The subject
heading of each one became more frantic in tone the more
recent they were.

The first one started with a simple, 'Where are you?'
and ranged from, 'Please just call' to 'I'll have to call the
police …' Carrie took a sharp intake of breath as the cursor
hovered over this last message. She felt herself pale, would the

police be after her? Checking to see that Birdy could not see the screen, she clicked on the message. Although Birdy was growing more confident with her reading, she knew that she would not be able to read all of it anyway. However, there was always the risk that she would pick out the key words: 'police' or 'kill' for example and she would announce to their captive audience that she knew what those words meant. Carrie need not have worried as Birdy's attention was still focused on her snacks. His message was short and concise but reminded her of how intimidating he could make her feel with mere written words.

> To: Carrie Waterson
> From: Jon Waterson
> Subject: re: I'll have to call the police
>
> *Carrie*
> *Come home and put a stop to this now. I will go to the police as I know you put some pills in my dinner last night. You really need to hide the empty bottle a bit better. Come home or I will go to the police and the longer you leave it, the worse this will be. Imagine our child knowing that you tried to kill her father. Think of that.*
> *Jon*

She swallowed hard. All her efforts of carefully crushing the pills, choosing a meal to cook with strong flavours which would mask the possible bitterness of the tablets and it hadn't worked. Carrie racked her brains for how many pills she had used, had she emptied the bottle? Why hadn't they worked? She considered whether they had been unsuccessful due to the expiry date – was that the reason? Looking towards Birdy, she gave her a weak smile and stroked her head. He was bluffing, he had to be. There would be no way he would want the police involved and was probably hoping she would realise she could not survive by herself. Maybe he was right. If she couldn't even do something as simple as administering enough tablets to ensure he wouldn't wake up, what chance did she have of providing a home for herself and Birdy long term? Carrie shook her head and deleted the message, her cheeks burning in shame and she moved to log out. However, almost instantaneously, another email arrived.

>To: Carrie Waterson
>From: Maggie Fuller
>Subject: re: I've left Jon
>
>*Oh, my darling! Of course I can send you some money. I am so happy you have been brave enough to walk out. You have often said how unhappy you are. You and precious Birdy deserve a new start.*
>*Carrie, I have to tell you, Jon has called. He said he woke up and you and Birdy had gone. Obviously, I've not told him anything as I don't know where you are. But you are safe. You know there is always a home for you here. When you are ready, come home.*
>*I know you need to get your head together and sort things out. I'm away soon as you know your uncle can't manage alone after he comes out of hospital but after two weeks, I'll be back home if you need me. In the meantime, I'll run down the bank now.*
>*Message me soon,*
>*Mum x*

Carrie allowed herself to stare at the screen for a while. There was no mention that Jon had spoken to her mother and informed her that her daughter had attempted to murder him. Of course he wouldn't mention this; Jon would plan himself how to deal with this. Carrie was interrupted by a tap on her arm.

'Mummy, what's wrong?' A concerned voice snapped her out of her thoughts. Carrie wiped her eyes on her sleeve.

'Nothing, sweetie. I'm nearly done here, are you ready to go?' She turned to look back to the screen and quickly clicked the tab for the latest headlines. Carrie wasn't sure what she expected to see but there were no stories regarding the disappearance of a mother and her child. She knew he had been bluffing. She guessed that he would have his own way of finding them.

As they walked back to the house together, Carrie made a mental note to explore the area once she had cleared her head a bit more. Besides, they were very short on funds at the moment so she would need to wait for the money to come through which prohibited them from doing much else. Once the money had come through, then they would have more freedom to plan what was next. However, as she was used to having Birdy at home as she didn't attend school, they had plenty of activities to do inside. Birdy seemed quite happy to return to the house and there were no complaints about being bored and wanting to go somewhere else. There were a few residents out and about on the street, but they did not acknowledge Carrie, obviously having no idea they were staying there temporarily. Anyway, would they want anything to do with them? Sadly, the days of knowing your neighbours' names were gradually fading. People tended to keep to themselves.

Birdy hurried to her room, possibly to see if the birds were still outside in the patio area. Looking around the room, Carrie made a point of tidying up. This was because she wanted to, not because she had to. She made herself a coffee with the intention of reading some of the paperwork which had been left so she had a better idea of how to run the place. It occurred to her that this was the first time in a long time where she was fully independent. After a while, she searched through drawers to find if there were any further keys. Not having access to the door downstairs was playing on her mind.

Carrie smiled as she saw her daughter sitting by the window playing with her bears. Part of it was a glass sliding door which they hadn't noticed before. As the area outside was so small, Carrie couldn't fathom why anyone would want to sit outside. The neighbour's house was so close that it gave the area a claustrophobic look.

'I'm just checking the door that we couldn't open where the boiler is,' she informed her and held up the bunch of keys as though she needed to show proof.

The wood-panelled door had once sported a blue gloss coat, but the paint had started to peel long ago. Carrie noted that the lock required an old-fashioned brass key due to the size of the keyhole sadly, none of the keys remotely resembled one of those on the keyring. She looked at the hinges which were rusted brown and wondered when the door had last been opened. Peering through the keyhole made her breath hitch as though she had no reason to be spying. It was bright on the other side confirming her suspicions that this was another way to access the outside. However, all she could see was another door through the keyhole, presumably the neighbour's similar back door directly in her line of sight.

Carrie sighed. There was no point worrying about this door as she doubted there would be any reason for them to require access during their brief stay. She rattled the doorknob again for good measure before retreating out of the room.

After dinner, Birdy decided to have another bath, Carrie presumed due to the fact that there was no pressure to get out and be ushered to bed. She sat next to the tub on the bathmat whilst idly moving a hand through the water. Every now and again, she glanced at the closed blind and wondered whether the neighbouring window was still obscured too.

She tucked a sleepy Birdy into her bed, Mr Bear clutched tightly in her grip. Her eyes were struggling to stay open and Carrie wondered whether she was just settling into their new routine here. Tomorrow they would venture out again, check her bank balance and emails. Once she was sure Birdy was asleep, Carrie decided to run herself a bath. She allowed her eyes to close as she lay in the tub.

She woke with a jolt as she heard a crackle from the light fitting. The bulb made an audible pop before plunging the room into darkness. The only light in the room was from the moonlight seeping in from the edges of the blind. Reaching for the towel, she paused as her vision became clearer. Unable to move now, it became all too apparent why she was able to see better. A light had been turned on in the bedroom from the house opposite. The person was back.

Suddenly very aware she felt vulnerable in the bath,

Carrie hurriedly got out and wrapped the towel around her before throwing on her bath robe. All the while, her eyes were fixed on the window. She allowed herself to edge nearer the window and moved the blind so she was able to see out. Carrie heard a gasp and realised it was coming from her. Sure enough, the curtains were open from the neighbouring window and there he sat, the person she had seen the previous evening, staring and waiting. She wasn't sure if he had seen her too and dared herself to look as long as she was able to without feeling nauseous. Why was he staring at her with such audacity?

'Mummy…'

'Jesus Christ!' Carrie jumped back from the window at the voice behind her. She squinted to focus on her daughter's face and could just about make out a worried frown.

'Sorry baby, the bulb went. Why are you up anyway? Do you need the toilet?' She flustered as she gathered Birdy up to put her back to bed.

'No, Mummy, something woke me up, a sound…'

'This is an old house, sweetie, old houses creak a lot by themselves, it's nothing to worry about.' Carrie hurried back into her room and settled her back into bed.

'Your hair is still wet,'

'Yes, I was in the bath. I had to get out as I told you the bulb went off. Are you okay, do you want me to stay with you for a bit?' Carrie felt breathless for some reason.

Birdy shook her head from side to side. 'I think I should be okay now.' She snuggled further under the covers. Carrie watched her for a few moments, grateful that she seemed unperturbed by the lack of light. She was just about to leave her to get back to sleep when a small voice piped up from the bed.

'Do old houses knock too, then?'

'What do you mean 'knock'?' Carrie was suddenly chilled.

Birdy made a fist and proceeded to tap on the bedcovers and made three muffled pats. 'A knock, like that.'

Carrie swallowed hard and chose her words carefully. She could feel the beads of sweat forming on the back of her neck and knew it was nothing to do with the thickness of the bathrobe. 'Where from, baby?'

Birdy pointed towards the door. 'From the room, the one you were looking for the key for. I got up to find you and heard it,' she repeated the tapping on her duvet in a pattern.

Carrie looked in the direction of her door and then back to Birdy. It was just an inquisitive question and Carrie did not sense any worry in her voice. Such a noise would seem quite innocent to a child, who would have no reason to question the source. Carrie on the other hand, had every possibility overwhelm her at once.

'Stay here,' she held up her hand as though she had to prevent Birdy from following her. Carrie stood at the open door before taking small steps towards the boiler room. She pushed open the door and decided that she needed that room illuminated as quickly as possible; she did not need the darkness adding to the whole ambience. Carrie was aware she was holding her breath as she stared into the empty room. Her heartbeat gave her the impression she was exceeding her regular resting rate. Just the sound of buzzing from the boiler was all she could hear. Carrie's throat tightened as she waited. She paused at the entrance to the room and strained to hear any other noises. There was nothing.

After a while, her nerves overtook the courage it had taken to investigate in the first place and she turned off the light before closing the door slightly harder than intended.

'There's nothing, honey.' She returned to Birdy, who remained in the same position as she'd left her. Birdy pulled a resigned face before turning back on her side.

'G'night Mummy.'

'Goodnight.' Carrie settled into her bed, her eyes refusing to shut as she stared at her door whilst straining to make out any noises. It took her a long time to get to sleep that night.

DAY 4

<u>New Message</u>

To: Carrie Waterson
From: Maggie Fuller
Subject: Money transfer

Hi Carrie
As promised, I have transferred some funds to your account. You do not need to pay me back, I am fully aware of how much you will need this for you and Birdy. I can't wait to see you both! If you could just tell me the city you're in...
Jon has called a couple of times but obviously, I have nothing to tell him. Stay safe honey and I hope to hear from you soon.

Much love, Mum xxx

Carrie let out a massive sigh of relief when she checked her bank balance. Never had she been so happy to see a row of zeros on her statement – in all the right places. This was a huge starting block for herself and Birdy and would mean that they wouldn't have to worry about money for a while. They would also be able to take their time planning what to do after their contract expired on 30 Dunberry Crescent. However, following the incident of the previous night, Carrie wondered if this might come sooner rather than later.

She'd checked the news headlines again for any recent stories regarding missing persons – nothing. Her inbox was filling up with messages from Jon since yesterday and she had no desire to open any of them. If he hadn't gone to the police the minute he realised she had tried to kill him, then the probability of him going now was slimmer. She had a sinking feeling of how the conversations had gone between Jon and her mother. He was choosing to play the wounded husband card, perhaps admitting that he did have some faults but if she'd only return home, they could sort them out together. The thought of him simpering over the phone turned her stomach. His last massage was titled, 'Come home'. For some reason, she found herself looking over her shoulder, even though that was a ridiculous idea. There was absolutely no way he could track her down. However, she still felt safer being inside and the daylight back in the house gave her some sense of comfort. She shook her head at the notion that sinister goings-on in houses were exclusive to when darkness fell. That was a naïve horror film plot.

Birdy soon settled in front of the television and before long, was giggling away. Carrie tapped her fingers anxiously against her mug. She got up from the sofa and saw that Birdy did not bat an eyelid. With the safety of the daylight, she decided to go to the locked door again, just to appease her worrying mind whilst she could still muster the courage. If there was any further knocking, she was sure to hear it.

The door was still locked. Of course it was. Carrie moistened her lips and bent down level with the exposed keyhole. A gentle breeze pressed against her eye and caused her to blink several times. She turned her head away for a moment as the cold air made her eyes water enough to distort her vision. Goodness knows what she expected to see as her range was limited to a small passageway. All she could see was the neighbour's door which was painted green and adorned with what appeared to be scratch marks. She dismissed any other possibility and resigned herself to thinking that they had owned a dog at some point. This was obviously the area it had been allowed to exercise it. Carrie smiled to herself. What on earth was she expecting to see?

Suddenly, she saw something move past the keyhole, momentarily blocking the light and breeze. It was quick enough to make her jump as she felt her heartbeat bounce inside her chest.

'Shit!' she exclaimed, scampered back as though she had just received an electric shock and found herself sprawled on the bare concrete floor. She put her hand to her chest as though this would push more air into her lungs. She became aware that her cheeks were damp and she was trembling. *For goodness sake!* She chided herself. *Look at you! All you're doing is looking through a keyhole and happened to see someone walk past. You can't cope by yourself; you are useless, just like he said …*

Carrie rubbed her face, aware that she was probably mixing dirt with her tears and would look a right sight to Birdy, so she cleaned herself the best she could. God, she was nothing like the weak, pathetic figure that had left the house a few days ago. *Screw Jon, I have already got us out.* Her shoes scratched the floor as she got up and dared to look through the keyhole again. There was nothing this time, just the same old view of the door again. It was every possibility that she had seen nothing to be of any concern. What did it matter if someone was in next door's garden? Since when had this been a crime? For all she knew, Agnes had been out hanging her washing in the nice weather. The whole timing of it was what had scared her, as though she had been caught red-handed. Carrie pressed her ear up against the door and could hear nothing. She was far too on edge for her liking. Her footsteps were deliberately loud as she closed the door and walked back up the stairs.

Birdy was still in the same position as she'd left her, unperturbed that she had been left alone and did not register Carrie's nervous disposition by what had just happened in the basement. Carrie looked at her for a few moments before an idea struck her.

'Birdy, will you be okay if I just nip out to next door? I just want to ask the lady about something.' She tried making her voice sound as light as possible. What was she supposed to say to her? *Just popping out to report to the old lady next door about spotting someone patrolling the outside area.* She toyed with the idea of taking Birdy with her but the prospect of having a fidgety child at her feet whilst she discussed the potentially awkward subject of being spooked by someone prowling the outside area didn't seem like a good option. There was no reason for Birdy to hear that conversation. Besides, she was only next door and would be a few minutes, maximum. Happy she had justified her decision, she waited for a response.

Birdy just nodded and didn't look away from the television.

'I've got the key, honey, don't answer the door to anyone, I'll let myself back in.' After a pause, 'Birdy?'

'Yes, Mummy.'

Carrie wasn't sure which she was answering to. Had she just heard the 'don't answer the door part' or just her name? *I'll be five minutes anyway,* she told herself and grabbed the keys. She had no idea what she was going to say but was sure something would come to her once the door was open. Agnes was it?

Their door had a large knocker in the middle, shaped like a lion's head. If the house was empty, Carrie imagined this would sound like a bass drum resonating throughout the house. In reality, it was probable they may not hear it at all if they were at the back of the house, or down in the basement … Regardless, she knocked a few times and took a few steps back, fully ready to dart back into her house. She reached the point where she needed to go or knock again; too much time had passed and she'd look ridiculous if she stood in front of an unanswered door any longer. They must be out, no … wait, *someone* was in.

'You'll get no answer, Miss,' the voice made her jump.

'Oh,' Carrie turned around, somewhat startled and saw the old school mistress lady behind her, the lady they had met on their arrival. 'Sorry, I …' Carrie racked her brains to remember her name.

'Valerie,' she seemed to read her mind. 'I say, you'll get no answer. Agnes goes out shopping once a week and visits the church on a Sunday. You'll not see her outside until then. Have you a problem in the house?' she gestured towards number 30.

'No, well, yes. But…'

'Agnes oversees the maintenance of the house. Organises the cleaning between tenants, arranges for repairs if need be.'

'Really?' This came as somewhat of a surprise to Carrie as she imagined this was a lot for an elderly lady to take on by herself.

'She schedules maintenance, doesn't do it herself.' Valerie seemed to read her thoughts again. 'So, you have got a problem?' Her manner was still fairly haughty as though she had the right to question Carrie knocking on the door.

'I was just wondering who lives here, I mean, I know Agnes does, but I wondered if there was anyone else. I saw someone …' she didn't know how to finish her sentence. *Spying on me in the bath? Roaming around outside the basement and knocking on the door?* There was no way she was sharing this with some nosey old battle-axe.

However, Valerie seemed quite willing to carry on talking. 'The house is owned by a lady called Maria Fisher. She's been working abroad for some time now. It's been up for rental for a number of years now, Agnes oversees the upkeep. No idea why she just doesn't sell it. I suppose the income is handy and it's worth a pretty penny now.' She mused. 'So if you do need anything, a note through the door is the best bet. She's quite quick at sorting things out.'

'No, there's nothing wrong, well, just a key I can't find but that's okay.' Carrie moved as if to go back to her house, now conscious that she had left her five-year-old alone. However, she couldn't pass up the opportunity to quiz Valerie about who else lived there.

'So it's just Agnes then?'

'George too. Her husband. But you'll never see him and he's the reason she won't answer the door. Early-onset Alzheimer's. However, that was many years ago. Goodness knows how he's faring up now …' she shook her head. 'Used to get very confused, poor soul. He was struggling with his hearing back then and had trouble getting words out that made sense.'

Carrie nodded. Her nerves felt marginally steadier.

That explained a lot – dozy old fool probably wasn't aware he was acting like he was a Peeping Tom as he sat in the room overlooking their bathroom. Watching and waiting. He was the one who was wandering around the outside area. Probably the only fresh air he could get that was in a safe zone.

'Thank you,' she muttered. 'That explains a lot. I'd better be getting back.' She let herself in with a shaking hand, Valerie still watching her. Was it a trait of someone her age to just stare with piercing judgemental eyes?

Carrie was glad to see Birdy unaffected by her absence. She ruffled her hair. 'Okay, precious?'

Birdy nodded. 'You missed a really funny bit, Mummy. Tom got the mouse but then he got away and splashed Tom with the milk ...' she trailed off, giggling at her own recount.

Carrie smiled back at her. 'I'm going to sort out some dinner for us.' She busied herself with their evening meal, relived that she could cross off some of the worries on her list. The figure in the window and beyond the door, the knocking Birdy had witnessed could now be excused away as Agnes's confused husband next door. Onwards and upwards, time to think about their future.

DAY 5

The bed felt comforting and she was tempted to stay in for a bit longer. Carrie looked at the alarm clock and pushed back the covers hurriedly. It was nearly half-past eight and she'd never slept in that late at home. Considering how uptight she had felt yesterday, it was no surprise her body had taken advantage of her comatose state to calm her down.

She wondered why Birdy hadn't come to wake her, at least ask for breakfast. Carrie went to investigate in her room and saw she'd resumed the position of playing in front of the patio door with her bears.

'Sleep well, honey?'

She nodded.

'I'll go and sort breakfast, give you a shout when it's ready.' Before she had time to wait for a response, she spied the door of the boiler room was ajar. 'Honey, did you open this door?' She was sure she'd shut it yesterday. 'Birdy?' she popped her head back around the door. 'Birdy, can you hear me?' she asked in a more hushed tone, wondering whether she had actually heard the question.

Disturbed from her playing, the child looked up, 'I did go in there, last night. The knocking was there again ...'

Carrie pulled her dressing gown tight around her neck. She hadn't heard a peep. 'How long did the knocking go on for?' she asked. She had a horrible vision of Birdy wandering in the dark, not knowing where the light switch was and then hurrying back into her bed.

Birdy simply shrugged, 'I don't know.'

'Well …' Carrie struggled for the right words to say. 'Maybe you should just stay out of there in the future. Just ignore the noise.'

'Okay,' she replied simply.

'We need to pop out again later. I need to message Nanny again and maybe we could go somewhere after?' she smiled. It was time to start relaxing a bit. They couldn't stay cooped up forever.

<u>New Message</u>

To: Maggie Fuller
From: Carrie Waterson

Subject: Thank you so much!

I received the money in my account. Thank you so much! I can't thank you enough, this will be a great help to get us back on our feet. House is fine, needs a makeover but it's spacious, just a weird old couple next door but nothing to worry about.

Speak soon, C xxx

Carrie turned to face Birdy, who was showing signs of exhaustion following their trip to the cinema, followed by the milkshake and burger diner and the toy shop. She held a new wind-up frog she had selected to add to her growing collection of toys.

'Not too much longer, sweetie,' she stifled a yawn herself and looked back at the screen. The reply was already there waiting to be read.

To: Carrie Waterson
From: Maggie Fuller

Subject: Re: Thank you so much!
That's wonderful honey, glad to hear you are more settled, you

sound it. I've got a feeling that maybe it's starting to sink in with Jon. I've not heard from him today.

Can you tell me where you are staying yet? At least you can give me a call?

Mum xxx

Carrie reread the message. *Stay and Snooze* properties were not fitted with a landline phone for obvious reasons. Now she could be a bit more flexible with money, Carrie decided she would buy a simple pay-as-you-go mobile. No contract meant no paperwork and she'd just use the Wi-Fi in the house. She replied, *Okay, I'll give you a call when we get back. I don't think it will be long before Birdy is in bed, long day for both of us.* She waited for a few minutes but it occurred to her that perhaps her mother had been distracted by something which was preventing her from replying. She logged off as the internet café was starting to fill and sooner or later, someone would need her seat. Carrie decided to go and buy a simple phone. It would be good to hear a familiar voice and she missed her mum now more than ever. She managed to persuade a sleepy Birdy that they just needed to visit one more shop and then they'd go home.

At the house, she settled her yawning child in her bed, the sky already growing dark. 'Did you have a good day, sweetie?'

Birdy nodded and smiled. 'Can you hand me Mr Bear, Mummy? He's the one who gets hugs at bedtime.'

Carrie looked around the top of the bed and then onto the floor around. 'Where did you put him?'

Birdy's eyes opened wider, more awake now. 'He was on the table,' she pointed to the end of the bed, a small oak table was positioned to the side of the patio door. However, an empty space stared back at them.

'Where is he, Mummy?' she rolled over to look over each side of the bed, eyes searching and was now on the verge of sobbing. A full-on breakdown was on the horizon. Birdy moved to sit bolt upright in bed.

'Don't worry, sweetheart, he won't have gone far,' Carrie searched around the bed, lifting the hanging duvet to look under it. It touched the floor surrounding the bed so would make sense for the bear to have slipped down and be hidden underneath. However, the space under the bed was clear. She went to the edge of the room and her eyes darted at all the spaces on the floor. By now, the tears had started. 'Birdy, don't be upset. Where did you see him last, where were you playing?' For a moment, she thought of the dusty boiler room.

'He was right here.' It was difficult to make out the words in between sobs. 'He was watching the birds with me.'

Carrie scratched her head. Stupid bear. Birdy had had it since she was a baby. She was in for a long night if it didn't turn up. 'Are you sure he's not upstairs, or in the bathroom?' Carrie paced the room, searching places she had already eliminated just moments ago. She had to be seen to care though, which she did. She left the room and darted up the stairs. A quick glance in the kitchen; nothing. The same in the bathroom and lounge. All the while, she could hear Birdy crying.

Pacing back around the bathroom area, she spied the closed door to the boiler room. It was the only room she had not searched. It had to be done. She opened the door and switched on the light. Scanning the room, she had no time to entertain more strange noises.

'Oh!' she gasped as the tatty bear sat propped up against the locked door. *Thank God* ... Darting over to the wooden door, she bent down to snatch the bear in her hands. 'I've found him, hiding in the room. What did I tell you about going in there? You shouldn't be playing in there.' She was aware her tone was harsh.

'I wasn't.' Birdy protested between breathy sobs. 'I didn't go in there, I promise.'

'Then how come ...?' Carrie paused, sensing the argument could go round in circles. She had left her playing in front of the window first thing in the morning. There was every possibility that Birdy had wandered into that room for a new space to play. Soon she was back in bed, clutching Mr Bear as though he were long lost treasure. Carrie moved to stroke down her hair and clammy face. 'All settled again, go to sleep now.'

Birdy sniffed and managed a weak smile. Carrie mirrored this and leant over to kiss her goodnight.

Upstairs, she relaxed back against the sofa cushions and poured an over-generous glass of wine before reaching for her new mobile. Her mother answered on the first ring, and they exchanged greetings.

'Sorry, I was going to ring earlier but Birdy had a problem with her teddy.' she breathed loudly. 'It's so good to hear your voice! You sound a bit tired, are you okay?'

'I'm fine ... fine, just busy packing ready to visit Uncle Al,' her mother reassured her. 'But you sound much more relaxed than the last time we spoke.'

Carrie told her some brief details about their house, what the area was like and how busy their day had been.

'So, can you tell me where you are?' her mother enquired anxiously. 'I could come and get you in a few weeks, when the dust has settled a bit.'

Carrie pondered over the question. Surely this wouldn't cause any problems. It was her mother, after all. She highly doubted the phone was tapped or anything.

'Okay,' she sighed after a while and recited the address. Her mother repeated it back to her.

Carrie's eyes welled up as she realised her mother was now away for a few weeks. 'So, you're ready for a few weeks with Al?' she tried to sound as upbeat as she could. The last thing she wanted to do was make her mother feel guilty about spending time with her own brother. She would be fine until she got back.

'Yes, packing like crazy!' She paused. 'Will *you* be okay? If you need me, I could just...' The break in the conversation was deliberate – Carrie knew she would be pushed to find someone else to help with her uncle.

'Don't for one minute suggest that you're not going!' Carrie joked. 'We'll be fine ...'

There was a long silence between them. 'Okay, if you're sure. I'll let you go now,' she replied. 'Use that money to get some bits for Birdy, I'm guessing you couldn't have left with much.'

'Thank you,' Carrie smiled. 'I love you and I'll call you when you get back.' She still held onto the phone after her mother had ended the call on her end. Had she sounded okay? Carrie thought she had sounded a bit preoccupied but reasoned this was due to how busy she was at the moment. She was very active for someone of her age and liked to have plenty of things to do. Maybe moving back to her mother's wasn't a bad idea after all. She was very near the coast and Birdy loved the sea.

Carrie must have had more wine than she thought as she slipped into a deep sleep very quickly. There were no visits from Birdy in the night and no other disturbances.

DAY 6

Her head felt heavy as she managed to force open her eyes. Carrie peered at the gap in the door from her bed and brought her hand to her head. *Did I really drink that much last night?* It felt as though she was nursing the beginnings of a hangover. She could hear movement from upstairs and realised that Birdy must have already made her own way up for breakfast. Puddles of milk surrounded by cereal would decorate the kitchen table and probably be waiting for her to clear away.

'Are you okay?' she asked, seeing that Birdy had settled herself in front of the television. 'You're up early.'

'I was woken up early.'

For one moment, Carrie was dreading to hear the mention of the knocking on the door again. Yes, she had managed to account for the figure in the window – a senile old man who didn't know whether he was coming or going but the noises were a different story. Knocking was purposeful, not accidental.

'I got too hot,' she interrupted Carrie out of the thoughts. 'My room was hot and I couldn't reach to open the window. Up here, the air is colder.'

'Hmm, I guess it is a bit warm in here.' She felt a nearby radiator and the heat quickly warmed her hand. It was well into summer and the last thing they needed was the heating coming on every morning in the middle of a heatwave. Carrie thought about turning off the heating program on the boiler, it should only be a matter of adjusting the timer. Very simple. Except that it then dawned on her where the boiler was.

'Any noises last night?' she tried to sound as upbeat as possible. 'Birdy?'

She shook her head.

Carrie smiled but wasn't convincing herself. Knocking sounds could also be attributed to old pipes too. But a thought crept into her head – they would surely be more regular and at the same time of day, when the heating and water system were scheduled, not at random times in the middle of the night?

Carrie walked carefully down the stairs back to their bedrooms. She would bite the bullet and go and look at the boiler herself. Yes, Birdy was fairly astute for a child her age and she had gained some knowledge other children wouldn't necessarily have from being home schooled, but she could also be a bit scatty at times and quirky. Carrie herself had not heard the noises. These had all come from the word of a five-year-old. She felt a bit guilty at disbelieving the word of her child. Still, she pushed the door cautiously but then after a few moments, dared to shove the door open wide. It appeared to look exactly the same as the previous night when she had frantically searched for Mr Bear. Whatever the noise was, there was a locked door which on inspection the other day, didn't look as though it had been opened for a long time.

She flipped down the cover for the panel on the boiler and saw indeed that the heating program was on. The timings suggested it was always on. To her dismay, Carrie couldn't even see a button to disable it temporarily. She couldn't recall having seen the instruction manual for the boiler. There had been no mention of it in the household manual either. The last thing she wanted to do was manage to turn it off and then struggle to restart it should they need it again. Carrie breathed deeply, wondering what to do. Then she remembered Valerie's appraisal at next door's ability to sort out the maintenance. She may never run into dear old Agnes again but a note through her letterbox would do.

Carrie wrote a short note detailing the problems with

the boiler and whether Agnes would be able to adjust the settings for her. She sat wondering what to do with the rest of the day. Should she start to get Birdy back into the routine of learning? Should they go out again and check her emails? Carrie was curious as to whether Jon had sent any further messages or whether he had given up. After all, her mother had said she hadn't heard from him yesterday. Perhaps a call to her was what she needed. After Birdy announced she would play downstairs, Carrie reached for her new mobile and dialled her mother's number. It was the only contact in the memory. She marvelled at how mobiles had changed from the one she had back home. This one would only accept and make calls and as she recalled from models she had in the past, this would hold its charge quite well.

She frowned as her mum's phone rang constantly. Perhaps she'd popped out for a few last-minute bits for her trip away, she reasoned to herself. All of a sudden, she heard an ear-splitting scream coming from Birdy's room. Throwing the phone down onto the sofa, she jumped up. Bolting down the staircase, she almost slipped at the bottom.

'For the love of God, what's happened!' She addressed Birdy, who by now was sitting facing the patio whilst wailing and pointing. Her breathing was ragged so it was up to Carrie to see for herself what was so upsetting. On the patio, she could see several dead birds and some in the process of dying.

'Oh, my goodness!' she exclaimed and craned her neck upwards to see if there was anything to explain this phenomenon. She resigned herself to the fact that it was very unusual for this to be a natural occurrence. She counted at least six birds; they'd all chosen this spot to die?

'It's okay, it's okay,' she gathered Birdy up in her arms. From the corner of her eye, she could just about make out a movement from the neighbouring window. It was as though it had been slammed shut quickly. Not able to link what that could possibly have with the death of half a dozen birds, she felt that they needed to leave the room. Pulling the curtain closed, she carried Birdy back up the stairs.

'What happened, sweetheart?' she asked, once they

were safely in the lounge area.

Her breathing was ragged. 'We were just playing...'

Carrie knew 'we' meant Birdy plus her stuffed toys.

'...and then they just started falling. Polly was one of them, she came to see me this morning.' The sobs were more controlled now.

'Did you see anything, from next door?'

Birdy frowned and shook her head. Carrie soothed her hair down and held her close. 'Maybe they were just poorly,' she offered quietly. 'Or maybe they were just tired and stopped for a rest and will fly away later.' She didn't remotely imagine this to be credible herself but wondered whether this would be believable to a five-year-old – one who desperately wanted to know that the birds would be okay after a while.

'Do you want to go out and get some fresh air?' she added quickly before Birdy had a chance to react to this. All of a sudden, the house felt stifling.

Birdy looked up at her and nodded slowly whilst sniffing.

'We'll go and get some ice cream if you like, I just need to stop off and check my emails again.' At the back of her mind, she still had a niggling desire to want to scroll through the messages again.

Outside, she reached for Birdy's hand before securing the front door. Carrie tried to look discreetly up at number 28, just to see if there was any movement. She shook her head as they walked in the direction of the shops. Further down the main road, a small school was signposted at the next left. Carrie reasoned that where there was a school, there was usually a play area not too far away. She was right. The park was spacious and a large play area was situated next to what looked to be a good picnic spot. As she pushed Birdy on the swing, she wondered about whether it might be time to enrol her into mainstream education, once they were more settled. She concentrated well at home when they worked together but Birdy needed to mix with other children as well.

'Just another few minutes.' She gave Birdy her five-minute warning, which seemed to work quite well at times when their departure was imminent. Carrie was relieved to see that she had calmed down since the events of earlier. Once they were at home, she knew she faced the grisly task of having to remove all of the feathery bodies.

At the internet café, Birdy clambered into the chair next to Carrie.

'Can I send a message to Nanny today on the computer?' She asked as Carrie logged into her email account.

'Sure, I'll help you type it if you want. But remember Nanny is away soon and might not see your message straight away,' her words stuck in her throat. Waiting for her inbox to refresh, she felt herself pale as the top email screamed out at her:

Maggie Fuller: CARRIE, OPEN THIS NOW!

She gasped and with shaking fingers, she managed to click on the link to open it.

'Mummy, is that from Nanny? What does she say? When can I do my message?' Birdy began to pull herself up so that she was kneeling on the chair. Carried found herself looking around Birdy's head as she momentarily blocked the screen.

'Please, Birdy!' she admonished her. 'Just let Mummy read it, please!' She added as a pouted face looked back at her. 'I'm sorry, sweetie, this just looks important.' However, Birdy remained with the same scornful expression on her face as she turned her head to the side in a temper and sank back into her seat.

Carrie was able to read the message in its entirety:

Carrie,

This is very important, Jon has been round to visit. He was here when you called and made me tell him your address. I'm sorry, he wasn't threatening or anything and said he just wants to talk to you. He was here for hours crying. I don't know what's happened between you two that made you leave, he didn't elaborate but said that you have a few issues and he is seeking help. I know you've been unhappy with him in the past, that's your business but he genuinely seemed like he wanted to sort things out.

I've not been able to call you as I stupidly dropped my phone down the toilet and couldn't recall your number. Call the police if you need to. Call me as soon as you get this message.
Mum xxx

Carrie looked at the time sent and saw that it was dated the previous day. She squinted at the numbers to make sure she was reading them correctly. According to her inbox, the message had been sent not long after she had sent the email thanking her mum for the money. If only she had stayed logged on for a while longer last night. She racked her brain as to when she had spoken to her mother last night. It was after this email. What was going on? Her heart sank when she realised the message was sent nearly twenty-four hours ago. It would not take Jon that long to get here from their house. Surely he would have arrived by now?

'Mummy?'

Carrie was unaware of how long Birdy had been trying to get her attention. She turned to face her and her expression must have said everything – Birdy did not ask again to go on the computer.

'We need to go home,' Carrie's voice was practically a whisper. She looked back at the screen, not sure what to reply. In the past, she had glossed over the worst of the abuse from Jon when speaking to her mother. Shame had prevented her from giving the full picture. She had always painted him to be a difficult man to live with at times, often with a temper and quite controlling. However, she had never given any details of her suffering. When she thought back over their relationship, the good times were also peppered with the bad.

Carrie quickly typed out a reply, not even sure if she would see it: *He's not here. I'll call the police if I need to.* She got to her feet and for a few moments worried that her legs would not support her. All of a sudden, she felt quite light-headed. They walked back together in silence, although Birdy seemed quite upbeat and almost skipped along the road.

'What are you looking for, Mummy? You keep

checking behind us.' Birdy's tone sounded irritated.

'Nothing sweetie,' Carrie mumbled back. She took one glance back behind them as she reached for the keys. Being so busy trying to find them, she hadn't seen Birdy scamper ahead to the rubbish bins. On top of one lay what looked to be a small book.

'Birdy, wait!' she called out to warn her, but it was already too late as she had picked it up. She stood and looked over her shoulder as Birdy lifted the cover carefully. Not sure what she expected to see, she was surprised abet confused.

'They're pretty, can I keep the book?' Birdy had already clutched it to her chest, claiming it.

Carrie pulled a face, 'Birdy, if it's been left on the bin, then I'm guessing it's rubbish and meant to be in it.' She sighed, weighing up the potential threat of it. It was an old album and surely innocent as it looked. 'Bring it in if you insist.' She dismissed this as something she didn't need to be overly concerned about. However, the idea of someone leaving a leather-bound book containing pages of several pressed flowers seemed quite peculiar. And to leave it right on top of her bin? She wondered if it were just a case of the person just hadn't bothered to open the lid and throw it in.

Inside, she pinched the top of her nose, feeling the start of a headache. Meanwhile, Birdy tucked the book under her arm as she picked up a piece of paper that was sticking out of the letterbox.

'Can have Cl ... i ... v...' Birdy clutched the paper as she struggled to read it. Carrie must have walked past it whilst she had been preoccupied.

'Let me see, baby,' she gestured for her to hand her the note. The writing was neat with sloping letters. *Can have Clive the handyman look at the boiler Monday if that suits you? Did call over earlier but you must have been out. Agnes.*

Birdy was waiting expectantly at her side. 'It's just someone coming to sort out the heating. We'll have to stay in on Monday.' Carrie mentally calculated the date and realised that tomorrow was Sunday. This Clive must be a very good tradesman if he was willing to call over at such short notice, the next working day for that matter. 'Go and watch television for a bit. I'll see what there is for dinner.' Carrie suddenly felt very tired.

She moved to the kitchen and rang her mother. The call was answered almost immediately.

'Carrie?'

'Yes, it's me …'

'Darling, I'm sorry. He just showed up and wouldn't leave. If I thought you were in any danger, I wouldn't have given him your address. You wouldn't believe how upset he was, broken I'd say. You've really given him a wake-up call.'

Carrie waited for her to say her piece. It had obviously been building up inside her.

'I couldn't call you or anything to warn you. Is he there yet?'

She shook her head but realised her mother couldn't see her. 'No, he's not here …'

'I'd thought he'd be there by now.'

So did I. Carrie thought. She had imagined the scenario. He would have left almost immediately. After Jon found out where she was, he would be hammering on the door at all hours, demanding to be let in. She would be cowering in the corner, and either give in to the fear or summon the courage to call the police. She was almost watching a slowing wheel of fortune as to which option this would settle on.

'It's not your fault,' she heard herself explain. *Maybe I should have specified not to give my address to Jon under any circumstances, to call the police if he shows up. He is a dangerous man … that is why I tried to get rid of him, to kill him and didn't want him to be able to find me, ever.*

Or was he as dangerous as she feared? He'd had a whole day to announce his arrival and so far had not shown up. Carrie went through the motions of further conversations with her mother. She did not mention how afraid of him she was. She gave her mother her phone number again, should anything happen to her phone and also reassured her not to come down. Her mother needed to go away as planned. If Jon did get violent, she did not want her mother to be in the firing line.

Systematically, she went through the motions of preparing the dinner for her and Birdy when a thought struck her; what if Jon had travelled down and was biding his time before knocking on her door? What if he was nearby, just watching and waiting?

The thought made her feel sick and clammy. Feeling nauseous, she found herself dry-heaving over the kitchen sink. This idea was surely more terrifying to know that he could be watching and planning his strategy carefully, ready to pounce. If she did leave and go on the run again, he would surely follow. Carrie was tempted to call the police. *What should I say? My violent husband is after me, but I haven't seen him as yet? He's on his way but for some reason, is taking hours to make the journey?* They'd think her stupid. She'd not contacted the police regarding his behaviour yet and doubted they would take this loose threat as seriously for a first-time offence.

Thankfully, Birdy was quite happy to go to bed at a reasonable hour. The curtains were closed tight even though Carrie had cleared up the patio area. She had managed to race down while Birdy had been preoccupied with her pudding. Holding the deceased birds as far away from her as she could, she had proceeded to dump them all into a black plastic bag which she'd tossed into the outside bin. Thankfully, the album featuring the pressed flowers had distracted her from the events of that morning.

However, being on her own after Birdy had gone to bed meant that she now started to replay the day's events in excruciating detail, reliving the horror at reading her mother's email. Carrie found herself starting to feel sleepy, so she laid her head back on the sofa.

She jolted awake as a small hand rocked her arm back and forth. For a moment, it took her a while to get her bearings, where she was, what time it was. It was now pitch dark and she was still on the sofa.

'Mummy,' Birdy shook her awake.

'What, what is it, baby? She mumbled groggily.

'I was sick in my bed,' her voice was small and strained. 'My tummy hurts and I can't get back to sleep.'

Carrie reached over and felt for the switch on the

side lamp. Her eyes were not fully focused, but she could still make out Birdy's flushed cheeks. She stretched over and put a hand to her forehead. 'You do feel hot, honey. Have you had a drink of water? Do you want to jump into Mummy's bed, and I'll sort your sheets out? I'll be there in a minute.' She forced herself up from the sofa as Birdy made the journey back downstairs. Her footsteps spoke volumes about how much energy she had as her feet dragged along heavily. Carrie shuffled to Birdy's room and was hit by the smell of undigested food. She held her breath as she quickly pulled the duvet back and exposed the under sheet. Stripping the bed, she decided to put the sheets outside in the patio area with a mind to sort them out in the morning. In the bathroom, she washed her hands and retrieved a nearby bucket, just in case.

Birdy had settled herself with the duvet pulled up under her chin. Her eyes looked heavy as though she was ready to drop off again at any moment.

'I've put the bucket there, just in case,' Carrie announced. She began to feel a bit hot herself and moved some of the duvet off her as Birdy snuggled close. 'Too much dinner?' She couldn't think of any other reason why she would be sick. Probably just one of those twenty-four-hour stomach bugs.

Birdy began to drift off asleep. She made a few attempts to string a sentence together. 'The noises were there again. The knocking woke me up again, Mummy.'

DAY 7

It was too hot in the bed, the heating had come on full force and Carrie could already see sunrays forcing their way through the gap in her door. It was as though the house's central heating was mocking her as it bellowed out its heat. She looked across at Birdy and reckoned that would be her for the day as her cheeks were still reddened and she felt clammy to the touch. She went to the bathroom and wet a flannel, half tempted to go back and sponge Birdy down but she found herself dampening her own face. There was definitely a heatwave coming, which was pushing away the rainclouds they'd had all week. Just what she needed – a poorly child running a temperature, a house like a furnace and Sahara Desert conditions outside.

Birdy still hadn't stirred after Carrie had been to make a coffee so she decided to jump into a cold shower in an attempt to cool herself down. Leaving the bathroom door open in case Birdy needed to be sick again, she went through the last words Birdy had said before drifting off to sleep. This was getting quite worrying now. One instance of hearing knocking sounds could be brushed off but now several recounts of the same occurrence gave her an uneasy feeling. However, Birdy was sick and this could be explained away by her delirious state last night.

Carrie dried herself off quickly and threw on the lightest clothes she could find. A trip to the shops for further supplies was definitely in order once Birdy felt up to it.

'Hey, how's my baby?' she cooed, pressing the flannel onto her forehead.

'My tummy still hurts.' Birdy moved to put a hand on top of the duvet in case Carrie needed any convincing.

'I've got you a drink, let me know if you feel hungry. Maybe you could try some toast later? I think you should stay in bed for today.'

For a moment, Birdy's eyes grew wide. 'Will you be here with me Mummy? I don't want to be left down here by myself.' Her voice wobbled slightly.

'You've nothing to be worried about.' Carrie shook her head. 'Whatever the noises are, you only seem to hear them at night, right? Well, it's the daytime now.'

'Please, Mummy, can I just lay upstairs on the sofa? I promise I'll be good.'

Carrie breathed deeply and looked at her sorrowful face. 'Okay, then. I'll set you up on the sofa upstairs.' If she were being honest, she would also welcome the presence of someone else, even if it was her poorly child. Having Birdy tucked away downstairs would prove to be a long and lonely day.

She smiled as Birdy lay comfortably snuggled under the duvet holding Mr Bear. The television played at a low volume. Carrie had not bought a thermometer but guessed that Birdy was running a low-grade fever. Nothing to worry about as she had managed to keep some fluids down her. Glancing at the clock, Carrie saw that it was almost eleven o'clock. Hadn't Valerie the old nosey neighbour mentioned Agnes went to church on a Sunday? Perhaps she could catch her whilst she was walking back. Carrie went and looked out of the bay window which faced onto the street; she could not see anyone in the immediate area but held onto the door keys, just in case she needed to dart out suddenly.

Several minutes passed before Carrie was interrupted by coughing coming from the sofa. She jumped up, already on alert. 'Are you okay, honey?' She feared Birdy was about to be sick again.

'Hmm,' she mumbled incoherently and fidgeted to get comfortable again. Carrie looked out of the window again and this time could see a figure slowly walking up towards the house.

'I'll be a few moments,' she informed Birdy, although she wasn't sure if she had dropped off to sleep again as there was no response. Carrie took the keys but secured the door in the latch as well. She waited for Agnes to get closer.

'Good morning!' she painted the best smile she could on her face as Agnes walked level with her, Carrie slowed her pace to match hers. Agnes's face morphed from deep concentration to what looked like a rehearsed greeting.

'Good morning to you too, dear. Everything running smoothly?'

Carrie nodded. 'Apart from the heat, but thank you for arranging someone to come so soon.' She added this last part as she did not want to appear as the nagging tenant who had found something to complain about after being there less than a week.

'Yes, it is quite hot, dear.' Agnes fanned herself down with an exaggerated swish of her hand.

Carrie was just about to correct her that she had been referring to the inside of the house as opposed to the outside but decided against it. 'My daughter is poorly,' she motioned with her head back to the house, 'but I just wanted to catch you before you went back inside.' She took a few steps away from the door. 'Um ...' She was not sure where to begin. 'My daughter has commented on a few strange noises during the night.' She smiled weakly. 'You know how children are, making things seem worse than they are,' Carrie laughed quietly at her own joke.

'Noises, dear?' She looked every part the concerned friend.

'Oh, just knocking on the door in the basement, where the boiler is. Not into late-night DIY, are you?' Again, she tried to sound as jovial as she could.

She waited for Agnes to respond but was just met with pursed lips and a frowning expression. Carrie wasn't sure if for a moment she had misunderstood the question or simply did not understand what she was saying. Thoughts raced through her mind on how to re-word this and move on from the uncomfortable silence.

'You'll find no one doing any building work around here,' she stated finally.

'Oh, well …' Carrie stuttered. 'I think I've seen your husband, in the top room?' she gestured upwards, even though the courtyard area wasn't visible from the street.

'That won't be my husband, dear. He's virtually bed-bound you see.'

'Oh, I'm sorry,' Carrie offered. She frowned and wondered how many answers she'd actually had from her conversation with dear old Agnes. She really was as scatty as when they had first met and had no reasonable explanations of the noises coming from the basement. 'No, there's definitely someone in the window.'

'That would probably be my old mannequin,' Agnes replied. 'I used to be a seamstress back in the day. All my things are still in my sewing room. That's probably what you are seeing.' She smiled widely. 'Go inside and see, dear. I'll show you from the window.'

Carrie moved her mouth to speak but instead found herself nodding along. 'The window, yes, okay,' she replied, flustered, and turned back to the house as Agnes stood waiting. Once inside, she saw Agnes pass by the bay window. Despite the fact that Carrie would have easily got to the bathroom before her by just simply walking at her normal pace, she still moved at double speed to the downstairs bathroom and pulled up the blind. She could hear herself breathing loudly as she waited expectantly.

After a few minutes, she wondered whether the old woman was simply stringing her along in an effort to get rid of her. And it had worked – outsmarted by a lady who had to be well into her seventies if not more. She went through their encounter again outside in her head. What had she actually gained from that? Agnes had brushed off her comments regarding the noises and Carrie still had no explanation of the source. She was back to now doubting her daughter's word again. She was interrupted by these thoughts as a light went on in the house next door. Agnes had pulled up her blind too and was now stood at the window, having dragged the mannequin so it now dominated the whole window. She stood with a smile on her face that Carrie could only describe almost macabre. She appeared as though she were holding up a trophy, a serial killer displaying their latest victim.

However, she had proved that the image in the window had been a dummy all along and not the dirty old pervert that Carrie had feared. It could indeed have been the slim figure she had seen in the window. For a moment, she felt like such a fool as she gave a half-hearted wave to Agnes and smiled. Seemingly satisfied, Agnes moved away from the window with the mannequin in tow. Carrie did not lower the blind and instead walked away. She did not want Agnes to see she was still mulling over the view and that part of her still was just not convinced. She was about to leave the bathroom when she had a change of heart. Checking to see what was now happening next door, she decided to lower the blind. Part of her still felt conspicuous with such an exposed view.

Back upstairs, Birdy had nodded off again. Carrie checked her temperature by placing her hand on her chest. She could feel the rise and fall as Birdy breathed deeply. So far, there had been no more sickness episodes. Carrie was relieved that whatever illness this was, it wasn't enough to panic and rush her to the nearest A&E or feel the need to contact an emergency doctor. But it did mean that they were confined to the house until she was back on her feet. In all that had happened that morning, Carrie's mind cast back to the feeling she had been pushing down since yesterday which was now bubbling up like a pressure pot. Jon still had not shown up.

The rest of their Sunday allowed Carrie too much time to think. She idled away the afternoon by watching television programmes suitable for Birdy, who had by now woken up again but was still not her usual self, whilst fidgeting anxiously. She was slightly disappointed when Birdy showed signs of wanting to go back to bed. Carrie had by now sorted out her room and tried her best to get rid of the smell but was secretly happy when she asked to share her bed again.

'Still feeling a bit poorly?' she sympathised with her. She didn't want to ask outright how she felt about sleeping alone in the room closest to the boiler room. Birdy simply nodded. She bent to kiss her head and gave her a tender smile.

Carrie ran herself a bath and reclined in the warm water. Staring at the closed blind, she could not see any light behind it. She allowed her eyes to close momentarily but then opened them abruptly to find the water was markedly cooler. Unsure of how long she had been asleep, she reached over and turned on the hot tap. The pipes complained as a rhythmic clunking sound was evident as the water flowed. *Great - dodgy pipes too*. Silently thanking God that she didn't own the house and this wouldn't be her problem after a few weeks, she turned off the tap. The groaning of the pipework stopped but a faint knocking took its place. Carrie froze, goose bumps forming on her skin even though the bath water had resumed a pleasant temperature.

Why did I doubt my own child? Of course she would not make something up like this. With her heart in her mouth, she reached for the towel and made short work of exiting the bath. She padded anxiously and stood outside the closed door. If she were likening her situation to a horror film, it would now surely be a foolish decision to go and seek the source of a strange noise in the middle of the night. The hapless victim in such films usually met their end here – disposed of by the crazy knife-wielding maniac hiding on the other side of the door. Her stomach knotted as she held onto the doorknob. Why shouldn't she go in? What was the actual threat with a locked door between her and next door? Was it so worrying to hear a few banging sounds from next door?

The boiler room had a musty odour to it and remained dark as she decided against turning the light on in case it woke Birdy up. She propped the door open to provide some light from the bathroom and avoid the inevitable 'door slamming shut by itself only to mysteriously open the next morning' scenario. As though she were measuring the room with the length of her feet, she walked in a straight line to the blue door. Pausing, she stood stock-still waiting for the knocking sounds. There was nothing. As she drew closer, shuffling sounds on the other side started faintly before becoming increasingly louder and nearer. Carrie held her breath as she pressed her ear against the wood – waiting.

She let out a gasp as it sounded as though someone was pacing on the other side of the door. The strides were getting closer together as though the person on the other side grew more frantic. The noise stopped as abruptly as they had started as Carrie took the shallowest breaths she could manage in an attempt to disguise her presence further. The noises had stopped but Carrie was convinced the person was still on the other side of the door, planning what to do next. It was as though whoever it was could see through the door and was watching her, waiting for her to leave the room. The silence hung heavily in the air.

She jumped as furious banging began against the door in the pattern of a drumroll. Paralysed, Carrie could only stand in horror as she whimpered quietly. It had been a while since she had been rooted to the spot in sheer fright, but she actually felt every part of her refusing to move away from the door. Her mind threw up images of a gorilla-sized man, using his full force to powerfully pound away on the door. Carrie could feel what she assumed were flakes of paint in her hair as they were dislodged from the surface. The hinges whined in protest. Her expression contorted into one of sheer panic as she didn't even acknowledge the trickle working its way down her leg and pooling at her feet.

The banging slowed down to resemble a metronome counting at one-second intervals. Carrie found herself entranced by this pulse – *bang, bang, bang, bang* ... Then, silence again. The only sound now was her breathy pants as she struggled to normalise her breathing. She placed a palm against the surface of the door and for a moment, imagined she'd felt it vibrating. Carrie had no idea how long she remained standing by the door; it could have been minutes or hours for all she knew. All the time, she doubted her sanity – had she just witnessed such a violent disturbance? For all she knew, this was how Agnes coped with the pent-up tension of having to care for an incapacitated husband. She recalled the pensive expression she had seen her wear while out walking in the street – the woman had a lot on her mind with a poorly husband to worry about. Everyone needed to let off a bit of steam every now and again, didn't they?

Carrie's focus soon began to sharpen and she found her feet were willing to move. She retreated out of the room, as quietly as she had entered, but all of the time her eyes were fixed on the door. Her reasoning began to kick in – this was not normal behaviour for a next-door neighbour to witness. It was quite frankly, disturbing, not one she wished to ever repeat. Once she had closed the door, she leant with her back against it as she put a hand to her mouth to repress her sobs. Embarrassed, she was now aware she had lost control of one of the most basic bodily functions she had always taken for granted. She covered her face with both hands and sobbed quietly. The house now stood silent again.

DAY 8

The banging started again but this time, the person on the other side managed to force their way through. The door had been rammed off its hinges and had fallen in pieces onto the floor. He emerged in a shroud of smoke as though the very ground had opened up beneath him and he'd crawled up through the depths of Hell. It had been easy to find her as Carrie had collapsed in fear, clutching at her chest as she struggled with every breath. He towered over her, teeth bared in a ghoulish grin before bending over as his hands found the side of her head and gripped it tightly as he squeezed. She felt her head throb as her eyes bulged. The laugh coming from him was the most terrifying thing though – he was actually enjoying it.

Carrie woke up with a start. A thin film of sweat covered her. She felt damp all over and for a horrible moment, feared she had wet the bed. Aware she was still shaking, she allowed the comfort of reality to seep in, the brightness from outside evident through the door. She had been dreaming, that was all. However, she had read somewhere that dreams could reflect the fears in real life, and this was certainly evidence of that. She had been petrified last night to the point of paralysis.

Birdy shifted in her sleep next to her as she lay oblivious to last night's events. Had she woken up, she surely would have been hysterical. Carrie decided to allow her to sleep but the movement of her getting out of the bed disturbed her.

'How are you feeling, sweetie?'

'A bit better,' she murmured, still somewhat groggy.

How can a child sleep so heavily? Carrie noted that Birdy had a bit of colour back in her cheeks and did not look as glassy-eyed as she had done yesterday.

'I'm getting up as I'm not sure what time the man is coming to look at the boiler,' she looked down on her daughter. 'I'll make you some toast?' She was relieved as Birdy nodded. Carrie returned her smile and went upstairs. She thought again of the previous night – perhaps it was time to cut short their tenancy and find somewhere else to move to. Whatever she had witnessed in the boiler room, she knew that she could not stay another night waiting for the same thing to happen.

Upstairs, Carrie looked around for her phone and frowned. She was positive she had left it on the sofa last night. She turned over a few cushions looking for it and tried to think where it could be. Okay, it didn't have internet access, but she might need to make a few calls. Birdy sat at the kitchen table, clearly struggling to manage one piece of toast. She chewed slowly and grimaced as she swallowed. There was no way she was up to sitting in the internet café whilst Carrie perused more properties for them to move into. And what was the guarantee that they would be ready now or at an affordable price as this was? Carrie realised there was no way she would get a refund for the rent on this house. She would be throwing money away which was something they could not afford to do at the best of times. Still, she needed to talk to Agnes and raise her concerns about the incident last night.

The knock on the door made her jump more than necessary. Carrie was aware her nerves were still on edge. She breathed deeply in an effort to mentally pull herself together as she went to answer the door. The two figures on the doorstep reminded her of a couple of cold-callers who had disturbed her and were most unwelcome. However, Carrie recognised Agnes straight away and saw a man young enough to be her son standing next to her. They were both smiling as

Carrie raised her eyebrows. She was surprised to see Agnes for a woman who supposedly hardly went out.

'Dear, this is Clive, who I told you about. He's come to look at the boiler.' She pointed in towards the house in a silent gesture to be let in.

Carrie shuddered at her greeting. 'Of course.' She opened the door wide and stood aside. Clive was old enough to be her father as what looked like once dark hair was speckled with grey flecks. His face looked quite weathered, suggesting he was quite outdoorsy or did a lot of work in the open air.

'Thank you.' He wiped his feet on the doormat, a symbol of civility rather than necessity; it was neither rainy nor muddy outside to warrant this. Carrie took it as a natural measure he took before entering another house suggesting that it came as second nature working as a tradesman.

'Mind if I go and take a look?' He nodded in the direction of the downstairs.

'Clive's been here before,' Agnes confirmed. This seemed to be the permission to go that Clive had been waiting for as he disappeared down the flight of stairs to the boiler room. Carrie was more than happy to let him go alone - *let him witness any strange goings-on.* Part of her guessed that all would be normal now in the room, it was daylight after all, but at the same time, half-expected to hear him call out regarding a strange knocking noise. Carrie was half-hoping that he would report hearing something, anything to confirm she was not losing her mind. However, the prime suspect or the person who would be able to provide the best explanation was standing in front of her. After a few moments, all she could hear were the sounds of him moving downstairs.

She was left to stand awkwardly next to Agnes, who had not moved but still stood with a fixed smile on her face. Carrie smiled back and cleared her throat a few times.

'Can I get you a coffee or tea?'

'That would be lovely, dear,' she replied as Carrie retreated to the kitchen area. Carrie could still see that Birdy was nursing the second piece of toast now.

'You can go and watch television if you want, leave

that if you've had enough.' Carrie followed her daughter out of the kitchen whilst the kettle was boiling, in case the sight of Agnes stood there would frighten her. She wasn't even sure if Birdy was aware they had visitors. Birdy gave her a fleeting glance as she walked past her.

'She's feeling a bit under the weather,' Carrie explained.

'Oh, poor sweet girl,' Agnes cooed. They watched as she disappeared from sight and soon enough, the noise from the television filled the silence.

Carrie fixed the most serious expression on her face as she could. There was no way Agnes was going back without providing some answers about last night.

'Agnes, last night, I heard what I could only describe as a disturbance ...'

Agnes was quick to reply and cut her off mid-sentence. 'Oh, they disturbed you, too, did they?'

Carrie's mouth moved to form some words before she managed to stutter. 'Th ... they?'

'We've had some bother for a few months now, local children, I think. They climb through the fence in our back garden and make the most awful racket. I do my best to secure the fence again, but it must be easy to force open repeatedly.' She put her hand to her mouth. 'I've called the police several times, I'll have you know but as always, they've moved on before the police arrive.' She frowned as lines of worry decorated her features.

Carrie stood, dumbfounded for a moment. She wasn't sure what to say. In any case, that had been an awfully quick knee-jerk response to her concerns. From the kitchen, she could hear the kettle bubbling to indicate it was ready.

'How do you take your tea?' she heard herself ask.

'Milk and sugar please.'

Agnes remained in the entrance as Carrie dutifully went to make a cup for her and Clive. She frowned as she reached for the teabags and sugar. That speech had been a little too rehearsed for the liking: *she hadn't even told Agnes what kind of disturbance she had encountered ...*

Carrie smirked as she decided to call her bluff.

Smiling to herself, she returned with two cups in her hands and handed one over. 'Agnes, I don't believe I told you what kind of disturbance we had last night?' She felt somewhat elated that she wasn't prepared to accept the brush-off by the old woman again.

Agnes regarded her and a scornful look had taken over her cheery expression. Her tone was clipped. 'You don't need to. It's the banging, isn't it? I told you, we've had the same thing before.'

Carrie was sure she heard a tutting sound at the end of her little speech and it hadn't escaped her that the 'dear' sentiment had been absent. Any confidence she had felt at the start of their conversation was rapidly decreasing. Again, she felt shot-down and dismissed of any legitimate concerns. It was almost as though she was to accept this back-handed comment, *oh don't worry about the banging, we hear it too…* Carrie was sure she paled as her memory replayed part of the incident from last night, she felt her cheeks heat up as she recalled the embarrassment of wetting herself. Nervous at not wanting any further confrontation now, Carrie shifted from foot to foot. She was somewhat relieved as Clive re-emerged from the downstairs.

'All fixed, Agnes. It's the same problem as before.'

Carrie looked back and forth at them as though she were watching a tennis match. She was waiting for the next serve. Agnes nodded her head, clearly understanding his reply.

'The boiler needs replacing,' Clive directed this to Carrie now. *Thank goodness he's taken it seriously*, she thought, *after all, it is* me *paying the rent on this place.* It might not be Agnes's house but she had been entrusted with ensuring it was safe and habitable for tenants.

'It's safe though, right?' she heard herself ask. She had visions of it exploding in the middle of the night.

He nodded reassuringly. 'It's not about to combust or anything.' He seemed to read her mind. 'If anything, it will just stop working one day. Just needs an upgrade, that's all.' He reached for his mug.

'Clive, we've had the trouble again with the local

children, do you think you could have a look at the fence again? My guess is some of the panels have come loose again. That will stop the rascals getting it.' Agnes made it sound as though she had asked this question already dozens of times.

He paused for a moment. 'Oh, yes the fence. Of course, I'll take a look at it.' He checked his watch, almost as though he was mentally figuring out if he'd have time today.

Carrie emitted a nervous laugh, 'I'm afraid I can't have that noise going on again, it was bad enough last night.' If the banging stopped, it might just extend her stay at this house a bit longer. There wouldn't be the urgency to find somewhere else.

'I can certainly have a look today, Agnes. If anything, I can secure the perimeter the best I can today even if it means I have to come back another day and make a proper job of it.'

Carrie noted how Agnes smiled and nodded in her direction. It was almost the smugness of, *see what I told you? We'll get this sorted* ... However, all Carrie wanted was for the noises at night to stop, she didn't care at what cost. Clive could rip the whole fence off and rebuild it for all she cared, as long as no one was able to get in. He smiled at her and replaced his cup on the side. For some reason, Carrie felt the urge to quiz him further about her weird landlady.

'Lovely cup, dear.' Agnes partnered her cup alongside Clive's. 'Well, if that will be all?'

'Umm...' Carrie paused, hoping that Agnes would shuffle off back to hers and she could catch Clive on his way out. Much to her disappointment, they headed for the door together.

Clive turned to face her. 'The original program for the heating and water has been restored. The heating should only kick in if it drops to a set temperature.' He placed his hand on a nearby radiator as if to confirm this. 'It's already much cooler.'

'Thank you,' Carrie drew her arms across her chest as she watched Agnes make her way to the house perimeter. It was as though she were walking a dog and dutifully waiting for Clive to come to heel before moving off. Carrie could see a white van parked in between their two houses and could only assume it belonged to him. She waited a few moments, nodding her thanks at the open door whilst he headed to open the back of his van. Agnes was slowly disappearing out of sight. Carrie couldn't delay it anymore and eventually closed her front door. She edged to the bay window so she would be able to see Clive even if he couldn't see her.

Birdy was still engrossed in the cartoons as Carrie watched Clive emerge with a toolbox from the back of his van. He went towards number 28. For a moment, Carrie had a longing to know what the inside of Agnes's house was like. She imagined it to have somewhat dated furnishing and possibly have that certain smell about it associated with an older generation. Not to mention a sickly old husband upstairs.

'Mummy, what are you doing?' a hoarse voice piped up from the sofa. Carrie was still standing by the window looking out onto the street.

'Nothing, baby. I'm just looking outside.' She pulled back on the curtain gathered at the side intending to drop it rapidly should anyone walk past. She had a good view onto the street seeing as the houses were all devoid of front gardens. Out of the corner of her eye, she saw what she had been waiting for.

'I'll just be out the front.' She didn't wait for Birdy's response and instead took the keys and put the door on the latch. Outside, despite the increasing temperature, she still felt a certain chill. She approached the man from behind as he rummaged in the back of his van. 'Excuse me,' she alerted him to her presence in case she frightened the life out of him.

He turned around to face her and for a moment, the look he gave her showed he wasn't glad to see her. His expression was blank and almost unreadable.

'It's Carrie,' she said and motioned to number 30.

'Oh, yes. Everything okay?'

Carrie faltered. She wasn't sure exactly what she wanted to say. 'I just had a few questions, if you have a minute.'

He paused and if she hadn't had been studying him,

waiting for his response, she would have missed the discreet glance he gave upwards towards the bedroom window. 'Of course. How can I help you?' His tone seemed more business-like than friendly.

'Um, well, I was wondering about the room the boiler is in.' It was the first thing that sprang into her mind and seemed an acceptable place to start, after all, he had just been in there.

'There is a door,' she continued. 'But I don't seem to have a key for it. I was just wondering, you know, in case these children come back and I… well, if I needed to go out there and have a word.' She was hoping he wouldn't size her up and wonder how she would sort out a group of unruly children. Her forced confidence wasn't fooling anyone and made a poor disguise for her mouse-like interior.

He seemed to ponder over her question. 'Hmm, I do have spare keys somewhere for when I do bits for Agnes. It's an old door lock, isn't it? I could have a look around for you if you like.'

'Thank you,' she smiled, slightly more relaxed and comforted that he was willing to engage in conversation without brushing her off. 'Look, I know you've worked for Agnes for many years, so she said. But last night, that was genuinely frightening, the noises I mean. I have a poorly child who thankfully was out cold by then, but I dread to think what would have happened if she'd been awake. Scared the life out of me it did.' She paused, waiting for his response and also thankful that she had managed to get all of that off her chest without interruption.

'Sadly, this isn't the best area,' he offered by some way of explanation. 'I'm guessing that once all the residents have left this street, then the houses will probably be demolished and redeveloped.'

Carrie nodded, not sure if where he was going with the line of conversation. 'You've known Agnes and her husband for a while then?' She waited for his response and for one horrible moment, was waiting for him to reply that Agnes's husband had died years ago and she wasn't sure who Carrie was talking about.

'That's right,' was all he offered.

'Hmm,' she pretended to ponder on this but could see that he wasn't willing to offer any more personal information about them. Perhaps she had overstepped the boundaries of casual conversation. Carrie decided to change the subject. 'So, the fence you are repairing, does it surround some kind of communal area outside? I wasn't sure if the locked door to the area outside was shared or …'

'It's kind of like a small outside area, yes,' he stated. 'The boiler room you have is an extension and part of the garden was compromised for it. You have a door leading to what's left of your garden. Agnes also has a door to the outside and there's a fence that separates the houses that back onto these. That's the one that's damaged. Agnes has neighbouring kids that clamber through it for kicks. Bored I reckon.'

'Okay,' she couldn't think on the spot of anything else to ask that wouldn't appear too intrusive.

'The key, I'll have a look and drop it round in a few days, assuming I can find it. I'm in the area again then if that's okay.'

'That would be great, thanks. I'll let you get on,' Carrie took a few steps back as Clive nodded to her. She looked up and down the street before turning back to the house. For some reason, her eyes flickered up towards the bedroom window of number 28. Her breath hitched as she could have sworn she saw some movement with the curtain. Carrie looked back to Clive who had by now, retrieved a plank of wood from the back of his van and was heading back to Agnes's. Carrie remained fixed to the pavement, frozen to the spot as Agnes opened the front door to let him back in.

Carrie finally made her legs work and hurried back into the house. For some reason, she felt clammy again and realised why. Once safely on the other side of the door, she closed it and pressed her back against it, tears prickling in her eyes. She recalled the other day when she had met Agnes on the street to enquire about the dodgy boiler. She had watched Agnes walk, no, practically *shuffle* back into her house; it had taken her for what seemed like forever. Carrie had made it downstairs to the bathroom in plenty of time waiting for Agnes to get upstairs and show her the mannequin in the window. Yes, she had been fast, but Agnes had taken what seemed like an eternity to get there. Therefore, a sickening feeling coursed through her. There was no way Agnes would have got from the upstairs bedroom window to the front door in that time just now. That meant one thing: she was being lied to about Agnes's husband who was supposedly confined to bed. If not, then there was someone else living at number 28. Someone else who had been conveniently left out of all conversations with regard to who lived with Agnes.

Mentally pulling herself together, she went back to see how Birdy was faring. She had managed to stay in an upright position to watch television. Carrie took this as a good sign as she had been barely able to move out of her supine position for most of yesterday. She moved in to embrace her daughter, already feeling more relaxed as her body warmth melted into her. Maybe she was overthinking things. As long as the noises stopped, surely it wasn't her business what went on next door.

A thought snapped her out of her pondering about Agnes. 'Birdy, have you seen my phone anywhere. You know, the small black one we bought the other day?'

She felt her head move from side to side.

'I'd better go and have a look for it,' she muttered to herself. She moved from room to room on that floor of the house, almost expecting the phone to make itself obvious to her. This was ridiculous – there was no way she would have hidden it so well. What was the point of buying a phone for emergencies if you couldn't actually find it?

Carrie paused in the kitchen and eyed up the empty wine bottle on the side. She knew there were two more in the fridge which she would no doubt be indulging in later. She let out a sigh of relief as she spotted the mobile on the kitchen worktop, tucked behind the bottle. For the life of her, she could not remember leaving it there. Never mind, it was not missing, which was all she was worried about. She turned it on, half hoping for a message from her mother but remembered that by now she would probably be in the thick of it, attending to her Uncle's every need. Carrie smiled to herself; what it must be like to have such a good support network.

The way things were going with Birdy, Carrie reckoned they should be able to get out tomorrow, even just to the shops to get some more clothes suitable for this weather. She decided today she would concentrate on tidying up the house a bit.

It was early evening when a knock on the door interrupted the calmness Carrie was starting to feel. She looked across to Birdy and then back to the door. For a moment, she toyed with the idea of simply ignoring it; after all, no one knew they were even there. Her blood chilled as she remembered there was another person who knew they were staying there. The knocking paused for a few beats and then started again. Carrie moved to get up, the constant memory taunted her, *now, we all know how this ended the last time you went to investigate a strange noise…*

However, this time on the doorstep stood Agnes with a plastic box balanced in her hands. 'Hello, dear,' she chimed. 'I've bought you and your little one a gift, I baked them myself.' She shoved the box into Carrie's hands.

'Oh, thank you,' Carrie replied, somewhat confused. Here was a lady who was supposed to only take on the role as her landlady and now here she was, presenting Carrie with a present. There was no need for her to open it now as she knew there were baked goods inside as she could feel the heat radiating through the box, yet she felt obliged to as she needed to acknowledge it. There was indeed a small pile of what looked like muffins. Their aroma told her they had been taken out of the oven quite recently.

'That's very thoughtful of you,' she added, her sentiments genuine. Perhaps dear old Agnes really was a harmless lady with enough time on her hands to indulge in some home cooking. It was very possibly her way of apologising for the gap in the fence which had allowed children to trespass.

'Just to let you know,' Agnes said, 'Clive did manage to secure the fence with the materials he had in his van so he won't be back again.'

Carrie emitted a small laugh. Relieved in the knowledge that the perimeter was now secure again but also, she entertained a small doubt as to why Agnes had felt the need to add that she wouldn't see Clive again. *What had she heard? He said he'd come round again once he found the key…*

'I'll be on my way, dear. Just leave the box on my doorstep when you are ready to return it,'

'Would you care to join us for one? We've just had dinner?' Carrie asked part out of politeness but also curious to entertain her for a while.

'No thank you, dear. I'd better be getting back, I'll let you enjoy your evening.' Before Carrie had even had the chance to respond to this parting, she had already begun the slow shuffle back to her house.

'Thank you again,' Carrie called after her. She frowned to herself and waited for a few moments before going back inside. She felt the need to study her walking speed again to reaffirm her suspicions about how quickly Agnes seemed to be able to get from one place to another.

'What's that?' Birdy asked once the door was closed. 'Can I see?'

'It's cakes and they smell delicious!' Carrie bent down to her level and opened the lid to tantalise her with their aroma.

Birdy's eyes widened. 'Mmm, they smell yummy, can I have one?'

Carrie laughed. 'Of course you can! It's good to see you're getting your appetite back.' She strutted to the kitchen with Birdy in tow, setting the muffins down on the table. They looked like small boulders in Birdy's hand as she immediately began to nibble on one. *Thank goodness she's thinking about food again,* Carrie thought to herself. She decided to pour herself a generous glass of wine and join her daughter with a muffin for herself.

Carrie walked back through to the lounge and was greeted by Birdy's scrunched up face. She held the muffin away from her and made an exaggerated look of disgust whilst simultaneously doing her best to rid her mouth of the taste.

'What's the matter, baby, are they not good?' Carrie was poised to take a bite herself.

'They have a bit of a funny taste, and I don't see any chocolate bits,' she complained as she set her muffin down pointedly on the table.

Carrie chuckled. 'You can't have chocolate chips in everything,' she laughed as she took a measured sniff of the muffin again. They had indeed smelt delicious when Agnes handed them over. Birdy watched as her mother took a bite, almost waiting for her to share and confirm her dislike of the taste. Carrie chewed slowly and then shrugged. Nothing tasted untoward to her, perhaps they were not as sugary as a young child would be used to. She thought back to a lot of the cakes on offer to children and reasoned their main ingredient was probably sugar. Birdy just wasn't used to someone else's cooking and Agnes possibly had her own healthy recipe in which she limited the sugar content.

'They taste fine to me,' she smiled, 'I think you're just used to the shop ones, that's all.'

Birdy continued to frown at the offending muffin and left it positioned on the table, she moved to sit on the sofa and crossed her arms as though the cakes were at fault rather than her.

'Oh, you're such a grumpy so and so!' Carrie exclaimed as she took a large bite of the muffin.

DAY 9

Her dreams were strange that night. She was in the boiler room, having gone to admire Clive's handiwork, except of course there was nothing to see as he had only changed a few settings on the panel. Carrie had felt brave as she approached the old blue door, her bare feet stepping on the shards of paint that had been dislodged the previous night following the vigorous banging. She winced slightly as the dirt on the floor dug into the exposed skin on the soles of her feet.

Her hands caressed the surface of the door as though she were trying to get a sense of the energy behind it. *Who are you?* she heard herself ask. There was no way she would swallow Agnes's justification for this just being 'children'. Kids don't plan this systematic campaign to scare the living daylights out of neighbouring tenants. Kids are too impulsive. This was planned and enacted with precision. This was playing on her fears of being alone and afraid and being built upon night after night …

Carrie's hands froze as the sound of scuffling started. She took on the pose of a mime artist who had paused his act for dramatic effect. Sliding her hands down the door, she bent down so that she was now level with the keyhole. However, this time she could not see the light on the other side. It was indeed dark, but she was not even able to see a small chink of moonlight. She could not feel the night air as the breeze found its way through. There was something in the keyhole preventing this. The only thing she could think of was that something had been shoved in the lock from the other side.

The voice did not make her jump as it would have done had she been awake. The sounds were indistinguishable at first. It was as though she was listening underwater. Low tones gave her the impression she was listening to a male voice on the other side.

'I ... see ... you ...' the voice hissed at her. These words were repeated on a loop so eventually, the sounds became more distorted as they blended into one another. Strangely, Carrie felt no fear.

The rough surface of the floor began to aggravate Carrie's skin as she knelt there. She winced as her knee grazed against the uneven concrete and shivered as the chill of the poorly insulated room cocooned her nightgown clad body, moving around her like some kind of spectre. She still had the feeling of tranquility as though she was floating but her senses were becoming sharper as sensations became more acute. This dream was feeling too real ...

The woman's voice was much clearer and snarled at the male voice. 'You can't be here, you mustn't be here.' Noises proceeded which sounded like a scuffle, as though something was being pushed or shoved with force. A struggle ensued on the other side of the door and finally, the sound of a single, heavy slap rang through Carrie's ears. All went quiet before a door eventually slammed shut on the other side.

Carrie gasped as she woke in her own bed. Her eyes shot open as she stared up at the ceiling, blinking to clear her eyes of the heavy film that seemed to coat them. Birdy lay beside her. The room was still too hot, and she reckoned this probably had to do with the fact that it had no windows, the door was only slightly ajar and there were two of them creating enough body heat to warm the room up. She would have to think about their sleeping arrangements going forward. Carrie put a hand to her forehead as she tried to rationalise her thoughts and make sense of her dream. How much wine had she drunk last night? She had certainly felt much more relaxed as a warm and fuzzy feeling had crept up on her with every passing glass. Her head had begun its telltale throb and she was aware that her mouth felt claggy. She rubbed her eyes with both hands as she struggled to sit up. She swung her legs over the side of the bed and put her bare feet onto the carpet. She half expected to see them covered in dirt from the boiler room floor and laughed at herself for entertaining such a thought. *Only in horror films, this had just been a very vivid dream.* The alarm clock informed her it was the wrong side of 9 o'clock which was exceptionally late for her. She went through the motions of going upstairs with the intention of making some coffee.

Carrie smiled at the sight of an empty bottle of wine on the counter. *This can't become the norm,* she thought. *I can't be doing with waking up feeling like this on a regular basis.* She was quite surprised at how heavy her limbs felt.

'You didn't wake me. Mummy,' Birdy's voice chirped behind her.

'Sorry, sweetie, you seemed to be in a deep sleep. How are you feeling, did you sleep well?'

'I'm much better,' she replied. 'Are we going out today?'

'Y'know, that was just what I was thinking.' She bent down to her level. 'I thought we could go shopping. Get some more clothes and maybe some toys as well …'

'Yay!' Birdy didn't even let her mother finish the sentence; the magic word 'toys' had clinched the deal.

'Grab some breakfast then and I'll just finish my coffee and then jump in the shower,' she walked through to the lounge area to put on the television. 'Which shop shall we head to …' she stopped abruptly as her toe made contact with the edge of the sofa. 'Goddammit!' she cursed, slightly louder than she intended and hopped around on the spot. 'Sorry, Birdy,' she addressed the stunned face now behind her. She bent to rub her foot. It was the worst place on the foot to bump and she was relieved to feel that she had just jarred it and nothing more sinister.

'What did you do, Mummy?'

'I don't know …' Carrie set her mug down on the table and carefully avoided the splash of coffee that had spread over the floor. *Jesus, can I not even walk in a straight line any more?* She tutted to herself and looked around at what had just happened. Yes, she'd had a few to drink last night but had been walking tipsy when she had gone to bed, not staggering even then. She shook her head slowly, confused, as she took a further look at the situation. The sofa was positioned with a clear protrusion into her route from the kitchen to the television. To get to the television, she would have to give it a wide berth to avoid colliding into it. This is exactly what she hadn't done as she hadn't needed to before. *Had it always been like this?* The sofa was now clearly out of alignment with the rest of the lounge furniture. It looked unmistakably out of place.

Carrie frowned, 'Birdy, did you move this?' she asked, whilst simultaneously using her strength to shove it back into place from one end. She had to use a considerable amount of effort and didn't even expect an answer; the question itself had been a stupid one. Carrie wondered if she had herself moved this whilst she was searching for her mobile last night. It was not an impossible theory. She certainly remembered looking under cushions. Maybe she had moved the sofa part of the way out in case it had slipped underneath.

'Maybe it was the fairies? Or the Boogeyman?' Birdy's smile was contagious.

'I'll give you the Boogeyman,' Carrie teased. 'Now finish your breakfast you little monkey so we can get going!' she made a show of chasing her back into the kitchen, much to Birdy's delight.

Carrie finished showering and waited for Birdy to clean her teeth before they left. She looked around at the house and noted that it was in a bit of a mess but she'd sort it out once they got back. As she picked up a summer hat that had been discarded by Birdy, she stopped herself and replaced it. Back at home, Jon had been most insistent on everything being tidied away in its proper place. The scene in front of her did in no way depict a messy house. It was fine as it was but still, Carrie justified her constant need to be clearing things away as just another by-product of Jon's influence.

In the street outside, the road was quiet as Carrie secured the front door and held her hand out for Birdy.

'Are you checking the messages today? Did Nanny send us any more messages?'

'No, I told you, sweetie. Nanny went away to help great-uncle Al. Remember I told you he's been in hospital? We might not hear from her for a while.' She decided she had no desire to check her emails to see if Jon had contacted her again. There was no way she needed him to dampen their spirits. At the back of her mind, she had parked the worry there of why he had not contacted her yet. If her mother was right, he had the address. Maybe it was the wake-up call he'd needed, and he was coming to his senses, accepting that she wasn't coming back.

They walked into a clothes shop; the bright coloured clothing in the window was displayed to appeal to children so Carrie thought this would be a good place for Birdy to choose something. Carrie ran her hands over some of the clothing on display. Jon usually chose Birdy's clothes or had a heavy say in what he liked her to wear, insisting she looked like the archetypical girl all the time.

'Do you see anything you like?' she asked. Birdy had paused by a display and then stretched out a hand towards the mannequins as she muttered something.

'What is it, sweetie?' Carrie moved closer and saw that she had a tear in her eye. 'Baby, what's wrong?'

'Daddy wouldn't want me to wear this,' she whispered. 'I'm not allowed, remember?'

Damn him, she thought. He's not even here, they'd been away for over a week and still he held this invisible vice-like hold on his own child. A child who was almost reduced to tears at the prospect of picking some new clothes that would meet with his disapproval.

'Daddy's not here,' Carrie whispered back. 'You can get whatever you want.'

'But when we go back home, he'll just shout and take them off me, won't he?' she now brushed away the wayward tears. Carrie looked away, her eyes filled at the sight of her child upset and by the words she was speaking.

'Birdy, look at me.' She put a hand on each of her shoulders and positioned her so she could look her square in the eye. 'Things are going to be different now, I promise you. And as for the clothes, Mummy is saying that you can buy whatever you want. You don't have to dress like a fairy princess all of the time.' She gritted her teeth in annoyance at what Birdy had endured in her short five years. What Jon wanted, he had got up to this point.

Birdy sniffed and managed a weak smile. She moved to hug her mother and held on tightly. Other shoppers moved around them but Carrie didn't care. If now was the time for them both to have an epiphany, then so be it.

'Come on, sweetie, you go ahead and choose,' Carrie smiled reassuringly. She followed Birdy who by now was wandering around the rails, stopping at various points and beaming.

'I've seen these clothes in that television show,' she smiled, 'can I have this one, Mummy?'

'Sure you can.' Carrie was glad she had picked up a basket at the door. The shop was relatively inexpensive and they were also fortunate enough to have the money Carrie's mother had transferred so they could well afford them. It was as though a weight had been lifted off Birdy's shoulders. Her spirits had elevated and she was coming out of her shell a bit more in the time they had been away. *Small steps*, Carrie reminded herself. *Just take each day at a time.*

After the successful shopping trip, they treated themselves to a large dinner, full of calories and sugar. Birdy's laugh was joyous, following her worries of that morning. Carrie looked forward to the future and hoped that there would be no lasting damage to the both of them as inflicted on them in the past. She watched as Birdy stifled a few yawns in succession.

'You tired, sweetie? I thought you slept well last night?' She was also feeling exhausted if she were being honest. They had been more active than usual today and the weight of a large meal was making Carrie even more sluggish. 'We'll stop off on the way home to get some more food for the week,' she stated. Birdy clutched hold of the bag of toys she had been encouraged to buy.

Carrie eyed up the wine bottles on display in the shop. She did enjoy a glass and acknowledged she was relaxing a bit more since they'd left home. She decided just one bottle wouldn't hurt. Jon had often frowned when she had reached for the bottle for a second glass, so she had tended to just stick to the one when at home. However, here she tested her ability to be able to refill her glass without the scornful looks. The increased alcohol intake made her slightly fuzzy and gave her a warm buzz, but it was not as though she was dependent on it.

Back at the house, Birdy placed her newly bought cakes next to Agnes's muffins. Her hand hovered over, as though she was seeking permission.

'Of course you can have one of yours,' Carrie laughed. She knew Birdy was waiting for the okay before she ate it. 'Although I thought you were ready to pop after all that pudding!'

'I still have a little bit of space in my tummy,' Birdy smiled as she pointed to the left side of her stomach. 'Just here.'

'I think I'll join you, sweetie, but then I might put the others in the freezer so I can give the tub back to next door.' She moved the box to one side and reached for her wine glass to fill the other hand.

They sat together on the sofa to watch the noisy show that had just started. Carrie could already feel how muggy it was in the room even though the heating was off – she had checked it.

'I thought maybe we could sleep upstairs tonight.'

Birdy cast her eyes towards the ceiling, 'you mean up above here?'

'Yes, the bedroom with the staircase.' She was referring to the open-plan bedroom which she was sure was once used for a lounge area previously but had probably been converted to maximise potential buyers so the owners could boast a three bedroomed property as opposed to two. Carrie had her reservations about the high bedroom. It was open, which meant no doors to stop the free flow of air. It did mean they would probably wake early as it was opposite the large bay window. The spiral staircase posed the threat of slipping down it in the middle of the night.

'Unless you wanted to go back to your old room?' Carrie didn't expect for one moment that she would agree but she could see Birdy was considering the question.

'Maybe I could,' she mused. 'The birds might come back again to see me.'

Carrie tried not to show her surprise. *If she had witnessed the boiler room incident, she'd never want to go near there again.* It was a small mercy that she had slept through the whole thing. 'You're sure?' She didn't want to talk her out of it in a way as she would relish the thought of a bed to herself again. Birdy was a bit of a restless sleeper at times and tended to fidget.

'My room is too hot,' Carrie stated, as though she needed further justification for changing rooms. 'And it's also a bit too dark, with no window and all.'

Birdy simply nodded, so Carrie took this as her seal of approval. She used the sofa for support and got up to rearrange the bedding to the upstairs bedroom. The spiral staircase made a statement regarding space-saving amenities, but it did ring alarm bells to Carrie with fire safety risks. She could not imagine bolting down it in the middle of a blazing fire. However, she reasoned with herself that the odds of a fire breaking out by itself were very slim. She didn't smoke or light scented candles and always made sure the oven was turned off before she started eating whatever it was she'd cooked. There was a small ensuite with a shower and toilet so no need to venture down at midnight for the bathroom.

Carrie was surprised as well as a little relieved if she were being honest at how well Birdy was coping with the changes that were being thrown at her. In the past, the separation anxiety she had suffered would often manifest itself at not wanting to be out of her sight. She took this as a sign that Birdy was starting to feel safe in her new surroundings. Carrie shook her head – if only she could share the same feelings. Yes, she did feel much safer than she'd felt in a long time, but there were niggles here and there at this house which meant she was not fully relaxed. However, as things were becoming more settled and there were reasons for the disturbances the other night, she reasoned with herself that her own reservations were partly due to the fallout from leaving a toxic relationship. She was bound to be on edge for a while.

Birdy gave a long, outstretched yawn once the programme had finished. She confidently strutted downstairs to her old bedroom to sleep alone for the first time in a couple of nights.

'Remember, I'm just upstairs if you need me,' Carrie moved the thin sheet over her.

'Upstairs and upstairs again,' Birdy corrected.

'Oh, yes,' Carrie pictured the wooden stairs leading to downstairs and then the creaky spiral staircase to get to the top bedroom.

'I could always shout from down below?' Birdy offered. 'You'd be able to hear me still.'

'That might be a good idea,' Carrie nodded. 'I won't have a bedroom door to block out the noise so I will hear you.' She smiled, feeling more relaxed that Birdy would not be poking her in the middle of the night. 'You give me a shout if you need anything,' she stood at the edge of the doorframe. 'I'll pull this door to a little bit but I'm right up here,' she pointed in the direction of the stairs.

Birdy nodded from the bed and turned over to face the wall after a few moments. Carrie took this as her cue to leave. She put a few things away upstairs before the urge to sleep got the better of her. They had enjoyed another busy day which Carrie put down to her sudden tiredness. Upstairs, she was surprised at how much light there was in the house, even with the curtains pulled over the big bay window. She sighed and remembered she had packed an eye mask with her clothes. She groped in the adjacent drawer to find it. Pulling it down over her eyes, she settled back in the bed.

Carrie woke. Something had brought her out of the deep sleep she had been in. It wasn't a jolt caused by a loud bang, but nevertheless, something had woken her up. She pushed her eye mask back and squinted into the darkness. It took her a few moments to get her bearings – she was in the high room and the bed was cold beside her. She stretched out her hand, half expecting Birdy to have climbed in during the night and she'd find her huddled up on the edge. But there was no one there, just the emptiness and cool sheets.

She couldn't see her watch to check the time, but the amount of light told her that it was either close to midnight or the early hours of the morning. The bed was comfortable but something sat uneasily within Carrie. She couldn't explain it, it was just a feeling she had. She strained to hear any noises as she slowly pulled the sheet up under her chin. Facing the banister overlooking the ground floor of the house, Carrie wrestled with the grinding knot forming in her stomach caused by the feeling that she was not alone. There was no reason for it, but she had the distinct feeling of another presence with her. She held her breath, too afraid to raise her head over the banister to look or to make any movements for that matter.

The house was still, devoid of any noise apart from her breathing; even that sounded too loud to her. Part of her wished for Birdy to be next to her, another person to share her thoughts of utter isolation. She had the desperate longing and need for someone to be beside her. As the minutes passed, these did not serve any comfort as she was still afraid to settle back to sleep despite the fact that the house was calm. Carrie considered the possibility it had been a noise from outside. She was now closest to the front of the house, so it could have been anything.

Her ears strained again – to hear any noise. The hum from the fridge, ticking clock, noise from a car or cat outside. It was just *too* quiet. Then, there it was, a slight shift in the sound pattern. Carrie heard the distinct sound of footsteps on bare floorboards. Barely managing to swallow, a hard lump formed in the throat as this was preceded by two sounds. They had a definite pattern to them, of something behind dragged or a foot being pulled with a limp. The steps became more frequent, as though someone or something was pacing in the area close to the front door.

A different sound broke this pattern. It had a shrill

quality about it, as though an alarm had been activated. It started quiet and increased in volume until Carrie sat up startled.

The screaming interrupted the noise, 'Mummy, Mummy!'

'Birdy!' Carrie gasped, as she reached for her dressing gown and threw the bedsheet off. Her feet tangled at the bottom. In frustration, she kicked the sheet to free herself and took large paces so she was at the top of the spiral staircase. For a moment, the room spun which made her think she had got out of bed too quickly. She took a few seconds to find her feet before descending as carefully as she could; the metal railings rattled as she grasped them for support.

Birdy's cries remained in the same place and sure enough, once Carrie had burst into her room, she found her sitting bolt upright, her sheet pooled around her waist. Her face was flushed and her hair plastered against her forehead. She continued to howl into the semi-darkness.

With no hesitation, Carrie put the light on and her eyes automatically narrowed to become accustomed. Despite the rude awakening, the light seemed to comfort Carrie with the feeling that it was safer. Things lurked in the darkness and shadows, light served the purpose to expose such things.

'Hey.' She sat on the edge of the bed and gathered Birdy into her arms. She pressed her against her body and was aware of Birdy's trembling. 'You're okay, everything is okay,' she soothed her, aware she was reassuring herself as well.

Birdy's breaths came in short pants and she struggled to control her sobs. Carrie wasn't even sure if she was fully awake yet. As she heaved in large breaths, Carrie feared for a moment she was hyperventilating.

'Breathe slowly,' she urged her, 'listen to my voice, everything is okay now, it was just a dream.' She rocked her back and forth until the sobs began to subside. After a few moments, their breathing synchronised as Carrie closed her eyes again.

Birdy shuddered in her arms as Carrie shuffled awkwardly so she was more comfortable. She held Birdy in her lap. 'Are you okay now?' she asked, her voice low to maintain the calming tone. She felt Birdy's arms tighten around her. Sensing that she was not ready to talk yet, she held her close and continued with the rhythmic, rocking sensation. Like a slow pendulum, back and forwards until she felt Birdy's posture begin to soften in her arms.

She sniffed as her breath hitched. Carrie felt clammy as Birdy moved out of her clasp.

'A bad dream, sweetie?' she asked, stroking down her hair.

Her blotchy face nodded back at her.

'Want to tell me about it or wait until morning?'

Birdy shook her head to both options.

'Let's get you tucked back in,' she made as if to move off the bed so that Birdy could snuggle back down.

'No, Mummy, can you stay with me?' her voice was urgent.

'Sure, no problem,' Carrie reached to turn the light off and let Birdy get comfortable before sliding next to her. She fell into her arms again.

'You won't leave me?

'No, I promise. I'll be here when you wake up. Go back to sleep, baby, because it's still night time.' After a pause, she added, 'You're perfectly safe now, nothing to worry about.'

Birdy mumbled something.

'Hmm? What was that sweetie? Mummy didn't catch all of that?'

'I said, you won't let him get me?'

Carrie felt herself emerge from the state of relaxation she had been drifting into. Her senses prickled again. 'Who, baby? Who is "he"?'

'The man,' she replied simply, with all the nonchalance as if she was pointing out a passing man in the street.

With every passing second, she did not respond, Carrie felt she was giving Birdy the impression that her comment had meant nothing, which she was brushing off dismissively. However, she was finding it hard to formulate the reply to go with. Voice her fears and she'd certainly scare the living daylights out of her child, disregarding the comment off-handedly would seem as though she did not care. She needed to find the balance. 'The man in your dream, honey?' There was no response as her breathing drew out and sounded heavier.

A weary mumble came from Birdy's mouth. Carrie couldn't be sure but had the horrifying realisation when she figured out what she'd said: *he's under the bed*. She stayed frozen in the same position for a while. Had she really heard that? Had her child just told her that a man was hiding under the bed they both lay in now? Again, her ears pricked for any sound out of the ordinary, the heavy breathing, a shuffle to move position. There was nothing and the room remained still. Carrie couldn't allow herself to relax and jerked several times as she drifted off. After this had happened a few times, her breath hitched as she made out a faint sound. It sounded like something clicking, up and down, in quick succession, before trailing off to a stop.

It was still dark and Carrie felt her head still fuzzy from lack of sleep. Her thoughts felt jumbled due to waking up early and so abruptly. She felt herself suspended in the state of not quite fully awake and not yet into a light sleep, just hanging, waiting to drift back off. She jerked slightly as the sound of another distant click pulled her back into consciousness before she was submerged again to sleep.

DAY 10

T he emerging dawn whitewashed any further night-time threats. Carrie woke to find she was positioned awkwardly, her limbs protested as she stretched gingerly. She lay in the bed for a moment whilst the sickening events of the middle of the night seeped into her thoughts. *There had been someone else in the house last night. Birdy was positive that there was someone under the bed.* She was convinced of this as the only other explanation she could think of was that the house was haunted. Carrie smiled at this thought − ghosts usually inhabited old stately homes, didn't they?

As she eased her arm from around Birdy, she wondered what scene would present upstairs. If she had indeed heard footsteps, she fully expected to see some kind of disturbance. She mentally tried to recall where she had left her bag and phone. *The bank card* − she only had the one and it would be a nightmare to get a replacement. She put a hand to her forehead, exasperated. The new one would automatically be diverted to her old house unless she could get to the bank that morning to make alternative arrangements.

Birdy stirred as Carrie sat up. 'Morning, sweetie,' she said guardedly. She didn't want to raise the subject of her nightmare in the hope she had been so delirious that her mind had already started the process of blanking this from her memory. She had been hysterical and there was no way Carrie wanted to force her to dredge up these thoughts.

'Can I get dressed straight away?' her eyes sparkled, obviously remembering their shopping trip from yesterday.

Carrie laughed. 'Are you sure you don't want breakfast first?'

Birdy shook her head and had already begun rifling through her new clothes, selecting her favourites by placing them to one side. Carrie looked at her, but couldn't help but turn her attention to the foot of the bed. She had been convinced that someone had been hiding under it last night. The gap under the bed was obscured by the hanging duvet but the space looked to be less than six inches; there was no way a person would have been able to slide under stealthily and then back out again without disturbing the both of them.

She had paused for a moment too long as Birdy stopped and looked up at her. 'Oh, I'm just seeing if I can spot Mr Bear, we don't want to lose him again.' She spied the tatty bear which had fallen over the side and lay on the floor. As she knelt to retrieve it, she made an over the top gesture of moving the duvet out of the way. Glancing as long as she was able to without arousing any suspicion, there was nothing to be seen, no protruding foot, and no wide-eyed maniac waiting to attack, after spending the night curled up under the bed.

She stood up again 'Is that what you're wearing today?' Carrie couldn't remember the last time she had seen her in jeans. It simply hadn't been allowed at home.

'Yes, but...' she paused. 'I think I'd like to wear my old socks if that's okay.' She indicated the white, frilly socks that she usually wore. 'I just like them, is all.'

'You can wear whatever you want, remember?' she rubbed her head. 'If you want to wear the socks with the jeans, go for it. I'll go and sort out breakfast.' She was glad Birdy would be preoccupied for a while downstairs whilst she planned to survey the damage upstairs. The more she thought about it, the more convinced she was about someone being in the house last night, therefore, she would have to be mindful of what she touched before she called the police. Upon leaving the bedroom, she spotted Birdy's wind-up toy frog positioned awkwardly on the floor. She vaguely remembered hearing clicking sounds in the middle of the night outside the room. Had the mechanism gone off by itself and used the energy pent up inside? She had visions of the frog bouncing along by itself last night. Anything could have set it off, it could have been dropped by Birdy at an angle yesterday and the build-up of pressure had forced it over by itself. She moved to pick it up and took it with her upstairs. There in the stark reality of daytime, sat one of her fears from the deadness of night.

She trod each stair carefully as she ascended to the ground level. Upstairs, she frowned. There was no damage, there was no forced entry or shattered glass and more importantly, her belongings were exactly as she'd left them. The door remained secure and nothing looked untoward. Had she imagined the whole thing? Carrie moved to the lounge area, slowly looking for signs of disparity. She scanned the room anxiously, waiting for the anomalies to become apparent, the flicker of recognition to substantiate her claims. Then, there it was – had the scatter cushions on the sofa been moved out of sequence? She was sure she'd left them as blue fluffy cushion, red in the middle and the pug cushion at the end. Now, the pug cushion was in the middle. Carrie put her hand to her chin to desperately try to recall how the sofa had looked before she had gone to bed. She looked around again and saw their shoes arranged by the front door. Had Birdy's been in front of hers or behind?

In the kitchen, her wine glass from last night sat innocently on the edge of the counter by the sink. Carrie was convinced that she had left this on the table in the lounge. The thought of calling the police slowly faded from her mind. What on earth would she say? *Yes, hello, I'm sure there was someone in my house last night. Forced entry, well no. What did they take? Well, nothing that I can see. But one of my cushions is out of place, I think. Did I have anything to drink last night? Well yes, a bit.*

'Can I have pancakes for breakfast?'

Carrie jumped 'Jesus, Birdy, you scared the life out of me!' She watched as Birdy's face morphed into a scowl. 'Sorry, I didn't mean to shout. Of course you can have pancakes.' She put herself on automatic pilot whilst she retrieved a pack from the cupboard, poured some juice and put the kettle on for some coffee. 'I'll be back in a moment.' She left the kitchen before Birdy had a chance to respond and took the stairs two at a time down to the bedroom area. She paused outside the boiler room door with her hand on the doorknob. This was the only other point of entry, wasn't it? Gingerly, she opened the door, fully expecting the rush of air to hit her flowing in from the now forced open, splintered wooden door. There was nothing. The room was just as she'd seen it before. Not wanting to be in there any longer, she made short work of going back to the kitchen.

Carrie cast her eyes over Birdy's choice of clothing for the day and for a moment, felt herself begin to tear up. 'You look gorgeous, sweetie,' she commented. 'Maybe you should think about a haircut soon, your hair is super long now.'

Birdy shrugged, 'I like it long.'

Carrie sat opposite her, tracing her finger around the rim of the mug. She didn't want to broach the subject of last night. Instead, she made a point of stretching over-exaggeratedly. 'Wow, I'm still achy after all the shopping we did yesterday; we must have walked for miles. I think I fell asleep straight away last night, what about you?'

'Me too.' That was all she managed to reply between mouthfuls of pancake.

'My feet are sore too,' Carrie frowned as this was actually the truth. Her feet were aching. She moved the chair back slightly and raised one foot to rest it on her other leg. The sole was markedly more painful around her heel. She squinted as she moved her foot as close as she could whilst at the same time, dipping her head slightly for a closer inspection. 'What the …?' She made her thumb and forefinger into a pincer grip and managed to extract what looked like a blue splinter. 'How did that …?' She didn't need to finish the sentence as she knew exactly what this was. It was part of the paintwork from the old blue door downstairs. Carrie was sure she had paled. It was highly reasonable that this had been in her foot from day one when she had first gone into the room. However, she had the sickening feeling that she had just acquired this recently. Surely, she would have noticed such an irritation sooner. She threw the splinter of paint into the sink in annoyance whilst ignoring the stark reality of how it had really ended up embedded in her foot; she could now add sleepwalking to her list of problems here.

'Can we go to the park today?' Birdy snapped her from her thoughts.

It took Carrie a few moments to register she had been asked a question. The only way she knew was by looking at Birdy's expectant expression indicating that she was waiting for a response.

'The park, sure we can. Why don't you play with some of your new toys for a bit whilst I get ready and pack a picnic for us?' She already felt much lighter at the prospect of being out of the house.

Birdy nodded furiously in approval and hurriedly finished her breakfast.

The walk to the park helped Carrie clear her mind. The temperature was already on the climb and it promised to be another sunny day. Birdy held her hand, her walk animated as she showed excitement for their day out. They moved among others but Carrie didn't look closely at anyone as the sea of faces blended into one another.

She settled herself on the picnic blanket watching as Birdy explored the playground equipment with delight. She leant back and closed her eyes, relishing the sun on her face. When she opened her eyes, she saw him. He stood a few feet from her, eyes trying to catch hers before moving any closer.

Carrie felt her muscles tense and jaw tighten. She felt like a cat that had been cornered and was reduced to sitting motionless in the same position until the threat moved away. He was standing on the grass next to her, hands up as if in defeat.

'Carrie, please,' he began, his voice soft.

She looked around almost in a state of panic. Where was Birdy? They needed to leave – now. Her natural defence mechanism would be to flee and leave everything exactly as it sat on the blanket. But she couldn't, she needed to find Birdy. This wasn't the safety of a house where she could slam a door in his face. It was too exposed and open. If she ran, this would surely result in a firm grip on her arm as she waited in a panic to cross a road on the way back to her house.

He approached her with caution as though she were an unexploded device that was due to detonate at any moment.

'Please, Carrie, I've not come to hurt you, I promise,' with every word, he inched closer. Carrie remained in the same position, but she began to draw her legs up as if to protect herself. She looked at him with wide eyes.

'What do you want, Jon?'

His mouth twitched into a brief smile as she acknowledged him by name. 'I've not come to harm you, I promise,' he repeated. 'I just want half an hour of your time and then I'll be gone.'

Carrie could see all of the movement around, all of the people in the nearby vicinity were just like they were. Couples sat together picnicking and enjoying the fine weather. She and Jon looked every part the happy couple. *If only they knew.* There were plenty of witnesses close by, adults and children who would be able to see and potentially hear if he started to threaten her. She nodded once in approval and watched as he strategically positioned himself on the edge of her blanket, ever so slightly encroaching on her space but at the same time, at a safe enough distance.

He gave her a weak smile again. 'Thank you. I won't stay for long.'

'How did you know I was here?' She knew full well how he knew but wanted to hear what he had to say.

'I got your address from your mum. I followed you here today from your house.' His expression looked sheepish and his eyes were cast down shamefully.

'And you've been watching me for a while now?'

He shook his head. 'No, I only arrived today. Since I found out your address, I didn't want to just turn up the next day. This is serious, Carrie. I've realised I need to get some help. I've already had a session with a therapist regarding my anger management problem. That's why I haven't come sooner; I've been at my appointment. I'm one hundred per cent being honest with you. This is me reaching out for help.' He breathed deeply as though he had rehearsed the speech many times.

Carrie couldn't answer, she didn't know what to say. 'What do you want?'

He looked around him and nudged a little closer, his voice low. 'Just your time for the moment to let you know I'm seeking help. I want to look for a way forward for us, you, me and … Bridgette.' He emitted a nervous laugh. 'Sorry, Birdy. I know you like that nickname.' His volume remained quiet as if he anticipated she'd have to inch closer to him to hear what he had to say. 'You leaving me, it made me see that I've not been fair with you in the past. It has made me see that we have problems in our marriage and I'm willing to do whatever it takes.' He smoothed his hands over his jeans. Carrie noted he had worn a light blue polo shirt to match. This complemented his sandy hair colour. In their early days, before Birdy, she had always liked these colours. He had planned his visit today well.

'Jon, I …' she began, 'I can't cope with you, us, anymore.'

'I know, I know, which is why I'm seeking help. I'm not asking you to come home with me today. I know you need space, which is why I'm giving you time. I just want you to know I'm here and ready to work things out.'

Carrie found the courage to look at him square on. For a moment, she didn't see the man she had walked out on over a week ago. She bit her lip in thought. This was too much for her to process.

'You followed us here then?'

He nodded. 'Yes, I ran into one of your neighbours, she told me you often came down to the park. I must have just missed you; by the time I got to the end of the road, I saw you crossing the street.'

Carrie hadn't heard half of the sentence, she had become fixated on the *ran into your neighbour* part. 'Which neighbour?'

'Uh …' he shook his head. 'Old woman, walked slowly. I can't quite remember.'

In her head, this meant either Agnes or the old schoolmistress lady, Valerie. Whichever one it was, they seemed to know an awful lot about her whereabouts.

'Mummy?' a small voice interrupted them. Birdy paused on her approach, 'Daddy?' she whispered. Her pace quickened as she ran up to him, a smile etched on her face. Jon opened his arms in a welcome.

'Wow, look at you.' He held her at arm's length to study her.

Here we go, Carrie waited for the comment, something to show her that he disapproved of the choice of clothing. It would be coded so Birdy wouldn't understand it, but it would be a clear message that he was not happy.

'You look … different,' was all he commented.

Carrie regarded him dubiously. He was ticking every box to show the sorrowful husband. But she could not let her guard down after everything they had been through in the past. Their whole journey here, in the middle of the night for goodness' sake, spoke volumes about the misery she had endured the last five years.

'Are you staying?'

'No,' Carrie heard herself snap. 'No, Daddy can't stay,' she added in a softer tone. Children could be so fickle. Less than twenty-four hours ago, Birdy had been fretting about her choice of clothes and here she was welcoming the very perpetrator who induced such feelings with literal open arms. Carrie wondered if this was a sign that Birdy was not altogether comfortable with their moonlight flit.

'I'm just visiting,' Jon affirmed. 'I just wanted to see you and Mummy.' He smiled back at Birdy again. Looking towards Carrie, he let out a sigh and checked his watch. 'I said I only needed a short amount of your time and I meant it. I'm going to give you space now to enjoy the rest of your day.'

'You're not staying?' Birdy piped up.

'No, I can't today. But maybe I can see you again?' He looked at Carrie for her approval. She pursed her lips, knowing that she would come across as the villain if she were to refuse his simple request.

'Can … may I give you my number?' he stuttered and reached into his pocket. 'I had to get a new mobile and have changed the number.' He handed her a small, folded piece of paper. She took it off him without looking at it.

Birdy wrestled with him as she giggled. 'Come on, Birdy,' Carrie voiced her annoyance. 'Daddy said he needs to go.' There was no way she would allow him to swan back in and pretend everything was back to normal. However, she reasoned with herself, if she did eventually divorce him, of course he would probably end up still in contact with Birdy.

'Come on, you heard your Mummy. I need to go.' He patted her and slid her off onto the blanket. 'May I visit you tomorrow?'

'Jon, I …' Carrie began. She gave him a look, *not in front of our child*. 'Perhaps I should call you when we're free.' This seemed to be a more practical solution.

'Or could we say I could see you tomorrow morning, but you call me if it's not convenient?'

Carrie's smile did not quite reach her eyes. She needed him gone now so she could think about everything he had said. *Therapy?* This did not sound like him, accepting he needed help from an external source. Jon had always been adamant he was able to sort things out by himself. Asking for help was a sign of weakness in his eyes. It seemed too good to be true.

'Give me big kisses,' he said to Birdy.

'Give Mummy one too.'

She allowed him to lean over to her but turned so he was only able to kiss her cheek. 'Thank you,' he offered. Carrie wasn't sure if he was referring to their parting or the conversation they had just had. He dusted off his jeans and paused to wave before walking back in the direction he had come from. Carrie stared as he disappeared from view. Suddenly, she wanted to be back home but at the same time, in the safety of other people.

'We need to be getting back too, sweetie,' she announced whilst hurriedly packing away their picnic items.

Making the journey back to the house, she found herself walking quicker than necessary, almost dragging Birdy by the hand. Carrie looked up and down the street, half wondering who had informed Jon of their whereabouts.

Back at the house, she found herself short-tempered and irritable. She chewed her nails as she sat on the sofa, pretending to watch Birdy playing. 'Why don't you go and play with your toys in your room?' she suggested. She didn't want Birdy to see the permanent scowl etched on her face. It surprised her that she was encouraging Birdy to go and play downstairs when she had been so keen to keep her within her range of sight. 'Mummy has a bit of a headache is all,' she added, even though Birdy had not voiced any complaints. Carrie rubbed her forehead as she watched her disappear from sight. It was late afternoon, and she felt a small glass of wine would settle her nerves now. How dare Jon turn up now, begging for her forgiveness as though the last five years had meant nothing? It was so easy for him to say he was seeking help, as though this was his ticket to waltz back into their lives.

She was snapped back to reality abruptly. 'Mummy!' An urgent voice summoned her from downstairs. Carrie jumped to her feet and didn't waste any time calling from the comfort of the sofa to ask what was wrong. She pounded down the stairs to Birdy's room.

'Look!' The child was pointing out to the patio area, a worrying tone to her voice rather than the alarming element to suggest an intruder of some kind. 'There, by the flowerpot.' They both pressed faces up to the glass to have a look. Carrie squinted and was able to make out a bird flapping on the cracked tile.

'I think he fell, I think he's hurt,' Birdy continued.

Carrie's eyes darted around and she couldn't help but look up towards Agnes's sewing room window. Just the one bird this time, not the flock which had sickened her before.

'Please save him, we have to bring him in before a cat gets him,' Birdy tugged at the door handle in an attempt to slide the door back.

'Okay, okay,' Carrie reassured her, even though there was no way a cat would be able to access the small, enclosed area. No, the only way in and out of this area was via her bathroom window or Agnes's sewing room window or through the door they stood against. To humour Birdy, she opened the door and stepped out. On their approach to the bird, Carrie could see that its breaths were shallow but nonetheless, it was still breathing.

'Did he just fall out of the sky?' Birdy offered, looking up.

'I don't know, sweetie,' Carrie replied. She had no explanation of why an injured bird had appeared outside her bedroom. Exercising great care, she scooped the bird up with both hands and held it as far away from her as possible, before drawing her arms closer to her after determining that it was in no position to attack.

'I think we should take him in,' Birdy chirped up. 'He can stay with us until he feels better.'

Carrie sighed and chose her words. 'Sweetie, I've no idea how to care for a bird. We don't even know what's wrong with him. It might be his wing and I've got no idea how to look after it.' She stood holding the bird, almost as though she was seeking permission to lay it back down.

'We can get a box, Mummy. He just needs to rest,' her voice was pleading yet demanding. 'Please, Mummy, he won't fly around, he'll be good.'

Carrie breathed deeply. She could see the desperation in her eyes and remembered the anguish a dead goldfish had induced back at their old house. If she put the bird back on the ground, it was sure to die. Perhaps a box might be a good idea. She'd get to it first in the morning and save Birdy the anguish of seeing it feet up. Birdy smiled as they made for the patio doors again. She raced ahead to find a suitable container.

'Here, he can lay in my shoebox,' she emptied the tissue paper from the box and stuffed a nearby tee shirt in the bottom. Carrie laid the bird gently on it.

'I think I read somewhere they need a heat pad or something. I don't know if we need to keep him warm or whether it's already warm enough.'

Birdy switched on the lamp on top of the chest of

drawers. 'There. He can sleep here until he feels better.'

Carrie hesitated and then turned the lamp off. 'I think it will be too bright,' she added after a while. 'It needs to be in the dark. We can put some holes in the lid until it recovers.'

'So I can keep him then?' Birdy beamed up at her mother.

'I guess so, just for the time being. It will probably only need a few hours to recover.' She smiled back at Birdy.

Birdy moved to throw her arms around her, this saying enough. 'I think I might call him Chirpy,' she announced. 'He can be my pet and I'll make him all better.'

Carrie put her hand on Birdy's head. If looking after an injured bird was all it took to keep her occupied and happy, then so be it. 'Just don't keep poking it,' she reminded her. She decided to go back upstairs and paused at the door, before turning to look back, smiling.

That night, Birdy was more than happy to settle in bed. She positioned the box safely on her chest of drawers in the corner. 'Mummy?' her small voice piped up from beneath the bedclothes.

'Yes, sweetie?'

'Are we going back home to Daddy?'

Carrie considered her words carefully, 'Mummy and Daddy have a lot to sort out.' This seemed to pacify her. 'I'll see you in the morning.' She pulled the door so it rested against the door jamb. Back upstairs, she went through the motions of watching television, even though none of what she was watching was registering. It was hard to focus on such mundane things when she had so many other thoughts buzzing around her head. She took one final look around the lounge before turning out the light, making mental notes where things were positioned. She could just blame her confusion every morning on the disrupted sleep or the new surroundings. The alternatives just weren't worth considering.

Carrie decided to make one final check on Birdy, just to make sure she hadn't impulsively decided to get the bird out of its box and put it in the bed next to her. Visions of her rolling over and squashing it in the middle of the night played on her mind. Thankfully, Birdy appeared to be fast asleep. In the distance, her ears prickled as a faint, scraping sound became apparent. It was too far away to be the bird in the box. Carrie's feet walked automatically to the door leading to the boiler room. The rhythmic clunking continued but didn't sound as though it was coming from the actual room. She opened the door and just the boiler greeted her, humming quietly. No, the sound was coming from the outside. Carrie walked as close to the door as she could before her nerves forced her to stop. She was unable to place the sound at first but after a while, it became more distinguishable – it was digging. The pattern of a shovel making contact with dirt before this was tossed aside continued for a few minutes, paused and then restarted. It was her first thought to call the police but then it occurred to her that since when had digging in your own back garden become an illegal activity? There was no reason for her to be concerned about this despite one downright and quite frankly worrying fact; it was almost midnight.

DAY 11

Asmall hand pulled her from her sleep. Carrie forced her eyes open and a forlorn expression stared back at her.

'What time is it?' she mumbled but suspected there was another reason Birdy had come to wake her as opposed to the other way around.

'Chirpy isn't feeling too well,' her features were creased sorrowfully. 'He's just sat in his box ...' her voice trailed off as though she was too upset to continue.

Carrie reached for her dressing gown. 'Well, he was quite poorly,' she reasoned with her. 'Let's go and have a look.' Carefully navigating the spiral staircase, Birdy had walked ahead and presented the shoebox to her. She lifted the lid slowly.

'See, he's just sat there.'

'Oh, sweetie. Remember he was quite poorly when we found him, I'm not sure if we can make him better.' She placed the box beside her and pulled a reluctant Birdy into her lap. Naturally, she cuddled into her and it wasn't long before her breathing pattern told Carrie the tears had started.

The rattle of the letterbox broke their calm. On the one hand, Carrie was surprised that they were receiving letters so early. On the other, a thought flashed through her mind – no one had this address to contact her, so why was she receiving post? She went upstairs, with a feeling that this was not simply a flyer for a pizza delivery company and she was right. A plain, white envelope sat neatly on the doormat.

'Who's that for?' A small hand went to pick it up.

'Don't touch it!' Carrie became aware that her voice was slightly louder than she'd intended. She hadn't meant to scare Birdy, it had just come out wrong. 'I mean, it might not be for us,' she added.

For some bizarre reason, episodes of crime programmes flashed through her mind, where a suspicious package was received and it was opened with extreme caution to preserve contamination. Carrie reasoned with herself that this could be one of those instances. This didn't look like a letter containing information about a local gym or diet plan, it appeared to be a personal letter for her, but unnamed. Birdy had wandered off in search of the television, now bored with the envelope on the floor and failing to see what the fuss was about.

'Can I get Chirpy so he can watch TV with me?'

'Sure, whatever,' Carrie responded too quickly. The actual question hadn't really registered with her. In the kitchen, she found a pair of kitchen tongs and used these to pick up the letter. She walked this back at arm's length as though it was a radioactive device. With all the strange things that had happened in this house recently, she was taking no chances.

A butter knife made short work of the sealed envelope and she took out the piece of paper slowly. It was folded in half, but she could see raised marks on the surface from the pen indentations on the other side. She congratulated herself on her decision to be overly cautious. If this was a threat in any way, her fingerprints were not on the letter. The note was simple, written in very neat cursive handwriting. It simply read:

Leave while you still can.

Carrie's breathing faltered, the sickening feeling that this letter was something to be suspicious of had proved to be right. What on earth was this supposed to mean? She looked around the immediate area, a sense of panic now prevailing over her. Everything appeared as she had left it. She moved to the lounge area and checked around as inconspicuously as possible without alerting Birdy that there was anything untoward. It was impossible to speculate on the position of the cushions as Birdy had the shoebox so it was nestled on top of the pug one. The blue one lay on the floor having been kicked off to make room on the sofa. Carrie was able to see her mobile and bag where she had left them. She darted upstairs – any sign to justify why she needed to act on this letter as though it were an emergency. Her clothes were as she'd left them, bedclothes askew since she hadn't made the bed yet. She perched on the edge of the bed, breathing hard. It took her a while to gather her senses together enough to get washed and dressed. Back downstairs, she contemplated the letter again whilst sitting at the kitchen table. She tried to push this to the back of her mind as she summoned Birdy to the table with her to attempt some kind of home schooling.

A sharp knock on the front door made her check the clock. It was still daytime, now afternoon, in fact, so she still had the safety of the daylight. It could be anyone, perhaps Agnes wanting her cake box back.

He stood smiling on the doorstep, arms behind his back. 'I'm sorry to just call over unannounced. I know we agreed you'd call but…'

'Jon … I,' Carrie stuttered.

'It's a nice neighbourhood here.' His smile widened but to Carrie also seemed desperate. Jon rocked back and forward on his heels and cleared his throat quietly a few times. Carrie looked into the house and then back to him.

'What do you want?' The question had come out a bit unwelcoming but on consideration, why should she be anything but?

His expression dropped slightly. 'May I come in? I know you said you'd call but I wasn't sure if you had lost my number.'

Carrie widened the door as he wiped his feet. 'I won't stay long. Just an hour, I promise. I'd like to see you and Birdy. I have my next appointment tomorrow with the therapist.' She nodded, sure he had mentioned the last part as his permission to enter. She shut the door behind him. Carrie noticed his eyes dart around the place, as though he was trying to absorb every minute detail of their living arrangements in the opportunity he had. Or perhaps he was covertly looking at the disorder in the room.

'How many bedrooms are here?'

'Two downstairs, one up,' she pointed to the high room.

'Looks lovely. Nice neighbours?'

Carrie shrugged. 'We've had a few issues.' She deliberately chose to be very succinct, not wanting him to know too much.

'A few issues?' He reached for her arm in a show of concern. 'Is everything okay?'

'Nothing we can't handle. Would you like a coffee?' She led him through to the kitchen. Their concerns were none of his business. Birdy had now taken the knock on the door as a signal to take a break in front of the television.

Jon trailed behind her, running his fingers over some of the surfaces he passed. Carrie pursed her lips, his subtle actions had not escaped her. She wondered whether he was checking the furnishings for dust as he did back at home; he had been most insistent for the need for her to be cleaning constantly. After all, he'd explained, it wasn't as though she had a lot of other things to do.

'What's that?' Before she could respond, he had picked up the letter on the table.

'Jon!' she exclaimed and her hand automatically shot out to grab the letter, 'I didn't want to touch it.' She tutted softly at him and lowered her arm. Carrie puffed out her cheeks and decided it was pointless stopping him from reading it now.

'*Leave while you still can.*' What the hell is that supposed to mean? Is someone threatening you, Carrie? Tell me.' His tone was urgent.

'It's nothing. Well, I don't know.' She sighed. 'Look, we've had a few problems with some neighbouring children, it's probably just them messing around.'

'You didn't want me to touch it, though? Were you

thinking the police would be able to pull some DNA off it?' he smirked. 'There's no way they would do that for a letter that's just winding you up.'

Carrie took the letter off him defensively and frowned. He was almost laughing at her. Jon saw her expression and took on his serious composure again. 'May I see it again?' He held it closer than necessary and re-read it, as though it were a page of writing rather than one line. 'It's very neat handwriting, almost too neat to be a child,' he mused. 'Carrie, I'm serious, if someone is bothering you…'

'… we come back with you? Is that what you're suggesting?' She stared at him, eyes unblinking. She took the letter back from him and folded it defensively. He had been very quick to downplay her concerns. Carrie put it on the kitchen worktop alongside her mobile and keys.

He looked at her and for a moment, she saw his eyes register her increasing bravado. 'No, I, well eventually I hope you will …'

'Jesus, Jon. I can't believe that's what you're thinking.'

He looked crestfallen and replied in a quiet tone, 'Well, it's what I want eventually. Don't you?'

'That is a long way down the line.' *If at all.*

'I'm sorry if I've rushed you,' his voice was almost a whisper. 'This has been a real wake up call for me and I've realised how much I miss you both. I just want things back to normal, well, not how they were before.' He gave a weak smile. 'The therapy I'm having. I'm positive it will change me to a point where you and Birdy do trust me again and will be safe with me.' He stopped and caught her eye, 'I'm really trying, Carrie, to get things right again.'

She put a cup down in front of him.

'Look.' He ran a hand through his hair. 'Is there anything I can do to help you? Do you need me to do anything? You said you'd been having some trouble?' He blew on his coffee before taking a sip.

'Just some problems with the neighbouring house. Banging at night, that kind of thing. Birdy's been fine and has slept through most of it.'

'Banging? Where's the banging coming from?'

'The basement room. There's a boiler in there and a door which leads to next door's back garden. It's mostly at night.' She saw that she still had his full attention. 'Like I said, the old lady next door blames the kids over the fence. They fixed the fence the other day.'

'And the noises have stopped?'

'Yes, well, no. I heard something last night, sounded like digging…' She was interrupted as a small figure stood at the door. Birdy held her shoebox proudly.

'Look what I have, Daddy!'

'Hello, gorgeous!' Jon opened his arms out in a greeting for her. 'What have you got there?'

'He's my pet. His name is Chirpy but he's not very well at the moment. I'm looking after him, though.' She carefully opened the lid to reveal the contents inside.

He peered into the box, 'I see,' he replied but his attention was still on Carrie.

'Birdy,' Carrie rubbed her brow with one hand, 'Daddy will be here for a bit, why don't you go and take Chirpy back to your room?' She was finding the whole set-up between them a bit overwhelming. Jon wasn't just some friend who should be able to come and go as he pleased. This was all getting a bit too normal.

'I want you to show me this room, Carrie.' He sat up in his chair. 'I just want to check the door, make sure you are safe. You'll let me do that at least, won't you?'

She considered this for a moment, 'I suppose so,' she said, resigned. Maybe he would spot something which would confirm that she had been worrying unnecessarily.

'I'm right behind you,' he called out. Carrie could hear rummaging in the dishwasher as though he were tidying away his cup. She raised her eyebrows: this was certainly a turn up for the books as he had never done this at home.

She waited at the top of the stairs as he hurried to join her. She would not allow him to be able to roam freely around the house and 'accidentally' end up in a different room whilst looking for her. Jon followed behind her down the wooden flight of stairs. As she passed, she found herself automatically pulling the bedroom door she used to sleep in, so it was shut. For some reason, she didn't want him to see where she had slept. They could hear Birdy in her room, half chatting away to the bird and also by the sound of it, rummaging through various drawers.

Carrie didn't falter outside the boiler room door as she would have done if she were alone. She opened the door and let Jon go in first. The first thing he did was crinkle up his nose as though the musty odour was too much for him. He stood in the middle of the room and turned in a small circle, his shoes scraping the loose concrete.

'This is the door?' he moved over to it.

'Yes,' she confirmed, although it was the only other door in the room apart from the one they had just come in from. Carrie wasn't aware if he had picked up on that she was deliberately avoiding moving any closer to the door. She just didn't want to be near it. He frowned at her as though he was reading it that she didn't want to be near him.

Jon pressed his hands against the chipped woodwork. He looked down at the doorknob and tried to open it. 'Do you have a key for this?'

'No, I mean yes, we should have soon.' She drew her arms across her body and shivered slightly. Out of the sunlight, this room had a real chill to it. 'The handyman is supposed to be bringing a spare around soon.'

'Hmm.' He cast a look over the door as though he was a surveyor assessing for damage. 'I can't be certain as to when this door was last opened. You have got a lot of loose paintwork, which is possibly due to age but would also substantiate your claim about the banging. I doubt it would take much knocking to shift this loose.' He mulled over the door for a few more moments as though something insightful would jump out that Carrie hadn't thought of.

'Carrie, look,' he sauntered over to her and grasped both of her arms with his hands. She shrank away instinctively from this hold which made him loosen his touch slightly. 'You have my number if you need it. Any more problems, you give me a call. I want you to be safe here.'

She nodded, more to appease him than anything. In

reality, she wanted to be away from the door.

He patted her arm reassuringly. 'I'll be off now. I promised you I would give you space and I meant it.' Back upstairs, he stood by the door. 'You have my number,' he repeated, more of a statement than anything else.

'Of course,' she nodded.

'May I call in on you tomorrow?'

'I'll give you a call if it's not convenient,' she replied and shut the door again once he had started his walk down the road.

Carrie leaned against the door as Birdy bounded towards her. She acknowledged straight away that Birdy had changed her outfit for the day. It was an odd combination of an old dress and jeans. She sighed; this was what happened if she left Birdy to choose her own clothes. She decided not to comment on it.

'Chirpy is feeling a bit better and said he would like a worm for dinner.'

She smiled and bent down to see the box. Inside, the bird did indeed look more alert. Its black, beady eyes searched around from inside the enclosure. 'Oh, sweetie, I don't think we can get him a worm. Maybe it's time to let him go?'

'No!' she stated, almost at the foot-stamping stage. 'Chirpy is not ready to fly away yet. He said he'd like to stay a bit longer.' Her face was pulled into a disapproving pout before she stomped off. 'He's going back to my room.' Her voice trailed off as she made for the stairs.

Carrie sighed as she went to the kitchen to think about their dinner. She took another look at the letter again before placing it towards the back of the kitchen counter, alongside Jon's number.

They ate dinner together at the table, Carrie noticed that Birdy every so often would place a few small pieces of food into a napkin.

'Oh, sweetie, no. You can't just give a bird anything to eat.' She pulled a face, imagining foodstuff being littered around the room and the inevitable bugs that would follow.

'Chirpy will leave what he doesn't want. Like he'd do if

he was outside.'

Carrie shook her head and decided it was a battle not worth fighting now. If the bird's health was anything to go by, she would surely be able to persuade Birdy to let it go tomorrow anyway. The scratching sounds were evident from the shoebox, indicating that it had found its feet again.

'Don't keep taking the lid off,' she warned. 'We don't want it to get out.'

'Chirpy, that's his name,' Birdy reminded her. She moved to gather the box up, 'can I go and play now?'

'You've finished your dinner?' She eyed up the plate, still with some food left on it. Carrie watched as she carefully folded the napkin and placed this on top of the box and pushed her chair back. 'Not too long until bed now.' She was speaking to Birdy's back now as she had already headed out of the room. Carrie busied herself with tidying up before eventually settling in front of a film with a glass of wine in hand. It was one she had seen before so she laughed in all of the right places but wasn't really paying full attention. Checking the time, she saw it was well past Birdy's bedtime. She went down to Birdy's bedroom, not sure of what she would find.

'He's feeling a lot better now,' Birdy smiled up at her as she put the lid back on the box. Carrie noticed she was having trouble aligning the edges of the lid with the box's rim.

'Remember what I said about the lid,' she warned her again. Carrie decided not to broach the subject of releasing it back into the wild tomorrow. Perhaps they could go to the park and do it there, though. 'I'm just upstairs if you need me.'

Birdy smiled and settled the box on the dresser for what Carrie hoped would be for the night. She snuggled down into her bed and had soon turned to face the wall. Securing the front door, Carrie took a last look, mentally noting where things had been left before turning off all the lights.

DAY 12

Carrie was aware of being woken out of a deep sleep as it took her a while to familiarise herself with the surroundings. She could hear the knocking again, but it sounded different this time. Groggily, she reached for her watch and illuminated the time. Seeing the early hour, she groaned and flopped back against the pillow. The proximity of the noise told her that the knocking wasn't coming from downstairs as there was quite some distance between the high room and the boiler room and besides, the door was shut.

The knocking was coming from the front door, the sound of a fist striking one of the panels rang through the house. Carrie almost screamed in frustration towards the door, *you have the wrong house!* as she assumed it was simply someone who had gone out for the night but had returned without their key. In their drunken state, they had confused her house with theirs. She threw the covers back in anger. What was she planning to do? Confront them? The idea was ridiculous, she would just have to wait for them to realise their mistake. In answer to her silent prayer, the noise stopped as abruptly as it had started. Carrie muttered under her breath, cursing in annoyance. She had been woken from a deep sleep in the early hours and it would undoubtedly take her ages to settle again due to the nature of the disturbance. She punched the pillow several times out of frustration as though that was the key to falling back to sleep.

Carrie stared at the ceiling again as the shadows threw some unusual shapes in the semi-darkness. She strained to hear any other noises but there were none. She took a sip of water from the glass and replaced it on the bedside cabinet and the sound of it making contact echoed around the house. Carrie frowned and froze in the position she was in. She was tired, the sound of the glass being replaced was a much louder noise than it should have made.

The noise of her own breathing and heartbeat pulsed through her. Away from her bedroom area, a distinct scraping sound sliced through the still night air. She couldn't place it but her imagination conjured up an image of a witch with long, bony fingers scraping her fingernails against the glass in the bay window. It sent a cold chill through her as she lay in fear. Her legs felt like lead, not that she had any intention of going down to investigate. It was no doubt just the branches of a nearby tree scraping against the window in the breeze. She justified this idea in her head before her subconscious reminded her that there were no trees in the nearby vicinity, and it was a calm night with no howling wind apparent.

The slow scraping continued, first travelling away from her and then back towards. It sounded as though it was focused on the front door before moving away to the bay window. Back and forwards like a slow pendulum. Finally, this stopped and Carrie allowed herself to exhale loudly. The noise was then punctuated by a loud bang on the front door before stopping completely. She moved her trembling hands to cover her face, her fingers wiping away the tears which were pooling onto the pillow. The disturbances, someone's sick idea of a joke was getting to the point of ridiculous now. Who in their right mind would do this and for what purpose? Crying freely now, she moved the duvet over her head and shook in the darkness.

She had closed her eyes, too afraid to open them again but at the same time, scared at what her mind would throw up at her. In the distance, she heard a faint noise. 'Just a minute, just a minute,' she heard herself mutter. The crying became louder and closer as Birdy tugged on her arm. She was standing over her bed now.

Wearily, Carrie opened her eyes as bright sunlight greeted her. She had fallen back to sleep somehow. 'What's the matter baby?' she slurred, still not fully conscious.

'He's gone, Mummy!' the wails were becoming more high-pitched. 'I can't find him anywhere!'

'Who's gone, baby?' she murmured again but her awareness was kicking in now and her stomach flipped as she dreaded the confirmation of what Birdy was so upset about.

'Chirpy,' she managed to sob.

'Oh, sweetie.' Carrie reached for her dressing gown again. 'What do you mean "gone"? A bird doesn't just disappear.'

'He's not where I left him, he's not in his box,' her drawling continued like a wind-up distress call.

Carrie had managed to haul herself into a sitting position. She figured out taking into account the broken sleep, she had probably had less than four hours sleep, if she had been lucky. Things were definitely going to take twice as long today without regular caffeine intakes.

'Let's go and have a look, a bird just can't disappear.' She followed Birdy downstairs as though she needed showing where to go. Carrie threw a glance at the front door – the source of the disturbance last night – almost in an *I'll deal with you later* stare. Birdy had made it back to her bedroom quicker as if this were the answer to finding the bird sooner.

Carrie rubbed her eyes. 'Where did you leave the box, honey?'

'There.' She pointed to the dresser. The lid lay to the side of the box. Sure enough, when Carrie peered in, the box was indeed empty apart from the old tee shirt and a few scraps of food.

'Did you have the lid on, Birdy? Be honest,' she looked accusingly at her, already suspecting what the answer was.

'I took it off,' she sniffed, long and loudly. 'Chirpy needed some air.'

'Oh, Birdy!' Carrie groaned exasperatedly. 'What did I tell you about the lid?' She looked around the dresser, half expecting to see the bird hunched up against the skirting board.

'Chirpy promised he wouldn't fly away.'

Carrie snapped at her, 'It's a bird, they fly, what did you expect to happen?' She didn't wait for an answer as she went through the motions of lifting up discarded clothes, toys and bedding in the search. 'This room is a tip,' she remarked, not expecting a response. Birdy was far too young to appreciate the need for tidiness. 'No wonder we can never find anything,' she muttered to herself. She moved to the bedroom door and looked in both directions. 'Well, I don't know where it's gone,' she threw her arms up in the air. 'I can't find it.'

Birdy put a bunched fist to her eye to suppress the tears but slowly began to cry again. Her shoulders heaved up and down as she fought to fight back the distress. Standing by the door, Carrie knew that she would have to undergo the rigorous search of the whole house, including rooms they hadn't set foot in for a while, such as her old bedroom. It would be like trying to find a needle in a haystack as she was sure there would be plenty of small gaps in the house for a bird to nestle into. However, nothing less would do. She had to show Birdy she was making the effort to find it.

'Okay, we'll start looking,' she announced. Birdy responded with a weak smile before wiping her face and joining in with the search. Carrie found that Birdy would either look in the places she had just checked or turn various superficial objects upside down to check underneath. She bit her tongue at several points as she eyed Birdy turning the lamp over and checking under a book on the floor.

The bathroom downstairs had been searched thoroughly. Carrie inspected around the marble bathtub, around the toilet and in their washing basket.

'How about this room?' Birdy was stood at the entrance of her mother's old room, the door now pushed wide open.

'Uh, we've not been in there for a while.' Carrie thought back to the previous day when she had purposely closed this when Jon had been here. 'Did you just open this sweetie? He couldn't have got under the crack in the door.'

'I pushed it open. And he could get under the door.'

Carrie crouched down and saw that, indeed, the gap was quite large from where the door met the carpet. She reasoned that at some stage perhaps there had been a mat or rug placed here or the carpet had been a higher quality to allow for such a gap. She breathed deeply, already growing tired of this search. 'Well, there's no way he could have got upstairs.' They were standing at the foot of the wooden stairs. She took one look at Birdy's face before adding, 'You go and look then,' and waved her hand in the direction of upstairs. As she scampered up, Carrie took one last look around. She had been avoiding it but there was clearly one room they had not looked in – the boiler room. It would have to be done; Birdy would work out that they hadn't looked everywhere if they didn't. She put her hand on the door, her imagination throwing up images of the bird on the floor, innards displayed for all to see. Perhaps she needed to check before Birdy.

Inside, nothing remarkable jumped out. The boiler hummed quietly and otherwise, there were no other distinguishable sounds. She dared to move into the middle of the room as Jon had so confidently done yesterday. A faint aroma piqued her interest, maybe Jon had been right to pull his expression of semi-disgust when he had stood there. There was definitely an odour that she couldn't quite place. Whatever it was, it wasn't pleasant and was enough to make her want to leave the room. Perhaps it was the onset of rising damp; the room didn't look the best with regard to insulation. She imagined it would probably suffer from damp during the winter months. Having no desire to upturn any items on the shelf which didn't look at though they had been disturbed for a while, she quickly backed out of the room. It was highly unlikely the bird would have made it under the door and then onto the shelves anyway.

Carrie joined the search back upstairs and then after that, into the high room. Between them, they unearthed nothing. No signs a bird had even been present in the area, no droppings or loose feathers. Birdy sat down on the floor, defeated.

'Where is he?' The pitiful wailing started again.

'Sweetie, I don't know,' Carrie moved so that she was sitting down next to her. She placed a soothing hand on her head as Birdy inched closer for comfort. Whatever the reason for her upset, her child was clearly distressed and this was the element that upset Carrie the most. She needed comforting and that was all Carrie would be able to do to rectify this situation. There was no way she could magic a missing bird out of thin air. They sat together for a while, Birdy still crying with all the demeanour setting in that they were never going to find the missing bird. Carrie held her tightly throughout. She had no idea of how long they had been sat there, the only indication of time was the fact that her legs were getting increasingly more uncomfortable by the second. Carrie moved Birdy a few inches away from her and studied her features. Her eyes were swollen with the number of tears shed and her cheeks were a blotchy pink. Her eyes still glistened as though they were about to overflow again.

'How about if Mummy fixes us both something to eat?' she suggested quietly. Her stomach had begun a protest but it was more about Birdy needing something else to focus on and take her mind off the lost bird.

Carrie didn't wait for an answer before carrying her off to the lounge and placing her onto the sofa. 'Shall I get Mr Bear for you whilst the pancakes are cooking?' A small head bobbed up and down in response. She was in exactly the same position when Carrie returned, staring pitifully at the television.

'Okay?' She passed the stuffed bear to Birdy and the sobs began again.

'He can't just disappear.' Her voice was high and squeaky. 'He must be somewhere?'

'Sweetheart, I don't know where else we can look, we've looked everywhere.' Carrie cast a look around the lounge to reaffirm this. 'Birds are very small and can fit in small gaps.'

'Then he must be in a small hole.' Her protest was broken and littered with breathy pants.

'Birdy, I …' a knock on the door interrupted her flow. Carrie didn't even pause to wonder who it could be, whether it was a charity collector or even a door canvasser, but anything would break the mood in the house. She checked the clock and saw that it was still relatively early. The fruitless searching around the house hadn't taken up as much time as she thought.

He stood with the same stance as the previous day, waiting like a vampire for permission to cross the threshold of the house.

'Jon,' Carrie breathed; maybe a change of familiar face would settle Birdy. She pushed the door closed behind him. 'We've got a bit of a situation.' She motioned with her head towards the lounge and continued in hushed tones. 'She's a bit upset.'

'Oh,' his expression morphed into one of concern as Carrie relayed their morning to him, that she had spent most of it on her hands and knees searching for the impossible.

'What a shame,' he over-sympathised. 'Maybe I could help.' Carrie watched as he wandered through to the lounge. She heard Birdy's whimpering start again as she had a new audience to hear her.

'Christ,' she heard herself mutter as she moved to join them. Birdy was sitting curled up on Jon's lap as he soothed her hair down with a hand. She heard it all again, the box, the lid and how Chirpy was fine when she'd turned the light out and nowhere to be seen in the morning. This event had now stretched into the afternoon.

'Daddy can help you look again, birds are very good at hopping around as well as flying,' his tone suited his captive audience. It was as though he was about to launch into a story. Birdy nodded, grateful for another willing member of her search team. Jon smiled as he allowed himself to be led by her small hand as they went to retrace Birdy's steps for that morning.

Carrie sank back into the sofa for a moment, she closed her eyes, still jaded from the disrupted night and grateful for a minute's peace. Suddenly, she sat bolt upright. Here was a man whom she and Birdy had fled from in the middle of the night and now she had given him a free rein of their supposed safe house. By manipulating Birdy with his simulated concern, he had successfully managed to worm his way back into her affections. Back at their house, he hadn't shown a shred of sympathy for the deceased goldfish.

She had no intention of sneaking up on them to eavesdrop on their conversation but was able to see into Birdy's room before she had actually reached it. He was crouched down on the floor, positioned so he had access to under the bed. Out of the corner of her eye, Carrie spotted the neat piles of folded up clothes on the high dresser. She noted they were the new ones that Birdy had chosen the other day, now nicely placed out of reach.

'Well, I don't think he's in here,' Jon got up from the floor. 'Let's check the other rooms on this floor, that's the most likely place if the bird is wandering around.' Carrie saw him make a beeline for the boiler room.

'The gap under the door is far too small,' she heard herself explain. 'And besides, I've already looked in there.'

Regardless, he flung the door open with the flamboyancy of a grand theatrical opening. The first thing to hit Carrie was the smell – the odour that had been lingering earlier was now much more pungent. It forced her to put a hand to cover her nose and mouth. Jon visibly shrank back too.

'Eww, what's that stink?' Birdy hovered by the door and pinched her nose.

'God, what is that?' breathed Jon. He spun around again to look for any obvious signs.

'I noticed something earlier and reckon it's damp or something,' Carrie explained. The last thing she wanted was him poking around in there, potentially disturbing whatever it was. However, in her mind, a thought began to creep in which she didn't want to entertain. The smell almost reminded her of something rotting.

Back upstairs, she made some coffee whilst Birdy was occupied making a few more half-hearted attempts to search the upstairs.

'There's no way a dead bird would make that kind of smell and so quickly,' Jon reasoned, once Birdy was out of earshot. 'How big was this bird anyway, a golden eagle or something?' He smirked at his own joke.

Carrie cupped her hands together to make a small space an egg would fit it. 'About this size.' She agreed with Jon but didn't want to admit this to him.

'Do you want me to have a word with your landlord about the smell?'

She shook her head. 'No, Jon, I do not.' Goodness knows what Agnes would think if a strange man she'd never met suddenly turned up on her doorstep and started rabbiting on about a strange smell. It would definitely arouse suspicion as to who he was. She paced exasperatedly. 'Why are you doing this? Why do you think it's your job to come and save us?'

He stared at her and for a moment and she saw his eyes change. 'Because you are still my wife...' His tone was harsh as though he resented being challenged on his feelings for them.

'Keep your voice down!' she hissed.

'And let's not forget you still have my child here.' He ran his hands through his hair. 'Look, Carrie,' his tone was calmer now, 'I get you need some space, I get it, okay? But like I've said, the least I can do is make sure you are both safe whilst you are away from home. Okay?'

Defeated and not wanting to start a full-blown row, Carrie sank further into her chair. She put her head in her hands, now emotionally and physically exhausted. Jon placed a careful hand on her shoulder. 'Look, why don't you let me make you something to eat? I'll leave whenever you want after that.'

She nodded. 'Okay, that would be … nice, thank you.' The day had proved exhausting and it was one less chore she would have to do.

He smiled. 'Right, you go and sit and watch TV or something. I'll rustle something up with what you've got here.' He quickly set about rummaging through cupboards before shooing her out of the kitchen. Carrie sat on the sofa with Birdy. Rewind about a year or so and this was just like the old times together.

DAY 13

The bed felt warm. Before Carrie even dared to open her eyes, she had a sickening thought to explain the temperature change. What if she's had another visitor in the night? What if they'd decided to ramp things up and bit and instead of simply banging on the door, what if they had now broken in and had dared to actually get in the bed beside her? He, assuming it was a man, would be lying down beside her, a menacing grin etched in his face, staring and waiting for her to wake up. Carrie calmed her breathing down before summoning up the courage to open her eyes. Fully expecting to emit a blood-curdling scream, she paused. Beside her, Jon lay breathing steadily.

The expected imaginary horror had merely been replaced with her reality. Careful not to disturb him, she crept out of bed and down the spiral staircase as quietly as she could. The last thing she wanted Birdy to do was stroll up and see them together. Carrie rubbed her head; yes, she had been tired last night but must have been so exhausted that she hadn't put up much of a fight for him to be in her bed. She figured the day to be Saturday, even though one day seemed to blend into another at the moment. Pulling back the curtain on the bay window a few inches, she was alerted to a scene outside. Carrie gasped as she saw Agnes standing outside her front door – this was not a day she had expected her to be outside. She had been informed it was Sunday for church and then Monday for shopping, as though these were the only days she was allowed to be outside.

Carrie moved back from the curtain into what she hoped was a concealed spot. Agnes was talking to a man who had his back to Carrie and from the looks of it, it was quite an altercation due to the animated gestures he was making. She was able to ascertain a lot from his body language and he appeared angry. Although the house was quite dated, the window panes were doing a very good job of making their speech indistinguishable, even though their voices were raised. Carrie froze as he gestured towards her house with a sweeping arm movement. His face was clear now – it was Clive the tradesman. She quickly dropped the curtain and pressed her back against the wall, praying neither of them had seen her. When she dared to peek back out, all she saw was him now sitting in the front seat of his van, a frown adorning his face as he prepared to drive off. Sure enough, his engine roared into life before he sped out of the parking space. Agnes by now had gone back into her house; Carrie had a feeling she had been looking at the wrong person the whole time and longed to know what Agnes' facial expressions had looked like during the argument. Had she been threatened? Had they had a disagreement over something? Whatever it was, it involved her house as he had pointed directly at her.

She was distracted by a noise from upstairs and guessed Jon was now starting to wake up. Carrie realised she had slept relatively soundly last night. In fact, she had not been woken by any noises at all. No banging or digging or imaginary footsteps. There had been absolutely nothing.

He took the stairs slowly and Carrie could see that he had already pulled on his tee shirt and jeans from the previous day. His hair was the tell-tale sign he had just got up. 'Morning,' he yawned. 'Did you sleep well?'

For a brief moment, Carrie saw him coming towards her to greet her properly. Anticipating this, she sidled past him quickly. 'I did, thank you.'

'It was fairly quiet here last night; I mean for a Friday night.'

And there it was: the subtle comment that there had

been no disturbances inside or outside due to his presence. Carrie drew her dressing gown tighter as though this was her shield.

'Jon, I think you should go, I mean before Birdy wakes up. I don't want to confuse her.'

He frowned. 'And what's to confuse her? Seeing her Mum and Dad together? Christ, Carrie, it's not even been two weeks and you're acting like I'm some kind of stranger to her.'

She held out her hand in defence. 'Jon,' she stuttered. 'I don't want an argument …'

'You don't want an argument,' he repeated, his voice taking on a sharper tone. This was the Jon she was used to – snappy and ready to challenge wherever he could. He took a few steps back and bit his lip thoughtfully, 'I'm sorry,' he stated, as though he was conscious that he had slipped out of character slightly. 'I didn't mean to shout.' He glanced at her but refused to make eye contact. 'I'll be out of here to give you some space.' He rushed past her to find his shoes and she heard him recite to himself what she presumed was a line from his therapy, one to calm himself down. 'I truly am sorry for raising my voice just then.' He was more composed now. 'It's difficult, you know?' He searched her eyes for forgiveness. 'I've overstepped the mark, I apologise.'

Carrie pulled her gown again and nodded. She was just glad to see him on his way out as she needed some space from him.

'May I call you again? Carrie, it's so nice just making these small steps, you know? Spending some time with you two away from the house. I really do look forward to these visits.'

'Yes, that would be okay,' Carrie's voice was small. 'If you are okay with the journey each time to see us.'

He looked at her for a moment as though he had not heard the question. 'Oh, yes. The journey. No, it's fine. Luckily, I've found a quick route by now. I stumbled on it by accident.' He laughed briefly at his own joke. 'I will call again unless you phone to say otherwise?'

Carrie nodded as she held the door open for him.

Anything to appease him just so he could get going.

'Right.' He nodded and walked past her. 'Tell Birdy I'll see her soon?'

Carrie simply smiled at him and closed the door once he was away from the house. She had wanted to slam at as soon as he'd set both feet outside but had feared this may flare up his temper. Upstairs, she stripped the bed in an attempt to erase last night, angry at herself for giving him the wrong impression.

Birdy wandered into the kitchen whilst she was bundling the sheets into the washing machine. 'Morning, sleepyhead, what did you want to do today?' She painted her best smile on her face, worried that the memory of the missing bird was still playing on her mind. 'I thought we could go out somewhere?'

'Is Daddy coming with us?'

Carrie paused; children had a way of just coming out with questions without really thinking about them. If she were an adult, she would have danced around the question for a while. 'He had to … go home,' she added tentatively. 'Did you want him to come?' Hoping this sounded like a casual enquiry, Carrie reached into the cupboard for washing powder.

Birdy simply shrugged, 'I guess I would have if you wanted him to.'

'Well, he had to go home,' she stated. 'Listen, before long we're going to have to think about what to do after we leave here.'

'So we're not staying here forever, then?'

'No, we only have this house for a month. We need to be thinking about where to go afterwards. I was thinking Nanny's for a bit?' She gave a genuine smile; Birdy loved her Nanny and she would always welcome them with open arms.

'I want to leave here.' Birdy scrunched up her face. 'It's very smelly in my room.' She folded her arms across her chest in protest.

It took a while for Carrie to register this before she remembered that Jon had pointed out a smell whilst they had been searching the boiler room. Sure enough, the smell hit her as soon as they walked down the wooden stairs and increased in strength the closer they got to the boiler room. It was as though it were seeping through the gaps in the door, ever closer to them like a thick fog. Carrie pushed open the door with her foot and held her hand to her nose.

'What *is* that?' she was sure the smell had got worse since yesterday. She couldn't quite place it in the surroundings, it smelt as though some rotten food was nearby. Carrie looked towards the shelving unit – perhaps something had started to turn on one of the shelves? She cast a glance over and could only see painting equipment, pots, white spirit and cloths. There was nothing that would produce such an aroma in a short space of time.

'Maybe it's coming from outside,' Birdy's voice was muffled as she'd made the exaggerated move of covering her mouth and nose with both hands and now spoke through these.

'It's possible, maybe they store their bins outside.' However, she didn't have confidence in her own convictions. Her own rubbish bins fitted outside the front door, and she could only presume next door's were the same. At the back of her mind, she still had the idea of finding the corpse of the dead bird, Chirpy, if they continued to investigate. Instead, she ushered Birdy outside of the door. She had convinced herself that now more than ever, was the time to move on.

'Maybe you should sleep with me in the high room?' She didn't want to encourage Birdy to sleep in her bed the whole time but couldn't imagine sleeping next door to the smelly room.

Carrie decided that a day out would be a good idea, just her and Birdy spending some time together. A trip away from this town was called for so they headed for the train station with a mind to travel a fair distance away. She felt she needed some space from Jon, the slowly decaying house and quite frankly odd neighbours. Carrie instructed Birdy to wait whilst she put the cake box back on Agnes's doorstep. For some reason, she didn't want her setting foot on the property. As though she were trespassing into a haunted house, Carrie positioned the box in front of the door before dashing back onto the pavement. As she did so, she had the strange sensation of eyes upon her. Carrie put a protective hand on Birdy's shoulder before looking up at Agnes's house. There were no signs of life from the upstairs window. The curtains to what she presumed was the lounge window were also still drawn. Come to think of it, Carrie couldn't recall ever having seen them open.

She cast one final look around the street as they walked off. There, she saw it, the tell-tale swish of a curtain from across the road told her that someone else had been watching her movements. It took her a while before she could recall the neighbour's name – it had been the greying lady she'd had a couple of run-ins on the street with – Valerie. Carrie pursed her lips as she recalled her harsh features. This woman had been another nosey busybody with nothing else to do than spy on her neighbours. They proceeded to the train station.

By the time they arrived home, Carrie was exhausted so she dreaded to think how Birdy was coping. She decided she was probably powered on adrenaline now, the excitement of their day still fresh in her mind. Birdy still had a bounce in her step as they reached the top of their street. It had been a busy day where they had decided to get off the train within walking distance of a museum and a sea life centre. Birdy had stared in awe at the different aquatic wildlife in their tanks. She had marvelled at the varying fish of bright colours. Carrie had given her a spending limit in the gift shop for more stuffed toys to add to her collection.

'Bath when we get back and then it's not long before you'll be in bed,' she informed her. Carrie stifled a yawn herself.

She sat on the floor by the edge of the bathtub idly trailing her hand through the water as Birdy sat surrounded by toys. Carrie got up quickly as she realised the blind was only half drawn. Just as she pulled it down to the bottom of the window, a small dark shape caught her eye. She gasped as she managed to see through the gap and then tried to discreetly move the blind to one side without attracting Birdy's attention or Agnes who may be in her sewing room. Thankfully, Birdy was otherwise occupied, running her wind-up toy frog through the bubbles.

Carrie inched the blind open with one hand and looked out onto the small patio area. She struggled to focus as dusk began to set in. The small object had been placed carefully onto the windowsill. She swallowed a lump in her throat as she realised this looked like a bird whose stillness informed her it was very much dead. It was a huge coincidence to be a bird that had died just as it landed on the windowsill. She put a hand to her mouth and swallowed hard. There was no doubt in her mind that she had found Chirpy. The brown markings looked the same and the same beady eyes were now permanently open. Somehow, it had got outside and then chosen their windowsill on which to die. She tried hard to rack her brain as to what Birdy's pet had looked like. Was this the same one?

'What is it, Mummy?'

Carrie dropped the blind. 'Oh, nothing, sweetie. Look, you should be getting out soon,' she placed a hand in the bathwater. 'Goodness, it's getting cold now.' She reached for a nearby towel and was grateful a willing Birdy got out.

As she towel-dried her hair, the image of the bird still sat in her thoughts. 'Birdy, remember I said that it's very important for you to keep the blinds and curtains in your room closed?' She felt her head nod as she dried her. While she decided what to do and when to go out and remove it, the best solution would be for Birdy to avoid the area for the time being. In a way, the smell was doing the job for them as it was too pungent for her to settle in the downstairs rooms.

'Grab your pyjamas and Mr Bear and I'll get you settled in Mummy's bed in the high room.'

Carrie watched as Birdy snuggled down beneath her sheets. She smiled lovingly and smoothed her hair with one hand. 'Did you have a busy day?' Birdy let out a long yawn as she nodded. Her eyelids were growing heavier with each passing second.

'Night, sweetie,' Carrie leaned in to kiss her and then turned at the top of the spiral staircase. Her eyes were already closed. It was still relatively early and Carrie did not want to go to bed herself for a while. She went back downstairs and stood outside the boiler room door, trying hard not to inhale fully. If it got much worse, she would have to call Agnes again to ask Clive to investigate. Upstairs, she sat on the sofa not really paying attention to the programme on the TV. She settled her wine glass on the coffee table before leaning back against the sofa and she felt her eyes start to feel heavy too.

Carrie woke with a start. Her limbs felt heavy and her head was foggy. She had an eerie feeling that something had woken her. Her ears prickled as she could make out a faint shuffling sound. As she was still lying on the sofa, she couldn't be sure whether it was coming from outside or somewhere in the house. Carrie felt her blood run cold as she clutched the cushion tightly, her breathing reduced to slow intakes. Something was just not right. Either someone else was in the house or the only other explanation was that it was haunted. She screwed her eyes tight like a child would, too petrified to go and investigate what might be nothing more serious than a window that hadn't been closed properly. Of all the disturbances she had encountered over the last few days, the action that seemed to have worked for her was for her to remain as still and silent as possible until the disorder passed. A thought taunted her; there was no way she could cope alone.

She lay on the sofa, now wide awake. Her heartbeat and laboured breathing were the only sounds apparent. Carrie forced herself to hear any other noises and eventually, the sound of the house's stillness rang uncomfortably in her ears. The silence was deafening. She wondered how much more she could take, how much fear could a person tolerate before they crumbled? Surely she must be teetering on the precipice of her own personal Hell by now. It was coming to the point that she did not like the person she was becoming. Jumpy, nervous and quick to doubt were her dominant traits at the moment. What was the cause of the disturbance now? What had woken her this time?

Carrie moved to swing her legs off the side of the sofa. She could not cope with living in fear for much longer. Goodness knows she had endured enough in one setting or another. With the remaining ounce of courage she still had inside her, Carrie got to her feet and inched her way towards the door. She felt as though she was made of glass – fragile and transparent with nowhere to hide. She wasn't sure what she expected to find or *wanted* to find. The figure of an intruder in her house? At least she would be able to justify all of the terror she had witnessed in the last few days. Carrie could not be sure who would attack first, her strength would come from the pent-up frustration at not being able to resolve this sooner. He would be alarmed at her frenzied attack and would flee the same way he'd gained access to the house in the first place. To her disappointment, there was nothing.

Her footsteps were light on each step down to the now unused bedrooms. Straining for any change in the sound, her senses felt heightened. Then, there it was – the break in the sound pattern as she could just make out a distant clicking sound coming from one of the bedrooms. Its rhythm slowed down with every passing second, like a wheel coming to a stop. And then, the silence again.

Pushing open the door to Birdy's old bedroom, the moonlight's blade pierced through the gap in the curtains spotlighting the cause of the noise. The wind-up frog lay innocently on the floor. Enraged, Carrie seized it and threw it back onto the carpeted floor where it bounced against the wall and ricocheted back off. It protested for a few seconds as the last few rotations of the mechanism were forced out. The toy came to a standstill a few inches from the skirting board. Reining in her outburst, she moved to retrieve the toy, fearing a dent in the paintwork. Bending down, she froze as a movement in her peripheral vision caught her eye. The outline of a fully grown person was sickeningly apparent as it too crouched to mimic her. Moments passed as she stared at the brazen onlooker for a while, daring it to move.

Carrie lowered her head so that her chin rested down as far as it could. 'For Christ's sake!' she muttered to herself as she stared into the mirror on the inside door of the wardrobe. Her tears stung her cheeks as she allowed them to flow. To be scared of your own reflection was reaching a new level. Unless you were afraid of the person looking back at you.

DAY 14

Regardless of the fact that she had stayed awake for most of the night praying for the morning to come, Carrie had managed a small amount of sleep but had still woken at an early hour. The summer morning began to creep in from around the curtains covering the bay window as she realised she had finally managed to fall asleep on the sofa. It had been a fitful and unsatisfying sleep. Her back felt uncomfortably stiff as she groaned into a sitting position. She took a few moments to appreciate the daylight, everything looked so different in the natural light.

Summoning courage, she plodded downstairs to have a look at where the noise had been coming from last night. In Birdy's old room, she remembered placing the frog back onto the bed and practically slamming the wardrobe door shut after her reflection had scared her. The smell hit her again and she wondered why it was so strong. To her horror, she spied the boiler room door to be a couple of inches ajar. Doubt clouded her recollection – had she left it open last night after she had got Birdy out of the bath? She recalled almost stomping off back upstairs after her investigation during the night and hadn't given the boiler room door a second thought back then. As she pushed the door open, the hinges creaked in protest and the door bumped against the wall. Not knowing what she expected to find, Carrie took a quick look inside and was disappointed to see nothing out of the ordinary. Nothing seemed out of place. It was something else to chalk up to her absent-mindedness.

Birdy was keen to play with her toys after lunch as Carrie sat at the kitchen table. She mulled over the letter again, weighing up the potential threat it posed. She traced the letters with her fingers – leave while you still can. Perhaps she was looking at this wrong – was it a warning as opposed to a threat?

'Mummy?'

The voice snapped her out of her trance.

'Mummy, I can hear knocking.'

Carrie shook her head, not being able to rationalise this statement.

Birdy spoke again. 'Someone is knocking at the door.' She hovered by the kitchen door and disappeared as Carrie got up.

He stood on the doorstep, smiling as usual. Upon seeing her face, he frowned. 'Carrie, you look rough. Is everything okay? Did you not sleep well?'

Carrie looked at him, her face pensive. She spotted movement behind him and spied Valerie across the road, taking much longer than usual to put rubbish in her bin. Not wanting to give her anything else to gossip about, she opened the door wider for Jon to enter.

'I'm fine,' she rubbed her eyes as though this would convince him. When she had got washed that morning, she had stared at her reflection and wondered whether she had always looked that haggard. The stress of all the events both here and at her old house was now startlingly apparent.

Jon stalled as he walked past Birdy, sat at the lounge table as she pored over some colouring sheets. 'Morning, sweetie, what are you drawing?' His voice sat almost a full octave higher than usual. He tilted his head to get a better look.

'Are those ghosts?' He let out a gentle laugh. 'It's not nearly time for Halloween.'

'Mummy says we have ghosts.' She didn't look up at him.

'Okay …' Jon frowned and stood up straight again. 'I'll just be in the kitchen having a coffee with Mummy.' As he backed away, he muttered to himself.

'She's just told me you think you have *ghosts*?' Jon spoke this word as though it were foreign to him.

Carrie shrugged. 'You know how quirky she can be, although I can't think of any other explanation.' She sighed as she sat down at the table, being upright required more energy than she had at that moment.

'You seem much crankier today,' Jon announced

'I'm just tired.' Carrie rested her head in her hands, grateful for the coffee.

'Noises back then? You said something like "there's no other explanation"?' He chewed on his lip thoughtfully.

'I'm just wondering,' Carrie got up and moved to check on Birdy. She quietened her voice, 'I'm thinking when you spent the night here.' She watched as a small twitch played on his mouth. 'There were no noises.'

He shrugged. 'And?' Jon fixed his eyes on her and let out a laugh. 'Oh, I see,' he replied, as though a penny had dropped in his mind. 'I spend the night here, and I might remind you, Carrie, of who came onto who there, and all of a sudden, your creepy night noises stop. I wasn't here last night and they're back. So clearly, this has something to do with me.' His expression morphed into a hard scowl.

'I'm just saying,' she hissed back in a controlled tone, 'that it's awfully convenient and a bit of a coincidence, don't you think?'

'Christ, Carrie.' He turned his head, exasperatedly. 'You really do need to get some sleep or help.'

She sprang in defence and put a fist on the table in defiance. 'Don't patronise me! Don't tell me I need help!' One look at his expression forced her to remove her hand and her eyes cast down to the floor. She stared at the floor feeling sheepish again.

Jon's voice was hushed but weighted, 'I think you're forgetting yourself.'

Carrie moved her mouth to reply, the words were cloyingly stuck in her throat. It was an effort to force them out. Everything she had been through – it was time she started to say what was on her mind. 'This letter,' she retrieved it from the counter. 'I think you wrote this ...'

'Oh, don't be so stupid. Why? For what purpose?'

'I think you're behind all of this. Trying to scare us so much that we'll come home.' Speaking these words that had toyed in her mind for the last few days convinced her. 'Where are you staying anyway?' Her mind flashed back to their conversation after he had stayed the night – he'd been a bit quick to answer with how he had managed to get to them with such ease.

He frowned. 'I'm at *our* house, where else would I be?'

Carrie turned away from him for a moment. She didn't want him to see her struggle to control the distress. As it stood, it was taking the last traces of courage she had to say the words and he was knocking them back as trivial frivolities. Carrie had new-found strength since leaving him; sure, this had dipped back and forth at times, but his presence now was moulding her back into the tense and highly strung figure she had left a few weeks ago. Her voice was quieter now. 'You seem to be able to get here very fast is all.'

'I set off early. I happen to be worried about your welfare, in case you hadn't noticed. I've taken time off work to sort things out between us.' His tone was waspish. 'What, you think I'm stalking you, is that it?'

Carrie shook her head. 'This letter I received. You were very quick to brush it off as being nothing to worry about.'

'Because you were. *You* brushed it off, I didn't want to worry you. You said it was just local kids messing around.' He brought a clenched fist down to strike the table then pushed his chair back to approach her. Instinctively, Carrie backed away and only stopped when the kitchen worktop prevented her from going back any further. She stood against it, her back pressed into it as the edge of the counter dug uncomfortably into her. Jon stood inches from her, his size dominating her. His face remained in a judgemental frown as he narrowed his eyes. This time, he did not remember to compose himself.

He moved nearer so his face was close to hers and spoke softly, 'I think you need to take a long look at yourself.'

His gaze moved to the worktops. 'Just take a look at these wine bottles. It's clear you've got yourself in the habit of polishing these off every night. What is it, a glass here and there to reward yourself after a long day? Then you have the nerve to imply I'd deliberately plan to scare you.' He shook his head, a look of disgust on his face.

Carrie blushed; it was true, she had been drinking slightly more than she had ever had. At home, he had not allowed her to drink so anything more than one glass every now and again so naturally any more was going to have an effect on her. But to downplay everything that had happened and blame it on her supposed drunken state? She had not simply imagined everything.

His mouth was inches from her ear so she could feel his warm breath against her face. 'You are not fit to be a mother. When you've had enough running away from me, I will be right back at home and I will take my daughter ...'

'You are not taking our child,' Carrie had started sobbing now as he was playing on her weak spot.

'Just think about it. Carry on drinking like this and accusing me,' he caught her eyes, 'yes, accusing. I can give an alibi for when I am not here, and you won't have much to fight me with when I go for custody.'

Carrie sniffed and wiped her eyes with her sleeve; her voice was barely above a whisper as her breath hitched. 'Everything I've given you over the years. You've had exactly what you've wanted. *I've* been exactly what you've wanted and so has Birdy ...'

Jon moved his hand, for one moment, Carrie feared the contact but realised he was moving too slow for it to be a slap. Instead, he put his hand so it rested on the side of her face. She half expected him to start stroking her face but his hand remained fixed in the same position. He gently forced her face upwards so she could do nothing but look at him. 'You are pathetic.' His words were slow and deliberate. 'You will come home and things will be exactly the way I want.' Jon moved his hand so that it now rested around her throat. His grasp was soft but flexed slightly. 'Is that clear? Carrie, answer me.'

Carrie stared back at him; the whites of his eyes were menacingly clear. If she was to shake her head, he would surely tighten his grip. She swallowed almost painfully as his hand prevented her. 'Yes,' she managed to reply.

Jon clenched his jaw as he retained his hold over her. He pushed at her throat and removed his hand but remained in the same position. 'I'll give you a week tops to hand your notice in here. Give your doddery old landlady your intention to leave and then come back home. And Carrie?'

Carrie swallowed in rapid succession as she blinked back at him.

'If you're not back by then, I will come back and forcibly remove you from here myself, do you understand? I'll drag you out by the hair if I have to.'

She nodded.

'And don't even bother to move on from here because I'll find out. It was ever so easy to track you down here, don't forget. Your mother just needed a sob story from me before she handed over your address.' He took a few steps back from her now and Carrie's shoulders visibly relaxed. For one moment, the look on his face, the absolute repulsion, it looked as though he was sickened by her. Again, she was nothing to him but someone to control.

The tears stung in Carrie's eyes as she watched him walk out of the room. He heard Birdy's squeals as he had obviously snuck up on her and surprised her. His voice was upbeat and at a distance now. She closed her eyes, her face hot with relief. Moving her hands to wipe her face, they shook as she struggled to compose herself.

'Carrie.' She heard his voice from the lounge, a summons rather than a question. Jon had his hands on Birdy's shoulders but his eyes were fixed on Carrie's. 'I need to go now.' He looked down at Birdy. 'But I was just speaking to Mummy and we talked about you coming home. Won't that be exciting?' His voice was jolly and playful again. His smile was infectious to Birdy as she automatically mirrored him. 'We'll all be together again,' he rubbed her shoulders. 'Well,' he puffed his breath out loudly and made an exaggerated glance at his watch, 'you and Mummy have a lot to sort out, so I need to be going.'

'So when will we see you again?' Birdy skipped behind him.

'I'll see you in a week, right Carrie?' His smile did not reach his eyes.

Carrie smiled weakly and held out a hand to Birdy. She swallowed, knowing she probably looked a mess. 'Let Daddy go now, sweetie.'

'Big hugs and kisses!' he crouched down to Birdy as Carrie opened the door. 'I'll see you real soon. I can't wait for us to be all back together again.' He stood up to face Carrie and leant close to kiss her cheek. There was little affection in it and it was almost a stamp of certification. He lingered for a beat too long before retreating, still with the same look in his eyes.

'One week,' he reminded her.

Carrie held Birdy close to her side as Jon waved back. He strolled back down the street, hands in pocket. She was sure there was a bounce in his step and she was sure he'd started whistling. Moving to close the door, she spotted it again. Valerie across the road could just be seen looking from behind her curtain. She looked across at the both of them and this time, Carrie let her.

DAY 15

Carrie stood in front of the bathroom mirror and wiped it free from condensation. She had soaked in the bath slightly too long and now felt light-headed from the heat. This coupled with her troubled sleep again last night when it had felt like she had done a lot of tossing and turning did not weigh up for a promising day. She had spent a lot of time since Jon left staring vacantly into space, managing a forced smile when Birdy had shown her a picture or asked a question. Everything she had set to accomplish since arriving at the house, of being a strong, independent single mother had all crumbled yesterday with Jon's cruel words. He was right – she couldn't make it on her own. She cursed herself at being so foolish to let him in again, all the promises of therapy had merely been a smokescreen for what lay underneath. After tucking Birdy into bed, Carrie had sat downstairs as the tears started again. She had reached for one of the cushions and had wailed loudly into it, sometimes sobbing in anger.

There was no plan for what to do next. Go to the police about Jon? Where was her concrete evidence that her life was in danger? He had even managed to win around Birdy's approval again in such a short space of time. Carrie smoothed cream on her face, donning a mask of her fragility internally. She would have to keep up pretenses for her child's sake for the time being.

They sat across each other at the kitchen table, Carrie

deep in thought as she held a coffee cup in one hand.

'Can we go to the park again today, Mummy?'

'Sure.' She answered too quickly but then realised a change of scenery and some fresh air would be a welcome relief from the stuffiness and sense of imprisonment inside. Poised at the front door, Carrie spotted the shadow from outside as Agnes walked past on her bi-weekly trip outside. Having no desire for idle chitchat to discuss the weather, Carrie moved away from the window and decided to wait until the coast was clear. She was half tempted to broach the subject of the smell in the boiler room but concluded this would need a lot of work in explaining and would no doubt take a while due to Agnes's apparent hearing loss. Perhaps a note through the door again would be the best solution. She was quite good at getting Clive to come around so quickly. Carrie made a mental note to write one when they got back.

She secured the front door whilst Birdy scraped her boots on the railing outside. Carrie had cast a fleeting look at her choice of outfit and had frowned at her selection of boots in the middle of summer but decided not to argue. There wasn't a cloud in the sky. Turning around, she saw Valerie's door open and instead of heading for her rubbish bin, she raised a hand for Carrie to stop and rushed over the road.

'Young lady, a moment of your time?'

Carrie sighed, from one elderly neighbour to another, she just wanted to be left in peace to enjoy the outing with her child, not pass the time on the pavement with a stranger.

Valerie's eyes darted up and down the street. 'I was hoping to catch you, I have seen you come and go for a few days but have always missed you. I didn't want to knock on your door yesterday as you had a … visitor.'

Carrie's mind cast back to Jon; any distraction would have been very welcome yesterday.

'I was hoping we could have a chat.' She looked around the immediate area again. 'Perhaps in my house?' She gestured behind her and reversed a few steps in a signal for Carrie to follow.

'Oh, really, we can't, thank you.' Carrie smiled

weakly. 'We have plans for the day and ...'

'I won't take up too much of your time,' Valerie replied, 'it's very important and ...' she faltered, again her eyes moved anxiously. Carrie looked down the street and wondered if she had been waiting for Agnes to pass and had deliberately come out of her house once the coast was clear. Now she was looking around like a cornered rabbit, fearing her imminent return.

'Okay, yes,' Carrie nodded. 'Yes, we can do that, Birdy?' She looked down at her, seeking her permission. During their conversation, Birdy had moved close to her side again, wary of this strange lady.

'Lovely, come this way.' Again she paced quickly towards her open door.

The hallway was decorated as Carrie expected. The floral carpet looked freshly vacuumed and a single pair of house slippers was neatly arranged at the bottom of the stairs. A small table stood opposite the flight of stairs and the shadow from the vase of flowers showed the surface to have been polished recently. All in all, it gave Carrie a vibe of the 1960s and she figured that the rest of the house would be decorated similarly. Figuring that Valerie was a lady who took care of her house, she found herself removing her shoes and tapped Birdy's shoulders to do the same. They padded into the lounge area behind their host.

'Can I get you both something to drink?'

The offer of refreshments gave Carrie the feeling that she had something to say that would warrant a visit long enough to finish a hot drink. What could a neighbour she'd barely said more than a few sentences to since she'd arrived possibly have to say? However, it was a welcome change of scenery, so she nodded.

'That would be lovely, thank you.'

'And for you?' She was bent smiling in Birdy's direction.

Carrie spoke for her quickly. 'Just juice, if you have any, will be fine.'

'Please, make yourselves at home.' Valerie waved towards the couch and retreated out of the room.

Carrie looked at the immaculate sofa, the floral carpet had spread into this room too and was accompanied by equally detailed wallpaper. She saw that Valerie had a liking for small china figurines. Politely, she perched on the edge of the settee and patted the space next to her.

Every part the gracious hostess, Valerie soon returned with a tray laden with a tea set and plate of biscuits. She handed a small glass to Birdy.

'Do you have a dog?' Birdy's finger pointed to a picture on the wall.

'I did. That's quite an old picture. I do have a couple of budgies now, though.'

Carrie saw Birdy's eyes light up as she let out an excited squeal. 'She loves her birds, any animals for that matter.'

'I used to have a bird. Chirpy was his name but he disappeared and we can't find him now.'

'Oh dear.' Valerie let out a small laugh. 'Perhaps you'd like to look at my birds?'

'Can I, Mummy?' Her small face glowed hope and her eyes glinted with excitement.

'Uh,' Carrie pondered. She was wary of Birdy wandering in this old lady's house, goodness knows what she might have further back there. For all she knew, Valerie was paving the way to kidnap both of them. Carrie shook her head, to pull herself together. 'If that's okay with you?' She allowed the question to hang in the air ready for Valerie to deliver on her promise.

'They are just in the dining room, come with me.'

Birdy was more than happy to scamper off the sofa after her. Carrie relaxed as she heard faint noises telling her that they'd found the cage and Birdy's excited chatter ensued.

'Lovely child.' Valerie returned after a few moments.

Carrie let out a small laugh. 'Yes she certainly loves her animals.' She moved to reach for her cup.

Valerie leaned back in her chair and regarded Carrie. 'So, how are you finding the house?' The loaded question; well this could be a very long visit. 'Oh, I know what you're thinking. You don't know me from Adam and here's some strange lady asking you about your business.' She crossed her legs, eyes fixed on Carrie. Still dressed in signature grey clothing, Carrie got the impression she probably dressed the same whether she was visiting friends or merely popping to the shops. Her stance took on the look of an interrogator about to probe for secret insights.

Carrie shifted in her seat, not wanting to meet her eyes. She dared to look up and saw a smile fixed on her face. 'It's well … we've had some issues.' That small sentence encompassed so much. It was a measured response seeing as she didn't know why she had been asked this question in the first place. Idle conversation or something much deeper, she had no idea.

'I remember seeing you when you arrived here,' Valerie pondered. 'When was that, two weeks ago?' She didn't allow her time to answer, 'I recall seeing a young woman and her small child arrive quite early in the morning. Quite nervous you were then, keen to make yourself invisible. It was as though you couldn't wait to get inside the house like you were trying to hide from something. I've seen you come and go in the last few weeks, just the two of you. Then yesterday I saw your gentleman friend and perhaps I've made a link myself between the two.' She paused, pleased at her observations.

Carrie swallowed, not knowing where to start. She allowed her to continue.

'You know, I used to be a headmistress before I retired.'

'I knew it!' Carrie heard herself say aloud, she faltered for a moment, 'I mean, you have a certain way about yourself.' She thought back to Birdy's reactions each time they had run-ins with Valerie. Sure, Birdy had had no formal schooling as yet but for some reason, she'd shied away from her. Carrie reckoned she gave off some kind of aura of being a figure of authority that Birdy had picked up on.

'How long have you been retired?' she asked politely. She studied Valerie's face and her voice trailed off, pleasantries fading.

Valerie's expression had dropped. 'You're in danger

if you don't leave that house.'

Carrie felt her jaw fall of its own accord. 'What did you say?' she heard herself ask meekly.

Valerie leant forward in her seat. 'Leave while you still can. Does that sound familiar?'

'The note, it was *you*?' she asked in disbelief, her voice barely above a whisper.

'Young lady, it was a warning…'

'It's Carrie,' she interjected.

'Carrie, you are in danger if you stay there. Trust me when I say this. But then I saw your visitor yesterday; is he an ex-husband? My guess is you left him but he's somehow managed to track you down. So I thought that maybe you'd come here to escape him; am I right?'

She nodded, an automatic reflex.

'So like I say, you are in danger if you stay in that house. But here's the problem I think you face – you are in danger if you leave.'

Valerie, as it turned out, had spent most of her working life in teaching. She had progressed through the school system quite quickly and when her own children were old enough, she had sought positions of school leadership. She informed Carrie that schools had changed considerably since her day, from the discipline through to the attitudes of children and respect to the teachers. Many decades in teaching had given her a certain way of looking at things and how she conducted herself to others. If her tone was formal, this had been gained from years of dealing with troublesome children. It was ingrained in her to be polite to children but always hold them at a distance. She wore grey a lot too as it commanded respect in her profession and was practical. Old habits die hard. She was also very alert and still had the natural skill held by teachers of being able to hold a conversation or undergo a task and still be acutely aware of what was going on nearby. Therefore, if she had been tending to the window boxes out front or putting the rubbish in her bins, she had the ability of knowing what was going on over the other side of the street.

She had also seen Jon arrive each time and also when he left. Carrie had blushed at this point, as though she had been caught out by her own mother when Valerie had realised he had spent the night. Moving to the room where Birdy had settled in, they watched as she still remained transfixed staring into the birdcage. She cocked her head, seeming to be able to communicate with the budgies who in turn, chirped happily at the attention. Valerie's house opened up into an airy space through the dining room and she had a small conservatory on the back of her house that she had filled with large plants which resembled a jungle scene. At the back, she boasted a small but well-tended garden.

'If you have no other plans, would you like to stay for some lunch?' she asked.

'That would be lovely, thank you.'

'We have lots to talk about,' she added as though Carrie needed any further convincing to stay. Birdy was more than happy to explore the back garden, taking care not to disturb the flowerbeds as she admired a bug house. The women sat on the outside patio as Birdy played.

'So, you were telling me about Agnes?' Carrie enquired.

Valerie nodded, 'I do certainly know a lot about her. I've lived in this house for as long as she and George, her husband, have lived in theirs.'

'Funny old lady,' Carrie mused. She brought her glass up to drink but paused mid-air as she saw Valerie's expression. She wondered if she too would be as cagey about talking about Agnes as Clive had been.

'Don't be fooled by her, Carrie. Agnes is a very different lady to the one you see on the street.'

'I've only ever encountered an old lady who has trouble with her hearing ...' she cut off her sentence as she saw Valerie shaking her head.

'Appearances can be very deceptive, as I'm sure you know.' She paused to look across her garden. 'Agnes shows you the lady she wants you to see.'

Carrie moved her head closer, expecting more detail than this. 'Go on,' she urged after a while. It was such a relief to find someone who could shed some light on this strange lady.

'Agnes is married and lives there with George.' Valerie nodded at Carrie. 'That's right, you've never met him and probably never will. He has been bed-bound for quite a while now.'

'And Agnes takes care of him all by herself?' she asked, shaking her head. 'Surely that's not possible for her, that's a massive responsibility for someone her age. Her mobility, I've seen how she gets around with my own eyes.'

'As I've said, the Agnes you see is very different from the one behind closed doors. Much sprightlier, shall we say. They had a son, Tony, I think his name was,' Valerie looked skyward as though she was trying to recall a distant memory.

'Was?'

'I say "was" as he was kicked out a long time ago. I haven't seen him since. Odd he was, short chap, would never meet your eyes if you got in a conversation with him.'

'Oh,' was all that Carrie could respond. She looked at Birdy; what would cause a parent to send their child to exile never to be seen again? For a moment, she longed to have Birdy in her arms and reassure her she would always be there regardless.

'Tony wasn't what they wanted in a son,' Agnes continued. 'They are devout religious types and strongly disapproved of his affair with Maria.'

Carrie frowned. The name Maria struck a chord with her, and she didn't know why.

'Maria is the name of the lady who owns your house. Anyway, Tony developed a huge crush on her, became infatuated with her – obsessed you might say. I think he had a problem with reading people and their non-verbal communication. I mean, what you or I may pick up on, say for example if you were getting a bit irritated with a person, he would misinterpret. That kind of thing. Anyway, he gave her everything he had, and I mean everything. Tony would constantly shower her with gifts here and there. She, of course, took advantage of this and destroyed him, financially and emotionally. Agnes didn't approve of their involvement, full stop.' She leaned in closer. 'She wasn't a religious woman, divorced.'

Carrie faltered, it was becoming all too familiar hearing about a controlling influence and not fitting into a style someone else had created. The disappointing and disapproving looks when she had dared to challenge anything with Jon in the past. All of a sudden, she didn't want to hear any more, it was too real. Yet, however, she was intrigued to know more.

'Her final parting gift to Tony was to accidentally run over his foot when she left. Poor thing never walked properly again afterwards, kind of walked with a limp if you can picture that, or shuffled along. Maria moved abroad after she'd finished with Tony. I've no idea whether that was her original intention, and she was just milking him for everything he was worth before moving on. It seemed just plain cruel if you ask me as I don't think she ever held any feelings for him, full stop. Agnes was furious with him after she discovered the full extent and blamed him for most of it, for being so stupid to fall for her. She banned him from the house and that's how it's been ever since. Maria rents the house out on short term leases.'

'Why doesn't she just sell it?'

Valerie shook her head. 'Negative equity, I think. She'd make a massive loss if she sold, especially when you take into account the area here. I doubt she would get the full asking price, anyway. She just can't afford to take a huge loss.' She looked around as if emphasising this. Carrie looked at the garden and thought back to the inside of Valerie's house. She had done her utmost to maintain a happy and peaceful oasis away from the crumbling surrounding area.

So many questions clouded Carrie's mind until one stood out at her. 'So, none of the tenants ever offer to buy the house?'

Again, the shaking of the head, 'No, I guess when you own a house just for rental you skimp a bit on furnishings and general upkeep of the house. I'm guessing it looks a bit tired in there. Agnes has also made sure that no one stays long enough to want to buy it. Any tenants that stay at number 30

… well, I don't know if you recall when we first met?'

'Well, I…' Carrie stuttered. It seemed so long ago, she had been tired after their long journey and couldn't recall what their conversation had been.

'I may have told you there and then that no one ever stays longer than a month. That is true, I'm afraid. If anyone has had a longer lease, there is always a reason for them to make an early departure. Quite frankly, I'm surprised you are still here. You've been here two weeks now.'

Shaking her head, Carrie was having trouble linking everything together. 'I don't understand what this has to do with me.'

'Agnes will do her damnedest to make sure that no tenants stay or ever want to buy the house, to spite Maria for what she did to her son.'

'The noises,' Carrie spoke aloud, 'they are from Agnes, then?'

Valerie simply nodded at her. 'It's very probable, or she's got someone to do it for her. Say for a small fee every now and again? Perhaps a friend she knows who would do any jobs for her, no questions asked. There are endless possibilities of what she could be capable of. Everything she can think of to drive you out of the house and never return. Subtle things I'm sure so you don't have anything concrete to go to the police about. Things that probably have caused you to doubt yourself or just brush it away as being forgetful.'

The pieces started to slot into place in Carrie's mind like a moving puzzle. The nightly noises were Agnes deliberately trying to scare her away. And guess what, she was succeeding. She had done enough to push Carrie to the edge and test her own boundaries when it came to fear. Carrie cast her mind back to all the strange occurrences she had encountered – the knocking, voices, movement of some of her personal belongings, the birds for heavens' sake! The arrival of the baked cakes that Agnes had been so keen for them to eat – Carrie entertained a bizarre thought that perhaps they had been laced with something. This seemed so unbelievable for her to even comprehend but at the same time, completely rational. Why, it would probably be very easy to obtain some medicinal drugs to slip into her baking. She recalled how she had woken up, limbs leaden, with a feeling that it was much more than just a hangover. Yet Birdy had been fine. But Birdy had refused to eat the muffins as she had baulked at their taste. Agnes had made Carrie question her own sanity and believe Jon when he brushed it off as her being stupid or confused because she had drunk too much wine.

They sat in silence for a while, the sun still shining but Carrie felt cold inside. 'You said I was in danger,' she asked finally.

'Somewhat. I don't know. The point is that you are not showing any signs of moving as far as she can see. That's a first from what I've seen. You must be stronger than she thinks.' She smiled at Carrie, 'Oh, I'm not saying everyone leaves the house screaming, running for the hills but it must be unsettling if you're staying there. I'm guessing it has been quite easy for past tenants to just pack up and leave. I'm just wondering how she will, shall we say, escalate things to get you out quicker.'

Carrie breathed deeply, unsure of how to respond. 'There's something that doesn't sit right with me,' she replied uneasily.

'Go on.'

'The banging.' Carried stated simply. 'It's difficult to describe but has at times seemed too … forceful to be her.' She chewed on her lip thoughtfully. 'I know you said she's much more agile behind closed doors, but this was something else. There's far too much power behind the knocks.' She paused and took a sip of her drink. The episode in which she witnessed the furious banging flashed in her mind. 'There was one time that I *heard* her.'

'Heard her? Doing what?'

'Talking to someone, I dismissed it as a vivid dream at the time, maybe it still is, I don't know.' She recalled the morning after this event and how she had fished a blue shard of the paint from the door from her foot. Carrie had at the time brushed this off to thinking she had begun sleepwalking and had inadvertently ended up by the old, blue door. But now she reckoned that she *had* been in the boiler room that night, fully awake, and therefore, *had* heard voices from next door.

'You heard her have a conversation with someone?'

'Yes,' Carrie nodded, 'I heard a man's voice.'

'And you are positive of this?' She didn't wait for Carrie to answer, 'Agnes's husband has been non-verbal for a number of years. And you heard a man's voice in the basement you say?'

'I'm sure I did ...'

Valerie made as if to get up, 'I've two spare rooms here,' she gestured to upstairs.

'I - I don't understand,' Carrie faltered.

'If you heard a man's voice coming from Agnes's then I don't want you in that house. Something isn't sitting right. Either Agnes's husband isn't quite as incapacitated as we've been led to believe or there is someone else there. That's the only thing I can think of. And I can't explain it, but I have a feeling you are in danger. Goodness knows how things could turn the longer you are there.'

DAY 16

Something felt different when Carrie woke up that morning. She couldn't place it at first but her head felt much clearer as though a fog had lifted. She put this down to the weight lifted from the toxic environment they had been living in for the last two weeks. Something was very wrong at number 30 and now she knew why: Agnes was deliberately plotting to get her to leave. In a way, she had achieved that already.

'You're more than welcome to stay here until you find your feet,' Valerie informed her over breakfast. 'What do you think you will do going forward?'

Carrie sighed. 'We'll probably stay with my mum for a bit, she's away at the moment. If I had known how this would all pan out, I'd have gone to her in the first place.' She paused.

'In my experience, if someone is fleeing a situation at their home, there never is a planned time. I'm sure something happened to give you a moment of realisation to get out?'

Carrie looked down into her lap. There were some details she felt foolish to say out loud. She rubbed her temple, 'I do need to pop back over the road and get some things. It's very kind of you to let us stay; I'd like that for a few nights, if that's okay with you?'

'Of course.' Valerie beamed back at her and then shifted in her seat. 'I'm afraid I can't offer to go into that house with you. I won't set foot in there. This isn't television

I'm afraid, where we go and investigate together.'

Carrie smiled, unsure of who would have been leading who if that idea were to transpire. 'That's fine, I'll be okay, just in and out really. Besides, for some reason, I was only targeted at night. I guess Agnes used the darkness as a disguise. It's probably for the best though, there is a strange smell coming from the boiler room. Now that I'm out of there, it is as though I've had a moment of clarity, everything is much more obvious now.' She looked at Valerie and was sure she had her full attention. 'I'm convinced there was someone else in the house at times. I brushed it off as a dream at the time or being too groggy and confused.'

Valerie's face was frozen in shock. 'You're saying you think Agnes was in your house at night? Were there any other signs?'

She breathed deeply. 'One night, I heard footsteps or shuffling, I'm convinced of it. Sometimes things weren't in the place I left them. I thought it was me, maybe it was …'

'That's impossible, how would she get in without you noticing? You say this was at night when you were in. You would have seen and heard the front door open. Surely you don't sleep that deeply?'

Carrie felt her blood run cold as she had ignored the obvious for so long. 'The cellar door,' she practically whispered. 'They must have that key. For goodness' sake, she's the landlady, of course she would have a spare set of keys to the house.' The room suddenly felt cold so she drew her arms around her. The feeling of being watched and having her privacy violated in that way, didn't bear thinking about what might have happened next.

Birdy seemed quite amenable at the thought of staying with Valerie for a few days. She was more than happy at having birds to admire and a garden to move around in. Carrie retrieved her shoes and mentally prepared herself for her mission over the road. She intended to gather up a lot of their belongings but not completely overwhelm Valerie with all of their suitcases and bags. She darted across the road.

Inside number 30, Carrie was surprised at how normal

everything looked. Nothing from the view of the doorway looked out of place, it was exactly as they had left it just the day before. She wasn't sure what to expect – graffiti plastered on the wall demanding they get out? Furnishing strewn everywhere in anger as she had not fled the house before now? All she could hear was the familiar hum of the pipes and buzz of the fridge. Beds were still made as she had left them. It seemed so ordinary that she really had to remind herself why they must stay at Valerie's now, for the image something portrayed could be very misleading.

Carrie was back over the road before she knew it. 'You're so kind for letting us stay,' she reinforced her gratitude again. 'You must let me repay you.'

Valerie waved her hand dismissively. 'It's no problem. It will be nice to have the company.' She helped carry the bags up to the spare room. 'Are you safe when you leave here, I mean, your ex-husband? He has visited you here.'

Carrie swallowed hard, 'He's still my husband. Jon is a … difficult man to live with, I had to get out.' She avoided eye contact for fear of being judged or questioned further.

Valerie patted her on the arm and didn't take the bait to ask more at that time. 'Let me sort out some lunch and then we can sit down. I've always been a very good listener.'

They sat at the garden table, the breeze gently ruffling the sides of the parasol. Birdy had settled herself on the lawn and had taken it upon herself to surround herself with books as she read to a captive audience of a circle of stuffed toys. Carrie smiled to herself.

'That's very competent reading for a child of five,' Valerie commented. 'You mentioned there has been no formal schooling?'

Carrie sighed; 'it wasn't what Jon wanted,' was a sentence which summed up their relationship. She took Valerie's silence as a cue to continue. 'We met at a New Year's Eve party a while ago. He was in a relationship with someone else at the time but for some reason, I still gave him my number when he'd asked for it out of earshot. I think I was flattered at the sheer gall that he had, the confidence to ask me out when his girlfriend was in the next room. I was quite naïve, I guess you could say, at the time and liked this dominance. I liked the control and was flattered.' She paused as she realised she still had Valerie's full attention. 'We went out for a date and he said he'd call. I had his number but was always too nervous to phone him, worried that she might answer or I'd catch him at a bad moment. So, I became one of those mistress types who wait by the phone. When I did dare to call, he'd sound distant and I would feel guilty. I think I was in love with him by then. It was always on his terms as to when he could see me. That was it, him calling the shots all the time. Sometimes, we would arrange a date and he wouldn't turn up. There would always be an excuse that I would accept. I began to feel grateful for the time we did spend together. I was forever wanting more than he could give. Anyway, after he and his girlfriend split, I moved in with him. I think she found out about us and came to her senses. Things moved along quickly. I was sure he was having affairs but could never confront him about them. I mean, when we had met, he was seeing someone else so why stop when we got together? However, if we were out and about and another man dared even look at me or perhaps ask for directions, he would accuse me of all sorts once we got back home. He'd accuse me of having affairs.'

'And did you?'

Carrie shifted in her seat. 'There was one man but it was quite short-lived, just before we had Birdy. I'd had enough of his behaviour and it was as though I was doing it to spite him. However, unlike him, I felt so guilty afterwards, so I did tell him. He was more forgiving of this than I expected. It was a silly mistake, but he's been far worse. Because I had just the one affair, this gave him permission to carry on doing the same. So, he did, and much worse. There was one time I found underwear under the bed. It was as though he was almost daring me to challenge him on it. I was pregnant at the time and just couldn't say anything, I was too sick or tired. I felt like he was punishing me with everything he said and did. When I had Birdy, he claimed to have stopped messing around.'

She looked down at her hands. 'It became very

intense between us just after Birdy was born. It was flattering at first that he wanted us to spend all of our spare time together. He would allow me to see my friends but there would always be a sulk afterwards, as though I had abandoned him. It was a slow drip feed, I guess, of what I was allowed to wear or whom I was allowed to see. After a while, it was easier to go along with it and avoid the fight afterwards.'

'And you say things got worse once you got pregnant?'

Carrie nodded. 'That was me pretty much housebound. He was desperate for a girl and I think deeply affected by his own mother's death – not that's any excuse for his behaviour. Birdy, like me, had to behave how he wished. If I didn't choose the right clothes, then he would do it for me.' She put her hand to cover her eyes and rubbed them to discourage the tears.

'Birdy … that's quite an unusual nickname?'

'I can't bear the name he insisted went on the birth certificate. Of course, he went to register the birth. The name on the certificate is Bridgette, after his mother.'

Valerie sighed. 'That will be quite simple to change if they're your intentions in the future. Children are able to bounce back very quickly after such a disruption in their lives, don't worry too much about that.' She passed Carrie a tissue.

'Thank you.' Her voice was quiet. 'Jon has a very good way of manipulating things and the way he speaks to me, not even having to raise his voice at times. He had a certain look and a tone. There was always a lot of belittlement in the way he spoke to me. A few days before we left was when he hit me for the first time. I'd had shoves and pushes before, always an apology to go with it of course,' she smiled in recognition of her own denial. 'That was it. One step too far. Birdy had accidentally got caught between us and was hurt.'

'Violence is never accidental.'

She nodded, 'I know, I know. It's a saving grace she doesn't attend school or I suspect I'd have a visit from the authorities by now. I just knew we had to get out and found the house to rent while he was at work. It probably explains why I've ended up in the worst house imaginable,' she let out a weak laugh. 'Talk about jumping from the frying pan into the fire!'

'Hmm,' Valerie pondered but she remained poker-faced, 'you'd probably have got something better if you'd had the chance to look around a bit more.'

Carrie fixed her gaze on a distant point. 'We left in the middle of the night after I crushed some pills in his food.'

'Some pills? Was it your intention to bump him off?'

Her voice wavered, 'I couldn't even do that right. It didn't work but of course he didn't go to the police about it, like I was supposed to feel grateful for that. I'd have probably been thrown in a cell, never to see Birdy again. I left with just two bags; I've walked out on everything with next to nothing.'

'That's not true, Carrie. You have left with your life.'

'But I've now put myself in a whole new situation here. And for what? He's found me again. He might claim he's started therapy, but I can see the old Jon is still there. It's as though he has this physical hold on me.'

'And you've been brainwashed.' She raised her eyebrows at Carrie. 'Am I right?'

Carrie nodded slowly.

'You need some time to think about your next steps before you face up to undoing everything he's put you through.' She looked up towards the sky. 'If I'm not mistaken, it looks like a storm is due. Goodness knows we need it in this heat.'

DAY 17

Not having to worry about odd behaviour in number 30 now gave Carrie a lot of time to reflect on what had happened. She wondered how much she could justify as part of Agnes's systematic campaign to get rid of her. The dead birds in the patio area had seemingly fallen from the sky but now she had the unsettling feeling they had been thrown from the sewing room window. Personal possessions not quite in the place she had left them – was this just another tactic to unsettle her? Carrie then turned her thoughts to the bird they had rescued from outside which had then mysteriously disappeared in near-perfect health, only to reappear on the windowsill dead a few days later.

The smell that had appeared in the boiler room – she had to agree with Jon that it was too pungent to be a dead bird. It was almost laughable to think that either rotten food had been placed just outside the wooden blue door or was concealed somewhere within the old paint pots on the shelf. One thing just sat uncomfortably with Carrie; this was too much to be the work of an elderly lady. It just didn't seem to fit. She was in two minds; should she confront Agnes with everything she knew and end this feud once and for all, or just move on and let the next unwitting tenant have all of this inflicted on them as well? The speed at which she had managed to secure their safety from Jon – what if the next tenant was in a similar position? What if they too were fleeing an unsafe situation at home? Valerie was right, it was time to start facing up to everything, including how much she had been brainwashed by Jon. Carrie knew she just had to sort this out.

She decided to go back into number 30 with the intention of picking up the rest of their belongings. Despite the fact that Agnes oversaw the arrangement of cleaning after each tenant, Carrie decided to clean the house herself. Subconsciously, she reckoned this was an attempt to erase her past, well, at least the parts she had control over. It would give her a purpose and who knows what she might uncover in the process. Maybe a hidden letter from the owner, Maria. Or some shred of evidence she could go to the police with.

'Valerie, are you okay if I pop out for a while?' There was no way she was willing to have Birdy back in that house.

'Of course, what are your plans?'

Carrie sighed, 'I might go and check my emails in the internet café. It's not far from here.'

'You go, we'll be fine here, won't we?'

Carrie bent to kiss Birdy's head and mouthed 'thank you' at Valerie. It felt strange walking down the street without Birdy at her side. It was hard to recall a time where they had not been together. She guessed this was why she was so comfortable with co-sleeping at various points during their stay here. They were almost one unit and it was very difficult to think about putting things in place to change this.

The internet café was fairly quiet as Carrie settled herself down in front of a computer. She logged on, not knowing what to expect, maybe an email from her mother from holiday to share some pictures? Her heart sank slightly when she saw there was nothing since they had communicated regarding the bank transfer and then the following message about Jon's arrival. Carrie reasoned with herself that there may be limited access where her mother was, or she was just simply too busy to message her. She had been half-expecting something considering the situation she knew Carrie had been left in. She had given Jon her address knowing they were having a few difficulties but then hadn't followed this up with a further email to see how things had developed. Carrie chided herself at being so self-centred. Her mother was entitled to time away from home without fretting over her fully-grown daughter.

She scanned over the emails Jon had sent her when he had been pleading for her to return home. The cursor hovered over the message before Carrie highlighted all of them to delete them all. This was her first step in moving on. She made a few searches of properties near her mother to rent as she was sure they'd be welcome but didn't want to outstay her visit. Her mother had always been an independent person and she didn't want to infringe on this.

On her approach to the house, she retrieved the keys from her pocket in readiness. Without a glance to next door for possible twitching of curtains, she let herself in and closed the door quickly behind her. She moved from room to room gathering their belongings. Donning a pair of rubber gloves, she began the task of half-cleaning and half-searching for anything untoward. As she knelt down in the lounge to clean under the sofa, a rattling of the letterbox stopped her in her tracks. Scrambling to her feet, she was at the door whilst simultaneously retrieving the envelope from the doormat.

He had his back to her but had definitely tried to time this drop off so he wouldn't be seen. It was the way he was scurrying down towards his van as though he had somewhere urgent to be.

'Clive,' she called out.

As he turned, she saw an almost worried expression on his face, anxious at being caught red-handed. 'The key,' he stuttered, pointing to the envelope in her hand, 'I managed to find you a copy.'

'I need to speak with you,' Carrie said firmly.

'I …I …' his eyes flitted briefly to next door's window. 'I have somewhere to be,' he looked at her again and then his eyes scanned the immediate area. 'Okay, okay,' he changed tack, 'I can spare a few minutes.' He hurried over, as though his movements were being monitored. Once he was inside, Carrie shut the door firmly behind him and stood with her back to it, a signal he wasn't going anywhere.

'What can I do for you?' His tone was had a forced breeziness about it as if he had managed to compose himself from their encounter outside. 'How is the boiler now?'

'We've moved out.' Carrie crossed her arms in front of her.

He ran a hand through his hair. 'Oh, I'm sorry to hear that.'

'Are you?' Her voice was deadpan. 'I'm sure you and Agnes are.'

He emitted a nervous laugh, 'I'm not quite sure what you mean. As far as my dealings with Agnes go, she calls me whenever there is a problem with this house, repairs and so on. I do a few odd jobs for her as well.'

Carrie tilted her head as he stood rooted to the same spot, his hands by his side, fingers fiddling with the hem of his polo shirt. 'Are you sure she doesn't ask you to do any other jobs for her?'

He shook his head. 'I'm not quite sure what you mean?'

Carrie exhaled deeply. 'I have reason to believe that Agnes wants the tenants out of here as quickly as possible. I'm not quite sure how, but I'm convinced you have a hand in this somehow. Then when I saw both of you exchanging words outside, this confirmed my suspicions. Need I continue?' She watched as he moved to sit down on the nearest chair. 'Yes, I thought you might want to sit down.'

His voice was quiet; it appeared he was steeling himself for a huge confession of guilt. 'You're right, I did have a run-in with Agnes a few days ago. She warned me to stay away from this house and I had no further business being here. I didn't tell her about the key. But I was told in no uncertain terms to keep away.' He paused. 'I'm not sure what she's trying to hide but I do know one thing. There was nothing wrong with your boiler.' He swallowed hard, as though this had been building up inside him for a long time. 'Agnes had asked me before you arrived to adjust the internal settings on the control panel and set them too high. You would obviously then notice it was running on high before informing her. She paid me to come over and reset the controls.'

Carrie perched next to him, 'And is this the first time you have done this?'

'No.' His head was bowed.

'The thing is, Clive, I think it's much more than that. I believe she has been deliberately causing a disturbance during the night. But something is bothering me – the banging sounds you both brushed off as neighbouring children seems a bit too far-fetched to me. They were also too strong to be made by a sweet old lady if you catch my drift.'

He held his hands up in defence, 'I've no idea what you are talking about. Agnes told me about the damaged fence which I went around to fix. It did have some broken boards so her theory could have been correct.'

Carrie shook her head again. 'There's no way she could have caused that kind of noise and impact. It was too strong.'

'It wasn't me, I am being honest with you. Like I say, I have no idea of what goes on in her house or why she wanted me to do this.' His expression seemed too genuine for him to have been lying. Poor Clive may have fallen on hard times for all she knew and was quite willing to do a few extra bits for Agnes, cash in hand.

'Who lives next door? I mean, with Agnes?'

He frowned at her and shook his head, 'I'm not a family friend or anything. I don't know what you mean. I do odd jobs for her every now and again. I walk through the downstairs of the house and if the garden needs seeing to, I can see to that too. But that's it.'

'I think you know more than you are letting on. She lives with her husband?'

'Yes – no, I mean, I've never seen him. I presume he's upstairs like you've been told. I've seen carers every now and again.'

Carrie put her hand out for him to stop. 'You've seen other people? Men? Women?'

'Look, I –' he shuffled his feet and shifted around in his seat, 'I'm not sure what you're getting at. Why the interrogation?'

'Tell me about this man, the carer you have seen, what's he like?' she waved her hand in a circular motion, 'appearance wise I mean?'

Clive puffed his cheeks out and looked towards the ceiling, 'Oh, I couldn't really say, stocky guy, mid-fifties, I don't know…' His voice trailed off. Carrie felt like a balloon was slowly deflating inside her. This description did not fit Jon in the wild assumption that somehow he had managed to worm his way into Agnes's house and played some part in all of this. Mentally eliminating every man who might have been responsible for the pounding on the door seemed her only option at the moment. She decided to change direction as the constant questioning was seemingly starting to unnerve him.

'So, this key you have given me, this will open the door to the outside area then?'

'Assuming the lock is okay, yes.'

'Then let's go,' she got to her feet but saw he remained in his seat. 'What are you waiting for?'

He remained in his seat and put a hand to his head. 'The fence. I'd think about it if I were you. I get the impression you think someone else is living there, or you are doubting Agnes's word of having a sick husband in bed. Let's say he's not confined to her bed as she says. Let's say he is losing his mind a bit and has a tendency to display erratic behaviour. Let's say he is behind the disturbances you have witnessed at night. If Agnes is lying about who she wants to keep *out* then I'd ask yourself this; maybe the question is who is she so desperate to keep *in*?'

DAY 18

Clive, as it turned out, was a jittery man who developed a twitch the more he was pressed for information. Before Carrie had said he could leave, she'd ascertained there was nothing else to get from him with regard to Agnes's family. He just didn't know or just wasn't willing to say. Carrie reckoned he was telling the truth and he simply had carried out odd jobs on request, cash in hand, no question asked. It wasn't his business to know why Agnes wanted the boiler adjusted and then set back. He would just dutifully turn up when called. Carrie rather suspected this had been going on for quite some time. That explained why he had given her the key so willingly, too; he had no knowledge of any potential threat posed if she did enter the garden space. Any night-time movements were alien to him. It was playing on Carrie's mind when she thought back to the altercation she had witnessed in the street between Agnes and Clive. Had she tried to warn him off at getting too chatty with Carrie? The more Carrie spoke to him, the more potential for him to let things slip. Perhaps the only thing she didn't want him to disclose was the fact that the boiler functioned perfectly as it was.

Carrie mulled over the key. She had taken it back to Valerie's realising that she had already been away from Birdy for a while and didn't want to take advantage of Valerie's goodwill. Almost every part of her sanity was screaming at her to walk away, throw the key away and never think of it again. Don't even entertain the thoughts of wanting to find out more. But a small part of her kept niggling at her. She just had a burning desire to sort this out once and for all, throw open the cellar door and see exactly what was behind it. Her consciousness summoned up images of chained zombies or a rabid dog tethered outside. She laughed these off but at the same time, feared the truth more.

She sat on the patio watching Birdy play outside. Their new house would definitely need to have a garden. This was something she would have to think about sooner rather than later. The day that Jon had threatened to come and get her inched forever closer, like a storm cloud on the horizon of an otherwise sunny day.

'I just need to finish packing all of our belongings at the house, most of it is just piled by the door. I need to ensure the place is left in the same condition as when we arrived,' she informed Valerie, who seemed more than happy to while away her time sitting crocheting as Birdy played.

'Be good,' she urged Birdy and needed to hug her tightly. 'I'm going to get the rest of our things.'

'So we won't be going back to live there?'

She pressed Birdy against her and inhaled the scent of strawberry shampoo. 'No, sweetie, we aren't staying there anymore.'

The street was always devoid of members of the public as though the one-way street was a deterrent for it to be used for anyone's route for walking. The other neighbours either kept themselves to themselves or left early in the morning and returned late at night. It occurred to Carrie that they hadn't really encountered anyone else since they'd arrived, certainly no one she had seen more than once. The house seemed more soulless than ever seeing as a large proportion of their belongings had already been packed away. She had given Valerie the impression that there was more sorting to do than there actually was. Carrie decided to do a sweep of every room to double-check there would no longer be any trace of them. She opened the freezer and saw the remaining muffins that Agnes had prepared for them. Removing them, she decided that it may be an idea to take them back with her as some kind of bizarre evidence.

It occurred to Carrie that she hadn't been through Birdy's old room since the smell had become too bad for her to remain in it. That would be her next room to sort out, to check if any toys had found their way under the bed. Downstairs was relatively dark as the sun had moved away from the window and gave the room a definite chill to it. Carrie frowned as her view became evermore shadowy. She turned around intending to switch on the light.

He stood blocking the doorway, his eyes distant without acknowledging her as his gaze was fixed on a point just beyond her. His stance gave the impression of being defenceless as he positioned one arm straight by his side while his other hand rubbed his arm. He rocked gently from one foot to the other and wore a tatty, stained jumper that looked a few sizes too big. His hand moved to scratch at already unkempt hair.

Carrie gasped and froze. She remained kneeling by the side of the bed, having just bent down to see under it. If she wasn't rooted to the spot, she wondered how successful she would be in running past him at full pelt to escape. Her throat felt as though it was closing and her vocal cords refused to cooperate as she willed herself to let out a scream. This would hopefully alert someone to her entrapment or at the very least, snap him out of his trance-like state so he would come to his senses. Who was this man? She entertained the possibility she had left the front door open and he had simply taken advantage of a seemingly empty property. However, everything about the way he looked told her that this was no passing person living on the street. He wanted to be there.

As the minutes passed, Carrie prayed the threat of the potential attack was also declining. He seemed too calm and unflustered to pose her any physical threat. The pair remained still in their respective positions.

He rubbed his arm in double time. 'I see you,' he whispered finally.

'Please,' Carrie croaked as she held one hand up. The scream was poised inside her.

'I knew you would come back.' He looked at Carrie

and smiled crookedly, revealing uneven yellowing teeth. Even though he had now fixed his attention on her, one of his eyes seemed unfocused.

Carrie cleared her throat, desperately searching for something to say that would not aggravate this intruder. She decided on a different approach, 'I have a tenancy agreement with Agnes next door, this is my house for the next few weeks.' Her voice wobbled slightly. It seemed an absurd thing for her to say, as though she were assuming his presence was due to a mix up with the rental agreement there. Her words hung in the air, seemingly falling on deaf ears. The horrible realisation that he wasn't in the house as a tenant haunted her. 'I think you have the wrong house,' she affirmed quietly, deciding to try a different approach. If he was here to harm her, wouldn't he have lunged at her by now? Unless his plan was to gradually toy with her first. Slowly, she moved to stand up. Even though she was on the other side of the room from him, she figured there wasn't much between them in terms of height, despite the stoop in his posture.

He moved a tattered sleeve to wipe his face, the cuffs looking as though they had been dragged through or caught in dirt and had not been rolled up or cleaned for a while. 'I knew you would come back and not leave me.'

Carrie shook her head slowly, not wanting him to register her confusion but at the same time, desperately trying to piece together a response.

'Maria.' His voice was faint as he smiled. He dared to inch a foot closer to her but withdrew suddenly, somewhat intimidated by her.

Light dawned in Carrie's head; she knew who this man was. 'Tony,' she replied in acknowledgement. She swallowed a lump forming in her throat. There was no other reasoning behind it – this must be Tony, Agnes's estranged son from next door. The son who had supposedly been exiled many years ago, a disgrace to his parents for his behaviour, only to suddenly return. But it didn't make sense; Tony looked as though he had been sleeping rough somewhere, had been staying somewhere else rather than the cosy house next door and had not been taking proper care of himself. It was possible he had been living rough and had only just arrived home. But she doubted this, it didn't sit well with her that he had arrived back at his parents' house very recently. Surely, she would have seen or heard something?

'I knew you would come back to me,' he repeated, holding a trembling hand out to her. 'Mother said no and to forget about you, but I always knew.' He summoned the courage to take a few steps forward; Carrie noticed a definite pull on one of his legs. It caused her to move back slightly as she scrambled to recall why the fact that he moved with a limp rang alarm bells to her. Recalling her conversation with Valerie, she remembered her mentioning Tony had had a run-in with Maria's car when she had fled. However, there was something else more unsettling. Then the pieces fell into place – it was one of the incidents of a disturbance in the middle of the night where she had woken up convinced someone else was in the house. She'd dismissed it at the time, not wanting to admit her life had been in danger while she had lain vulnerable in bed. Night time intruders: this just didn't happen in real life, where a stranger would enter your property just to stand and stare. This was every bit more terrifying than being burgled. The intent to cause uneasiness and self-doubt was much more disturbing and chilling than a midnight theft.

The thought sickened her as she forced herself to face up to the reality – this man had been in the house before while she and Birdy had slept in their respective rooms. This man had watched them as they slept and had been seen by Birdy after she woke. Carrie had dismissed this as a nightmare at the time. She suddenly felt so exposed. Her first instinct was to overpower him somehow, never to return. But he hadn't attacked them during his last night time visit, so should she assume the same for now?

Thoughts bounced around her head, and one stood out, *he thinks you are the object of his unrequited love, Maria.* This is why he would not physically attack her. Maria, who was supposedly far away in another country while Tony still mourned her departure, holding a torch for her after all this time. Having no idea whether Tony now held resentment towards Maria, Carrie was unsure what his next move would be.

'Where are you staying?' was all she managed to ask. She frowned at her choice of question, for all the responses in the world and that was the one her muddled thoughts had chosen for her to say.

Tony pivoted on the spot and pointed in the direction of the boiler room. This came as no surprise to Carrie as though she had expected it. Of course that was his point of entry into the property. He must have got the spare key from his mother.

She was now stood by his side. 'Show me.' This man was her entry into the mysterious space she had longed to see into before but at the same time, had also dreaded. The fear of what was behind it was now being presented to Carrie, albeit her guide was probably the reason behind all of the fear in the first place. Here in front of her was the reason behind all the anguish and torment she had faced in the last few weeks. However, he came across as being quite vulnerable which caused her to wonder about his part in all of this. Was he just a pawn used by Agnes in her plot to rid number 30 of all tenants?

The blue wooden door was still ajar. The key sat pushed into the lock. Behind the door, was a small, sheltered area that looked like a passageway from number 30 to Agnes's. Looking left, this opened up into a small garden surrounded by a tall fence. By the looks of it, repairs had been carried out on it recently. The small grass area was uneven and beyond this, an area had been dug in the soil; they stood looking into this and Carrie reckoned it easily measured six-foot wide. Even though the area was soaked in sunlight, its appearance still made the area feel dank and miserable. They remained side by side gazing into the hole.

Carrie felt as though she were having an out of body experience. Inside, a voice was screaming at her to get out, *you've gone into the garden led by a strange man that not so long ago, had been standing over you, watching you in* your *own house. Now look at how he has manipulated you.* Strangely though, his whole demeanour and manner told her that he wasn't intending to harm her. For some strange reason, she felt very calm. She hadn't been losing her mind, as she had feared. The house had not been haunted and despite what Jon had implied, her illogical thoughts were not the result of too much wine. Carrie heard approaching footsteps behind them and turned around while Tony remained with his back to the house.

Agnes walked quickly up to them, she had one hand outstretched, her voice was urgent. 'Tony, you shouldn't be out here.' Her eyes darted to Carrie nervously. She moved to usher him inside.

'It's okay,' Carrie tried to reassure her, 'he was just showing me this.'

'Well, he shouldn't be wandering around outside by himself, he knows this.' She grasped his arm to which he immediately withdrew.

'No!' He squirmed and appeared to shy away from Agnes. He moved his arms to shield himself.

Agnes breathed exasperatedly. 'Now see what you've done,' she muttered at a low volume. Carrie wondered whether she had been supposed to hear this. She frowned, here was a woman acting completely out of character from the old lady she had met in the street a few times. The doddering old lady who had stood in her house while Clive came to adjust the boiler settings. She wondered which one was the real Agnes and which was a façade.

'Tony has learning difficulties,' she said, as if his behaviour needed some kind of justification to it. She succeeded in moving Tony a few paces towards her.

'Wait!' urged Carrie, 'Agnes, you owe me.'

'Owe you what?'

'Owe me what?' she repeated back to her. 'I know,' she gestured with her head, 'about the house and how you want rid of anyone who lives there. Clive told me.'

The woman froze as if Carrie's realisation of the truth was a great shock to her. Carrie moved to obstruct her passage back into her house. 'I know what you have been doing to drive me out of this house and I'm now guessing how you've been using your own son to help you with this. Things are starting to make a lot of sense now.' She stood her ground firmly.

Agnes's eyes searched for anywhere to focus on away from Carrie. 'Things aren't as they seem,' she replied, rather too ambiguous for Carrie's liking. 'My priority is my family and keeping them safe. Now if you'll excuse me, there are things I need to be doing.'

Carrie breathed deeply. 'Fine,' she replied in defeat and stood to one side, she caught Agnes's arm on her way past. 'I will call back tomorrow, and Agnes? You will answer the door to me and we will talk. I think I deserve at least that, don't you?'

DAY 19

Carrie sat at Valerie's breakfast table while she absentmindedly stirred the sugar into her coffee. From the corner of her eye, she could see Valerie's expression, informing her that she had been doing this for longer than necessary. She placed the spoon on the table.

'I went back to the house.' Since returning from there the previous day, Carrie had had the urge to spend time with Birdy. Something in Agnes's words had rung true with her – her priority was keeping her family safe. She hadn't wanted to confess to Valerie that she had been into next door's garden and encountered a strange man with a complex backstory and information that could explain all of the oddities she had experienced in the last few weeks. The reality of what had happened and being able to put a face to all of the disruptions seemed somewhat of an anti-climax to Carrie.

'Why do I not like the sound of where this is heading?'

'I saw a man there. He was in my house.' She raised her hand as she saw Valerie's mouth open. 'It's okay, he didn't hurt me or anything.'

'Who was this man, Carrie?'

'It was Tony...'

'That's impossible,' she interrupted her and went to the sink with her empty plate. 'He hasn't lived there for years.'

Carrie shrugged. 'That's what you've been led to think but, believe it or not, I get the impression he's always been there. I think he's been the cause of a lot of the upset I've had there. I don't think he means any harm; I don't think he's … all there if you catch my drift.' She tapped the side of her head to emphasise her point.

'He was never the sharpest tool in the box when he was there. I think that's the reason why he was duped by Maria so easily.'

'I want to go back,' Carrie stated. 'I want to find out more. At the very least, I think Agnes owes me an explanation.'

Valerie shook her head and stood next to her. 'Carrie, I urge you to proceed with extreme caution. You've no idea how this could go.'

'I'd like to go back.'

'Are you asking for my permission or seeking my approval?'

Carrie drummed her fingers on the table. 'I don't know,' she confessed. 'I really don't. All I do know is that I want answers and to know whether their next tenant will face the same problems I have. This needs to end now.' She stood up level with Valerie. 'Please, I didn't want to go behind your back. All I'm asking is if you could keep Birdy safe for me until I leave Agnes's.'

Carrie stood on the doorstep of Agnes's house, looking up and down the street. She gave the knocker another tap, half expecting nothing to stir from inside the house. Determined, she stood her ground, refusing to move until the door was opened.

A shuffle from inside the property told Carrie that someone was approaching the door. It opened a crack which Agnes's face filled. She didn't look surprised to see Carrie and opened the door wide to allow her to enter. Feeling nothing like an explorer about to unearth worldly treasures, Carrie went in. She wasn't sure what she expected to see on entry into her house. In a way, the décor wasn't a great deal different to Valerie's – it had an older generation's touch to it. It was architecturally different to number 30 and boasted a hallway on entry that featured a staircase to the right. The hallway was dark, but Carrie could see the décor was a dark pink colour. There were a few paintings on the wall and a circular mirror, framed in gold leaf. The smell wasn't as she expected and had a subtle woody scent to it. Agnes led Carrie through to the lounge area and motioned for her to sit down.

'You met Tony then?'

'Yes, although I'm sure it wasn't your intention for us to bump into each other following his trespassing into next door. Granted it's not my house but I am entitled by law to stay in there for our agreed time.' Her tone was overly harsh.

'Tony … has difficulties when it comes to boundaries and expected behaviour,' Agnes explained.

'And that excuses him entering my house? What if I had been in at the time? I'm afraid the law sees this as trespassing and entering unlawfully. Maybe we should call the police and ask them what their take on all of this is?'

'So you weren't in at the time?'

Carrie frowned, she wasn't sure if Agnes was playing the ignorance card, or she was being strung along. All in all, this was a very different lady in front of her, just like Valerie and implied. 'We have left the house. I thought you knew this. And don't for one moment pretend like you don't know why. I want to hear from you why it is your single-minded objective to get tenants out and ensure the house forever remains for sale.' She leaned back in her chair.

'You sound as though you've been speaking to Valerie, I can't think how else you could have come to these conclusions so accurately. I'm afraid she does make it her job to get involved with other people's business. We've not exactly seen eye to eye over the years so it stands to reason that she would take the first opportunity for a good gossip.'

Carrie clasped her hands so that they were in front of her positioned on her legs. 'Tell me who has been banging on the door separating the houses up until now.'

Agnes moved her hand to her mouth and her gaze wandered off. 'I think that was probably Tony. I am sorry, it wouldn't have been to scare you. We don't always see eye to eye and I'm guessing it was following one of those times.' She breathed deeply as if considering her words. 'This goes back a long way to when Maria used to live there.'

'So you made up a story about unruly children too then? It was never children in the first place, was it? Please, go on.' There was no way Carrie was going to let a few sentences end the conversation.

Agnes continued, 'That's not entirely a lie. We have had children taunting Tony in the past. He seems to be an easy target which explains why he prefers to stay inside now. It's all too much for him at times. Maria was a lady who bought number 30 following her divorce. She was nice to Tony, which he relished. I mean, here was a confident, attractive lady who would actually give him the time of day. But the way she ... conducted herself she was very, shall we say, unsavoury to folks around here. Of course she caught Tony's eye, I'm not sure if that was her intention. Tony has been living here for most of his life. He tends to struggle with other people, how to interact with them, that kind of thing. If Maria was flirtatious with him, sadly he read that the wrong way.'

She paused. 'Tony had a very good job where he worked from home, oh, computers and that kind of thing,' she waved her hand. 'Pretty soon, he was buying her little gifts and such, which she would take and thank him more than necessary. Well, this just encouraged him and soon the presents became more expensive in value. All the while, she just let him, not a word to discourage him. She led him on in every way possible. When she'd had enough of him, it absolutely devasted him. She dropped him like a hot potato.'

Carrie rubbed her temple, feeling somewhat sorry for him.

'Maria would often entertain other men at her house.' Agnes pulled a face. 'Oh, we'd see them come and go, the way you or I would change a pair of socks. One particular time, she made a very public display of affection in the street with one of them. Unfortunately, Tony saw this. He became very aggressive towards the man. Started screaming that she was his girlfriend. He got a few punches in and this got him in a lot of trouble as someone called the police about the noise. Probably that Valerie who lives over the road. Well, of course the charges were dropped, I imagine Maria wasn't too keen on being publicly shamed at how she had humiliated and controlled Tony. She moved abroad and decided to rent the house out.'

'And you became the landlady?'

Agnes smiled wryly, 'yes, I did agree in the end. I wanted her gone as much as the next person did. We agreed on a small cut for me if I upheld the maintenance and so on. Because she left in such a hurry, she couldn't put things in place for anything else. Sadly, she could never find a buyer due to the large loans she'd taken out against the house. Those men needed a lot of pampering too.'

'And she has no idea of your campaign to ruin her?'

Agnes whistled through her teeth. 'It's not a campaign as such. But no, she wouldn't be aware of how unpleasant it is to stay there if you catch my drift. Maybe it's just something I need to do as payback in my own way. She, on the other hand, has just accepted that it will always be up for rental. The fees paid by tenants are regular enough to keep her head above water, I'm guessing. She just hasn't got the funds to renovate the property.'

'And your part in this is making sure the average stay is short. The quick succession of tenants doesn't give a very good impression for any potential buyer.' Carrie laughed to herself. 'So where does Tony fit into all of this? How has he come into play since I moved in?'

'My dear,' Agnes addressed her full-on. 'By some coincidence, I'm afraid you share a remarkable physical similarity towards Maria. Tony is just desperate to see her again as he is convinced it is his fault she left. But why wouldn't I want the house empty? If Tony has a free rein of the garden to come and go as he pleases, then this is for his own good. If he wishes to do gardening at a late hour, he should be able to without the neighbours complaining. It's what he needs to keep his mind in order. I want number 30 to be empty so he won't be judged. I don't want people spying on my son.'

These words chilled Carrie. She had no desire to hear her suspicions confirmed – Tony had been banging on the door in an attempt to get to her. It may not have been his intention to alarm her at the time, but it had put the fear of God into her when it had happened. Reading between the lines, she was willing to bet good money that he'd been allowed access to the key and had wandered in and out of number 30 whenever he wished. Perhaps he would touch her furnishings or sit in the chair and pretend he was waiting for her to arrive home.

Agnes seemed tenacious and willing to stand her ground as though this was her son's right to behave in such a manner. Carrie wasn't sure how much more sense she would get from probing her. Agnes broke the silence. 'Now, if you will excuse me for a moment, it is time I tended to my husband.'

George had a designated bedroom at the front of the house. The curtains were permanently drawn as Carrie was informed he had sensitive eyesight. The hospital bed dominated the room but it was flanked with medical equipment and what looked to be a mobile unit to provide him with concentrated oxygen. As well as the bed, the room housed several storage units with some medical paraphernalia on top. The bed had two chairs on either side, one was occupied by Tony as he sat slumped over the bed, gently holding his father's hand, his head bowed. He did not look up to acknowledge who was in the room.

Agnes went around the bed, adjusting what Carrie saw to be a feeding tube and repositioning his breathing apparatus. 'He's taking this badly,' she informed Carrie. 'We have been offered a place for George at a hospice, but he wouldn't want that. George's wishes were to remain at home, you know, until the time comes. Sadly, he is not going to get any better.'

'You manage this all by yourself?' Carrie asked in disbelief. The mammoth task this must pose for her, plus a son requiring his own care.

'Oh, I have carers who come in. But it's my job to look after him. I made my vows after all. In sickness and in health.'

Tony stirred, as though he had been woken from a

sleep. He smiled when he saw Carrie stood over the bed.

'Hello Tony,' Carrie greeted him, smiling. There was no point showing any resentment towards him. She had a feeling he wasn't fully aware of the result of his actions towards her.

'This is Carrie,' Agnes confirmed, 'from next door.'

Carrie looked between the two of them. It was almost as though Agnes had already talked with him to explain that she was not Maria.

'Hello C-Carrie,' he nodded towards her and spoke as if he had trouble with the initial consonant.

She couldn't help but start to feel a twinge of sorrow laced with her confusion toward this family. With everything that had happened, she had learned that there was more to a story than meets the eye.

Agnes snapped her out of her thoughts as Tony turned his attention back to his ailing father. 'He's got it in his head that his father will be laid to rest out the back,' her voice was low. 'He's taken it upon himself to dig a hole for when the time comes.' They both turned to look at him.

They walked back downstairs together, Agnes leading the way. 'Now you know the truth, are you still staying at the house?'

'No,' Carrie answered far too quickly. 'No, my ... daughter is settled where we are at the moment and I don't want to uproot us again. As it is, we'll be moving on soon anyway. And besides, there is a funny smell about the place.'

'Ah, again, I do apologise for Tony's intrusion. You must appreciate that with his fragile mind, he just got a bit overwhelmed when he thought you were her, you know, Maria. Normally he moves around the garden area at night, likes to look at the stars, and must have found the key to the door. As for the smell? I'm not sure, possibly a gift hiding somewhere for you which has now turned sour.'

'The same with the birds then?' Carrie shook her head, not really needing any further excuses. She could marry all the oddities now to this vulnerable man. They stood at the door for a few moments before rushing footsteps came down the stairs.

'I have some flowers for you!' Tony declared and promptly disappeared back into the kitchen area. He returned with a neat bouquet which he thrust in Carrie's direction. They looked to be an assortment of flowers picked from a garden. The arrangement looked familiar as Carrie recalled the book of pressed flowers that Birdy had found not so long ago. The book that had obviously been left as a gift for her to find. He did not meet Carrie's eyes as he grinned shyly and brushed the tip of his shoe against the other foot.

She turned to leave but turned around suddenly. 'We are planning to leave in a couple of days, I don't know if you needed to…' she checked behind Agnes, 'warn him again?'

Agnes simply nodded at her.

Carrie felt much lighter in spirits as she crossed the road back to Valerie's. She raised her eyebrows at Carrie's arrival.

'You were right about her, Agnes, being completely different that is.'

'I'm just surprised you made it out in one piece,' she muttered.

'Tony isn't quite all there and her husband, well, it's not a good outlook for him.' She paused, 'I don't know, I just feel that a lot has been cleared up. It's as though I have closure, if that makes sense.'

'Absolutely, if you feel more at peace with the situation, then so be it.'

Carrie settled back and settled her gaze back onto Birdy. For a moment, her heart ached. The time for them to leave in one way or another was becoming more imminent.

DAY 20

'I've got an idea.' Valerie mixed the pancake batter with a certain skill that only an accomplished baker would. Her eyes were anywhere but the bowl as she had shown delight at honouring Birdy's request for pancakes for breakfast. Carrie reckoned she was pleased to have someone to cook for other than herself and genuinely enjoyed it. Carrie was first to admit she overused a microwave and was not very skilled at cooking from scratch until it came to Birdy's pancakes where she was more than happy to do. Birdy was thriving on home cooking and even helped at various points.

'Oh?' Carrie asked as she proceeded to set the table.

'Well, you mentioned staying with your mother when she returns from her holiday. Rather than find a new house for the time in between, I wondered whether ...?' she motioned with her head, not wanting to say the words out loud in case Carrie had other plans and it would upset Birdy if she had to decline the offer.

Carrie smiled. 'Oh, Valerie, we've already taken up so much of your time, I couldn't possibly impose on you for much longer.' She pondered over this offer briefly. 'However, it has been so lovely staying with you.'

'Then I will take that as a yes then, it's been a pleasure having you both here. And this little one is a delight!' she beamed at Birdy and handed the whisk over. 'You said yourself your mother's arrival back is imminent so it's not like it will be forever.'

'That is so kind of you,' Carrie touched her arm, 'I'm so very grateful. If we were to move on, I'd have been forced to find another *Snooze and Stay* rental like the one over the road. It would be just my luck that my next neighbour would be an axe-wielding serial killer or something!' she chuckled at this small joke.

'And Jon, what are your plans for … you know?'

She inhaled sharply, 'I think I will have to tell him we need more time to sort things out, that I am not ready to go back just yet.' Carrie did indeed feel more confident in herself now that the situation over the road was sorted out. She recalled her state of mind following Jon's last visit and the fear started to nudge its way in again. Her stomach flipped at the thought of confronting him.

'Good for you.' Valerie smiled at her. 'And well, if things do get a bit, shall we say, heated, there is always a number you can call.'

Carrie nodded, knowing full well she may have to call the police on him if things did get out of hand. She had a couple of days until he was due back. She didn't want any of her worries to reflect on Birdy, but glancing over at her, she was engrossed in whisking the batter mix. It may be time to start involving the police with Jon. Part of her did miss him, which she hated herself for, but a growing part of her had finally reached the limit of what she was prepared to put up with. Every time Carrie had crossed the road back to the other house, she had been conscious that she was being watched. What if he was tracking her movements, just watching and waiting, ready for his self-imposed deadline which loomed closer? The last thing Carrie wanted to do was get Valerie caught up in all of it. She had a horrible feeling their next meeting was not set to go smoothly but resigned herself to cross that bridge when she came to it. The more time she spent away from him, the more her confidence swelled inside her. The minor setback with him recently had given this a nosedive.

Birdy stood on tiptoes as she peered over the frying pan marvelling at the cooking pancakes.

'Shall I try and flip it?' suggested Valerie.

'Yes!' she exclaimed, 'Mummy never can. She tried once and it landed, splat, on the floor!'

'Ooh, you cheeky monkey, that was supposed to be a secret!' she grabbed Birdy from behind and started to gently tickle her. She squealed in excitement and wiggled away from her touch.

'Okay, here I go.' Valerie held out the pan at arm's length whilst Carrie gathered Birdy into her to create a bit more room. Birdy let out an excited screech as the pancake flipped in the air and landed almost perfectly in the pan.

'You did it!' She proceeded to clap her small hands in quick progression before sitting down at the table while reaching for a knife and fork.

'You don't waste any time!' Carrie laughed.

'That's quite all right,' Valerie slid the pancake onto her plate.

'What are we doing today, Mummy?' Birdy asked through a mouthful of pancake.

'Manners, Birdy. I'm not sure, I think we might need to get a few bits at the shops,' she looked in Valerie's direction. 'You are more than welcome to come with us.'

Valerie shook her head. 'No, I'll be fine, you two go and spend some time together. I've got a few bits to sort out around here.'

She nodded. 'No problem,' and realised that this was probably the most active Valerie had been in a long time. The poor lady was probably longing for a bit of peace and quiet. 'When you're finished then, sweetie?' She rubbed Birdy on the head.

'You like staying with Valerie?' she asked Birdy as they walked down the street again.

Birdy nodded her head enthusiastically. 'She's funny. And she has pets.'

Carrie smiled. At the bottom of their street, she took a fleeting glance back out of habit rather than caution. Birdy did not register this, so she decided not to dwell on it. They crossed the road together. 'I was thinking we could get a nice present for her, what do you think she will like?' Birdy tilted her head and started to chatter, offering ideas that weren't exactly practical or ideal. At the back of Carrie's mind, for some reason, she thought about whether to buy a gift for Tony. According to Agnes, Maria had done nothing but take from him. If she reversed this and gave him a gift, then it perhaps may break the cycle and make it clear in his mind that she was not Maria once and for all.

They browsed a nearby shop and moved around the displays. 'I don't think Valerie would like that,' Birdy scrunched her nose up as her mother had stopped to admire some models on the solar system. 'That's the space, isn't it?'

Carrie nodded and she picked up one of the models, remembering that Agnes had mentioned that Tony liked to look at the stars at night. This would be an appropriate parting gift to which she had given some thought to, but it wasn't overly sentimental.

'Valerie likes the animal models, Mummy.' Birdy's voice was more distant as she had moved to another display and proudly stood alongside some china figurines. She was careful not to touch and pointed a small finger at one.

'Is that one you'd like to choose for her?' she carefully picked it up and moved it closer to Birdy so she could inspect the colours.

'Yes, I think she would like that one.'

'Okay, we'll buy that too.' Carrie balanced the two purchases together.

'Who is that one for?'

'Oh,' Carrie pondered, 'just for Agnes and her son next door. I went to see him,' her voice trailed off, not wanting to go into too many details. 'His dad is poorly, and I thought this might be nice for him.' She breathed deeply, maybe this was the time to have a conversation with Birdy about their future.

'I was thinking sweetie, are you happy to stay with Valerie for a bit longer before we go and stay with Nanny?' She watched as small eyes lit up and her head bobbed up and down. 'About Daddy,' she faltered and cast her eyes down, 'Mummy and Daddy have a lot of things to sort out. I'm not sure if we're … ready to move back home yet.'

Birdy shrugged and puffed out her cheeks, 'I guess that's okay.'

'That's sorted, now, let's go and pay for these.' They spotted the queue for the checkouts and headed in that direction. Just a mother and her child shopping like anyone else. They could blend in amongst the crowd, hard to single out as anything other than ordinary in the swarm of people. A person would have to be looking very closely to spot them.

Valerie, as it turned out, loved the ornament they had selected for her. Unbeknown to Carrie, she was collecting a particular set, and this was one of the pieces she was missing.

'Every time you look at it, you can always think of us,' Birdy declared as she positioned it next to the rest of the collection.

'Listen, I …' Carrie got to her feet. 'There were a few more bits and pieces over the road to bin. Like food in the cupboards and fridge I forgot to do yesterday. Then I'll be done and won't need to go back again.'

Valerie nodded, pre-empting the question. 'That's fine with me.'

'I won't be long.' She addressed them before heading out of the room. Close to the front door, she retrieved her bag from their trip out earlier which contained Tony's gift. She wasn't a hundred per cent sure if she were doing the right thing but set out anyway.

The sun was beginning to start its journey down as the late afternoon rolled in. No longer shining onto the street, the orangey glow from behind the rooftops shone brightly into Carrie's eyes. Momentarily dazzled, she put a hand to shield her eyes as she fumbled for the key with the other. It hadn't been a lie – there were food items in the fridge which Carrie determined could indeed go in the bin. She went around with a bin bag, putting any other items that could be thrown out alongside them, old newspapers and magazines that were pointless to go with them. Satisfied that the upstairs was now clean and clear, she headed back downstairs to the two bedrooms.

The smell was still lingering but didn't seem as strong. *A small gift he may have left for you* echoed in Carrie's mind but she did not want to dwell on what this might be. She stood outside the wooden, blue door with the key in her hand. The key that she had so desperately wanted but ironically, in the time Clive had taken to retrieve it, the door had been opened anyway. Unsure if she should go and knock on the front door or just have a peek around the door into the garden, she opened it. It was a solid, old-fashioned type which was heavy to move. Carrie appreciated the sturdiness of the door as she shuddered and recalled the pounding that had been inflicted on it not so long ago.

He was sitting on the back doorstep, tracing patterns in the loose dirt with a finger. Carrie remembered his tattered and dirty clothes and reckoned the cuffs had probably become grubby from this repeated activity. Tony did not look up to acknowledge Carrie's presence.

She took a few steps towards him, not wishing to startle him. 'Tony?'

His head snapped up and an instant smile adorned his face.

'Carrie, remember me?' She clutched her bag tighter in her hands. 'How are you today?'

'Good,' he nodded.

She took a seat next to him, thinking that he might feel a bit more comfortable if she wasn't towering over him. He seemed quite content to sit alongside her. Carrie wasn't sure if he was struggling to think for something to say or was just happy in the silence.

'I have something for you.' She held the bag out for him to take and he hesitated. For one moment, she feared she'd made a horrible mistake – what if he got the wrong impression like Agnes said he had with Maria? 'It's a gift,' she stated, 'from one friend to another.'

'Thank you very much!' he gushed and clutched the bag as he beamed widely.

'Aren't you going to open it?' she laughed quietly. This was quite typical of how Birdy would react to a gift, sometimes more overwhelmed at the thought of receiving a present rather than what it actually contained.

He fumbled with the carrier bag and took out a small, flat box. Carefully, he eased the lid open. Carrie saw his expression change as he was now faced with coloured tissue paper. Moving this to one side, the present had been positioned carefully due to its fragility.

'It's a mobile, see?' Carrie moved to release the string and hold up the decoration. She saw Tony watch in awe as the slight breeze caused the planets to spin as though they were orbiting the sun. 'That's what it does,' she explained. 'If you hang this by your window, the wind will turn them.'

'It's beautiful!' he exclaimed as his eyes lit up. 'It's the best present I've ever had.' Carrie wondered whether he might actually start crying with emotion but he appeared too elated to shed any tears. 'Thank you ...'

'Carrie.' She finished the sentence for him to reinforce the fact that she was not Maria. Carrie wondered in all the work it must take for Agnes to care for her sick husband, whether Tony was adequately looked after. It must be very hard on her. They sat in silence as the planets moved around again fuelled by the wind speed. After a few moments, he slowly replaced this in the box.

'I'll look after it forever,' he beamed at her and leaned in towards her before retreating just as quickly.

Carrie smiled and lifted her hand slightly to give warning of her intention. She placed a hand on his. 'You're very welcome.'

The shuffle of footsteps didn't cause Carrie to look up straight away as she figured Agnes had opened the back door so discretely, she hadn't even noticed. Or she had been so engrossed with her thoughts that it was just one of those things that occurred and she needed a few moments to process. Whatever it was, the noise informed her that they were no longer alone.

He stood in front of her, having walked through the boiler room and therefore, through her own house. Jon stood blocking the doorway, eclipsing it. His expression was one of scorn and almost judgemental. Her eyes moved up, starting with heavy-looking black boots to jeans and a checked shirt.

He could almost be mistaken for a workman which caused Carrie to entertain an absurd thought that he had kicked the front door in. Seeming to register this, he held up a key.

'I took your spare.' He smiled as he said this as though it had been perfectly acceptable for him to do this. 'You left it on the kitchen worktop when I was visiting you.'

Carrie felt her thoughts multiply and jumble in her head but her mouth was too slow to process anything.

Menacingly, his voice remained at the same hushed tone, 'I know what you're thinking, we agreed on tomorrow.'

She started to respond but only managed a faint sound at first. Clearing her throat several times, she asked, 'Why are you here?' All the while, the fluttering inside her stomach had begun bubbling, slowly rising.

Instead of bending down to address her at her level, he remained standing but did inch closer, increasing his intimidation and preventing her from getting up without colliding with him. 'I had a feeling that you might need reminding. However, there is no harm in you coming a day earlier.' He looked down into the garden as though he was expecting to see Birdy at the other end. 'I see from inside you're all packed up,' he declared.

Carrie remained sitting, unaware that she had slowly started wringing her hands; her fingers shook as her palms began to feel clammy.

'So there's no reason to stay around here any longer. If you just get your bags together and we can all be on our way.'

'Jon ... I ...' she stuttered. This caused him to frown at her, feigning confusion at what could possibly be preventing her from leaving with him right now.

'Where is my daughter anyway?'

'She's not here,' Carrie replied firmly. 'We don't live here anymore.'

'Hmm,' he seemed to ponder her response and looked in the immediate area. 'You're right, it's not too safe here. That fence, although it's been repaired, looks like someone could scale it no problem.' He turned back to face her. 'Doesn't it Carrie?'

She moved her mouth in response, her mind a

confusion about what to think, what to believe. Who was the real enemy here? What part had *Jon* really played in this the whole time they had been here? 'It was you? All this time, you were the one behind it all?' she asked in disbelief, unable to accept the obvious suspect had been known to her all along. It was Jon who had been intimidating her this whole time?

'Maybe some of the time. You mentioned you'd heard knocking sounds in the night, which wasn't me, I might add, but why shouldn't I take advantage of someone else's plan to scare the living daylights out of you?' he smirked. 'God, you're so easy to get jittery. Maybe I did bang on the door and your neighbours' for good measure now and again. Imagine how easily I got away with it when you started rabbiting on about wayward children? Carrie, you made it far too easy for me to slip the spare key you left lying around into my pocket and return it a few days later. And that stupid pet bird you let our daughter have,' he shook his head at her.

'It was you,' she replied, angry at being duped this whole time. Maybe some of the odd behaviour had just been Agnes or Tony leaving her odd presents but Jon's hatred towards her was far worse.

'I did say to you no more pets. Besides, it was on its last legs when I let it go. How was I to know it would actually peg it of its own accord? It was really easy to let myself in through your front door once I'd seen you leave for the day. I thought I'd just leave it in a place for you to find it. On the windowsill was just fine. Then by some weird coincidence, it turns out you have an oddball neighbour living next door anyway. So where's the harm letting him take the blame?'

Carrie shook her head at him, as she struggled to find the words to condemn his sick and twisted behaviour. She had been so blinded, the way he had described Agnes as a 'doddery old lady'. How would he have known this unless he had seen her with his own eyes, out on the street perhaps whilst he waited for Carrie to leave the house and track her whereabouts? She had been right – he'd used the time wisely between finding out where they lived before actually confronting her in the park that one afternoon. And as for therapy, she doubted he'd even approached a doctor at all.

'Who's your friend, anyway?' He nodded in Tony's direction, his voice tinged with arrogance as though he had the right to know.

Carrie turned to face him, unsure if he had been too polite to say anything or too socially awkward to remove himself from the growing tense atmosphere. He still sat with his eyes cast down, unaware that Jon had now referred to his presence.

'Hey, I'm talking to you,' Jon raised his voice as he looked down on Tony, who in turn, slowly raised his head. 'Are you talking to my wife?' his pitch raised in faked ignorance. Tony remained frozen in the same position, obviously intimidated at being put on the spot and interrogated as such. Carrie reckoned he was probably having trouble with how to react to such an obvious question. In his mind, of course they had been talking.

Jon turned his attention back to Carrie. 'Is this what happens when I'm gone?' he gestured his head towards Tony. 'You hook up with the nearest man in your sight? Really Carrie, I think you could have chosen a *little* bit better.' He smirked to himself.

Carrie bit her lip. 'He's just a friend.' Her voice was small and meek.

He nodded at her and with no preamble, moved swiftly to grasp her arm and pull her up. More out of surprise than pain, Carrie let out a squeal. 'Get up now and get your things!' His voice was raised now as though he had finally had enough of the small talk. His hand twisted her arm as she fought to release his vice-like hold. As she struggled to release herself, he seemed to interpret this as insolence. 'I said get up!' he shouted whilst simultaneously releasing his grip. The sheer force caused Carrie to tumble back onto the step once more.

'Move now!' He raised his hand over her head and Carrie narrowed her eyes as she saw the inevitable blow coming.

'No!' Tony caught Jon's arm and suspended it inches above Carrie's head. He held tighter as he managed to get to his feet. They tussled with each other before Jon gained the advantage and shoved Tony backwards. He crashed into the ground and lay flat for a moment. Carrie gasped and instinctively moved towards him, fearing the worst until she saw him raise one hand to prop himself back up.

'Get your freaky boyfriend away from me!' Jon boomed. He reached for Carrie's arm again and this time succeeded in hauling her to a standing position. He hastily raised his hand and struck her across the face, Carrie shrunk backwards like a cowering animal. The resounding noise of the palm of his hand hitting her cheek reverberated around her head. She raised a hand to cover the stinging area on her face.

'Get inside, you worthless whore!' he spat the words out as though they lay unpleasantly in his mouth.

Carrie's vision was a blur through her tears. She could see him looming over her, ready to strike again as though he was squaring up for a fight. Tony, in his frightened state, had managed to get up and move away. She saw him scurry off down the garden, obviously too afraid to rush past them and hide in the safety of his own house. Carrie wouldn't have blamed him if he had. Jon was a powerful man and Tony was clearly outmatched.

Jon managed to shove Carrie back into the boiler room. Without a glance back, he reached for the doorknob, ready to seal them inside and steal Carrie's sanctuary from the outside. With the fear etched on her face, she watched as Jon froze suddenly, his face morphed into a surprised expression.

Carrie was not sure what she became aware of first – his motionless features or the clang of the spade hitting his head with a powerful force. Either way, he managed to remain standing for a few moments, wobbling back and forwards with anyone's guess as to whether he was destined to fall forwards or back. His centre of gravity shifted as he moved one hand up to his head, before tumbling backwards. Before making full contact with the ground, his head bounced off the bare concrete before slumping to one side. As his limbs sprawled outwards, the puddle of blood gradually seeped out from under his head, inching ever so slightly wider.

She was aware her breathing was coming in short pants as the tears continued to course down her face. Carrie looked at the doorway, where Tony stood poised with the spade like he was a batsman at a baseball game anticipating the next pitch. His eyes were wide circles as his jaw trembled. Slowly, he lowered the spade and adjusted his grip on the body of it so that he held it by the handle. Moving it so it was parallel with his body, he averted his gaze away from Jon onto Carrie.

'No,' she heard herself gasp as she scrambled down so she was crouched next to Jon's motionless body. The dark, red patch which haloed his broken head had now reached its maximum range. She could see his head had tilted to one side and stared in shock at the exposed skull as though she were examining a shattered eggshell. Carrie held onto the front of his shirt covering his chest and bunched her hands into fists, forcing the material to twist. She had begun sobbing now, deep, uncontrollable howls as she mourned the man he had once been, perhaps glimmers of which may have emerged again.

Tony broke the silence and shuffled his feet, 'I didn't … he was hurting you, I didn't mean to …' His voice cracked in several places. Carrie looked up at him as his eyes searched for validation for his actions and affirmation that he wasn't in trouble. He dropped the spade and it too tumbled forwards before clanging onto the floor. Tony's hands moved up to his head as he paced frantically.

Carrie had blocked out every sense as she leaned with her head rested on Jon's chest. The rise and fall had ceased long ago. She inhaled the scent of his aftershave as her sobbing ebbed away. She slowly opened her eyes, suddenly feeling very tired. Within her sight, Tony had sunk down so that he was resting against the wall, quietly murmuring to himself, his voice muffled as he pulled his knees up and bowed his head. With no concept of time, the boiler room had grown cooler and darker. A single sound invaded the silence as a distant door squeaked open.

She didn't run in as Carrie would expect. It was almost as though the scene in front of her didn't come as a shock to her or perhaps she was just too detached from the situation. Agnes stood in the open doorway as though she were surveying the wake of a mini-tornado. She looked across from the pitiful sight on the floor – Carrie now cradling her dead husband's head to her vulnerable son, slowly unravelling due to his actions.

'What have you done?' Her voice was barely above a whisper. 'Tony, what did you do?'

The only word he could manage to utter came out on a loop, 'no, no, no.' He shook his head from side to side. Her feet scraped the concrete floor as she stood by his side. Fearing she may snap him out of his trance with a slap across the head, Carrie breathed hard and moved to a kneeling position.

'Agnes, no,' she croaked and reached out her hand even though she did not make contact. Her arms were streaked with blood and her hands were dirty and grainy. 'It wasn't his fault.'

'Wasn't his fault?' she repeated sharply. 'Look around you, my goodness, these things don't just happen, the police …' she crouched down, suddenly gasping for breath.

Carrie dragged herself over and shuffled next to them, Tony sat with his head bowed whilst Agnes clutched her chest. She placed a hand on Agnes's shoulder. 'Breathe,' she urged as calmly as she could muster. Rubbing her hand on Agnes's cardigan, the coppery smell began to invade her nostrils overwhelming the usual damp smell from the room. 'This was not his fault,' she repeated. 'He only did what he thought was right. Jon, my husband is a violent man …' She paused, acutely aware she was referring to him in the present tense. 'He attacked me, Tony was just defending me.'

'I very much doubt the police will take on that view.' Her tone was sharp as she struggled through her tears. 'They'll take my boy away,' she wailed as though the pain of this was too much to bear. 'My husband is not long for this world and now I'm going to lose my son too.'

They sat as a trio. Carrie looked back onto the body sprawled on the floor. The more she looked at him, the more the image of her husband faded away and she was left staring at an aggressive man who had been attacked due to his own ferocious behaviour. Maybe he hadn't deserved what had happened to him and how things had unfolded but there was no way Tony deserved to be punished. Yes, she had loved Jon but could only imagine how the rest of her life would have panned out if there had been no intervention. Her pity became anger – for believing Jon when he said he would change and for her own stupid naivety in falling for it. Everything she had struggled so hard to suppress during their marriage began to push to the surface. Every excuse she had made for him, he was having a hard time at work, they were struggling with money, he was upset due to his mother's death … It was excuse after excuse as she justified his behaviour and just took the verbal abuse and subtle taunts, a slow drip-feed of controlling behaviour. Her own mother had always said that one day she would wake up and see the light – suddenly the room had never looked brighter.

Carrie raced over to the side of his body and screamed at him, she beat her fists on his chest and pounded, weeping in anger. His body shook due to the force as she continued until she had nothing left. Sobbing over his body again, she felt strangely removed from any emotion.

'Don't blame yourself,' she addressed them. 'He was a controlling man with a lot of issues. He does not deserve your sympathy or guilt. I am the stupid one for putting up with him for so long.' She pushed his wayward arm away from her as though she were swatting away an annoying insect. Agnes by now had moved to place her arms around Tony, still lost in his own world as he struggled to rationalise the situation.

'Tony.' Carrie crouched in front of him. 'Look at me.' She was aware that eye contact posed a challenge to him at the best of times but placed a bloodied hand under his chin. She forced his head up and his eyes flitted to her. 'This was not your fault.'

He entertained a weak smile before casting his eyes down again.

'We have a body,' Agnes moaned, 'we have to call someone.'

'Or do we?' Carrie replied.

'I don't understand?' she faltered. 'Are you suggesting we just leave him here?'

Carrie shook her head. 'No, but I'm just trying to think if anyone knows he came here.' She racked her thoughts and could not envisage such a conversation he may have had with a friend as *just going to get my wayward, disobedient wife back from her self-imposed escape, back soon!* She smiled briefly at her own joke.

'Then what?' Agnes pressed, the urgency in her voice apparent. 'What could we possibly do to change this situation?'

'I have an idea.'

The white noise rang in Carrie's ears as she walked on autopilot back to Valerie's house. The night had begun to set in as she cast no shadow on the street. She walked, head bowed, no one around to witness her appearance. Had it been light, they would have seen Carrie's face streaked with tears, dirt and blood. Her hair had become a tangled mess, trousers were so very dirty from constant contact with the ground. Her clothes were equally as pitiful, ripped in places but the dark, red patches gave them a more chilling quality. All in all, it looked as though she had crawled her way out of a deadly situation, on her hands and knees fighting for her survival. Perhaps in a way, she had.

Birdy had been tucked up in bed long ago as Carrie let herself in quietly. Once she saw Valerie who had rushed into the hallway, anticipating her return, she sank to her knees and sobbed into her arms. The hallway was dark but Valerie must have been able to see her appearance but didn't make any acknowledgement of this. She simply offered her presence as a comfort. Her sobs came in long heaves, one blending into the next as she shook in the aftermath of the day.

'He came back, I don't think he ever really left,' was all she could manage to say after a while. She felt Valerie stir as though she was nodding. Her hand rhythmically soothed her hair to flatten its dishevelled state.

Carrie had spent the last few hours almost in a trance-like state. They had moved with purpose, automatically working together to clear up every trace of Jon's visit over the road. Working in relative silence, Tony had lifted Jon's top half of his body and Carrie had manoeuvred his legs out of the boiler room. She had seen Tony grit his teeth under the dead weight of Jon's corpse as they navigated their way through the garden. Placing his body on the edge of Tony's recently dug hole, Carrie had taken on the task of pushing him in. They stood for a few moments, almost in a silent prayer to mourn his passing. Carrie then took on the task of using the loose earth nearby to cover his body as Tony used the spade to gather more from the surrounding area. Before too long, the repeated task of shovelling and flattening the earth, they had eventually managed to level the ground in place of the hole Tony had made.

It hadn't crossed her mind whether the neighbours were outside in their gardens. And what would they have thought if they were? There was Agnes's crazy son outside doing his digging again at any old hour. They would excuse it as normal for him. Carrie took one last look back at their garden, it just took on the appearance of being recently tended to and if anything, looked a bit more orderly. Some strategically placed grass seed and a regular watering every day would yield results in no time.

Agnes had spent the time on her hands and knees applying bleach to the stain on the boiler room floor, scrubbing and dipping the brush back in as the evidence of the assault there gradually faded. It was a mammoth task for a lady of her advancing years but she didn't show it or let up in any way. She showed no signs of fatigue apart from wiping her brow with her sleeve every now and again. Agnes had just been fuelled on by the determination of protecting her son. Carrie had taken the bucket from her with a mind to emptying it down the nearby drain. As the water splashed down, she understood Agnes's actions – the things a mother would do to protect her child.

The three of them stood outside in the passageway between the two houses. Agnes nodded at her, signalling their job was complete. Tony had gone inside first, his pace heavy-footed as though the exertions of the day still weighed on his mind.

Carrie placed a hand on Agnes's arm, knowing it was dirty but equally, her cardigan was just as filthy. 'Agnes,' she said as Tony disappeared from sight. 'I left a few days ago and I was never here, is that understood?' She looked at her straight in the eye, 'I was not here,' she affirmed.

Agnes nodded, the sheer exhaustion now catching up with her. 'You were an unremarkable tenant who kept herself to herself. I barely saw you. You had a small issue with your boiler which I sorted. After that, I had no further dealings with you.'

Carrie nodded back at her. 'When you set about clearing the rest of the house, you'll find no trace of us. I've spent the last few days cleaning away any evidence that we were ever here, do you understand?'

She nodded back at her.

Carrie spent a lot of time scrubbing at her skin over-enthusiastically even though she was clean. She was desperate to rid herself of the feeling of sticky blood and dirt on her, as well as wanting to free herself of any memory of that day.

Once she was semi-satisfied she was clean on the outside, she dressed in light pyjamas and brushed through her long hair.

Valerie stood over her with a pair of scissors. 'I think this is for the best, don't you?'

In the reflection of the bathroom mirror, Carrie nodded as Valerie took to her long hair with the blades. Her long hair had been long overdue for a cut but this was another symbol for the change she felt inside and out. She began to feel a transformation emerging – she was no longer the victim of an abusive marriage. It was time for a fresh start.

DAY 21

irdy had eyed her cautiously from across the kitchen table. It was as though she was aware that something was different but couldn't quite place it.

'You look different,' she exclaimed finally.

'Do you like it?' Carrie asked, touching her newly cut hair, to which Birdy returned a nod.

'It's nice. What will we be doing today?'

Carrie breathed in deeply. 'Well, sweetie, that is what I wanted to talk to you about.' She watched as raised eyebrows greeted her. 'I think it's time we left here. We need to leave today.'

Valerie sat stoically next to her. They had spent a lot of the night talking, deciding what Carrie needed to do next. It hadn't been all too comfortable listening to it for Carrie's liking but there were things she needed to face up to now that Jon was out of the picture. Maybe it had taken a stranger's take on the whole situation to make Carrie admit to the absolute hold that he had had on her. Things she had been afraid to do in the past, she was no longer under his control for any more. But there were things that would be more gradual and take a while to undo, she had just been too afraid to confront him and stand up for herself during the course of their relationship. The prospect of being alone for real rather than running away was also a realisation that was starting to sink in with Carrie.

'Where are we going to?' Birdy asked.

'Well, I was thinking we could go to Nanny's house to start with and maybe then think about getting our own house in the future.'

'Nanny's?' she squeaked excitedly. 'For real?' The glee adorned her face but then dropped slightly. She turned to face Valerie, 'I will really miss you, though. Maybe you could come with us?' She tilted her head.

Valerie let out a small laugh, 'I would love to, but what about my house? This is where I live.'

'Hmm,' she pondered. 'Well, we'll just have to send you lots of postcards and you can come on your holidays to us.' She leaned in slightly. 'Nanny lives by the beach you see.'

'Okay, Birdy, we need to look at all the things in your room, decide what to take with us, up you jump.' Valerie smiled at her and set about clearing up the breakfast table. Carrie knew she needed some time with Birdy so followed her upstairs. She folded some of her clothes and made separate piles of older items.

'Is Daddy coming with us?' Of course she was bound to ask the question sooner or later seeing as it had only been a week ago since his last visit. Prepared for this type of question, Carrie shook her head.

'No, he won't be coming with us.' She stopped what she had been doing and sat down, patting the bed next to her. 'Mummy has decided that it would be best for us. and you, if we don't live with Daddy again. Sometimes when parents aren't happy together, it can make their children sad too.'

'But I will still see him?'

She thought for a few moments to choose her response carefully. Everything that Jon had put the two of them through, if only she knew the full truth, maybe her fierce loyalty for him would change. But children were very accepting and forgiving. She only knew things that were told to her directly and saw what Carrie had allowed her to see. The crying she had done behind the locked bathroom door often during their days together had been kept from her deliberately.

'Daddy would like some time by himself for a while,' seemed to be an acceptable answer. 'Listen, this will be an opportunity for us both to have a new start.'

Birdy frowned, which caused Carrie to wonder whether she needed to rephrase the statement.

'Some of the things that happened at home. We don't have to live the same way anymore.'

'So we don't have to be quiet when Daddy is watching his programmes or I don't have to eat all of my vegetables?'

Carrie smiled at her innocence. She picked up one of Birdy's dresses. 'I mean you don't have to wear these anymore, unless you want to, that is.' Birdy shuffled towards the pile of clothes and fingered some of the material. 'And you don't have to use the name Daddy gave you anymore.' This had been the one thing she had been building up to saying to Birdy for a while now, just waiting for the moment to be able to say it, without fearing the wrath of Jon. But he wasn't around anymore and they would be free to choose.

She looked across to Birdy and saw a single tear had escaped, then joined by several more. A small finger went up to her eye in an attempt to stem the flow. She kept her head bowed as she continued to fiddle with the folded pink dress.

'It's okay,' Carrie whispered to her. She put a hand to her hair and smoothed it gently. 'You can get a haircut too, if you want. But I know you do like long hair.'

Birdy's expression twisted into trepidation and sadness. 'But I'm not allowed.'

'*I* say you are allowed,' Carrie replied firmly.

Birdy sniffed several times. 'What name can I have then?'

Again, Carrie took her arm to make contact with her, reassure her that everything would be okay from now on. 'You know what?' Her voice was a whisper. Birdy nodded at her as her breathing shuddered as the tears subsided. 'It's going to take me a long time to get used to things, too,' she explained to Birdy. 'Being with Daddy for a long time, he had a way that he liked things and I had to like them that way too, I'm not sure how much of this you will understand …' Carrie shook her head, 'I have let you down and not been the Mummy I should have been to you.' Her voice was quiet as she felt her own tears build up. She wiped her eyes quickly. 'I

should have said no, I should have got us out before now.'
She breathed deeply and looked up, 'Birdy, look at me.' They
locked eyes as Carrie continued. 'Some of the things Daddy
said to you weren't true.'

'What kind of things?'

'You know. You can say it.' She kept her eyes fixed
and encouraged her by nodding. 'It's okay to say it now.'

The voice which came from her child was small but
determined. Said quietly at first, Birdy repeated it. 'I am a
boy.'

Carrie nodded. 'You are a boy.' She placed the dress
on the pile of girl clothes. The newly bought items more
identifiable as clothing suitable for boys sat next to it. Jeans,
tee shirts and shirts that Birdy had expressly chosen during
their shopping trip, the ones that Jon had discreetly tried to
remove when he had visited while helping look for Birdy's
pet.

Jon's mother had died shortly before Birdy was
conceived. He had taken it badly but was so desperate for
their first child to be a girl, so she could carry his late
mother's name. When Birdy had emerged as a healthy baby
boy, this was not enough. It was not enough for him to have
the unconditional love of a child; he wanted his daughter.
The slow move to control this had begun just after they had
got home from the hospital. He had refused to change the
nappies and had been himself to register the birth, emerging
with the name Bridgette on the birth certificate even though
it clearly stated the born gender on it. Keeping Birdy off
school to be educated at home avoided the inevitable
comparisons of gender, avoided the questioning from
teachers and other children as to why Birdy had long hair or
dressed like a princess. When the arguments had erupted, Jon
had simply stated that their child would be free to choose
what to identify as the years went by. Carrie had always
harboured the fear at the back of her mind that he had never
meant this and would secretly arrange for treatment for Birdy
citing gender identity issues. Jon was insistent to the point of
extreme anger if Carrie ever referred to their child as a 'he'.
Always *he* was a *she*, even to the point of carrying on with this

in front of Carrie's mother. She would frown and play along with this if it meant Carrie's life would be that much easier, being careful where she could to avoid using pronouns.

'Cut it off,' Birdy pointed to his hair, 'I do like long hair but boys have short hair.'

'If you are sure, I just want you to be happy. Valerie cut mine.'

'I am sure,' Birdy collected some jeans and a tee shirt from the pile of clothes and his hand hovered over the white, frilly socks. 'I do like these though.'

Carrie laughed. 'Wear them, then, it's no problem.'

Valerie made a lovely job of sorting out Birdy's hair. Not only was it long, but it was also quite untidy too as Jon had only allowed short trims now and again. As Birdy had always worn long hair and been dressed very femininely in public, no one ever had any reason to suspect he was anything but a girl. How appearances could be deceptive. Valerie had worked out almost from the word go that Birdy was a boy. Carrie put this down to one of her innate skills as a shrewd observer of all that happened around her. She also had avoided referring to Birdy as a girl during their stay with her and would always compliment Carrie on her well-mannered child. She had explained that during her life working with children, she had always encouraged self-expression. However, a gender forced on a child for another purpose was altogether different.

Carrie and Birdy stood in the hallway, waiting for the taxi that would form part of their long journey to the coast to stay with Carrie's mother.

'I can't thank you enough, for everything,' Carrie embraced Valerie as her voice wobbled with genuine emotion.

'You're very welcome, and you, too, Birdy.'

Carrie hesitated, 'what will you tell people? I mean, people who may come around perhaps, looking into number 30 across the road? That sort of thing might happen over time. Who would you say stayed there?'

Valerie shrugged, 'I will say what I saw on the day you arrived. I saw a woman with long hair arrive. She was accompanied by her daughter, also with long hair, maybe aged around five years old? They kept themselves to themselves. I barely saw them really. And then one day, they left. If they ask any other questions, well, I'll just throw them off track.' She took hold of Carrie's shoulders with her hands. 'And here leaving my house aren't the same two people. I see a young woman stood proudly, brimming with confidence with her young son.'

They were interrupted by the beep of a car horn from outside. Valerie blinked back her tears. 'Now you two, be sure to have a safe journey.'

They walked to the taxi together as Carrie settled Birdy in and sorted their luggage in the boot. She turned to Valerie and hugged her again. 'Thank you.'

Valerie nodded and raised a hand as the taxi drove off to the end of the street. She took one last look at the house across the street before going back inside.

DAY 26

The letter arrived a few days later. It read:

Dear Valerie

We are having the bestest time ever with Nanny! Her house is blue and is near the sea. In the morning, I can see birds out of my window, how are your birds? I play on the beach every day as it is so sunny and can go in the sea as well. I eat lots of ice cream and pancakes (but not as good as yours!).
We are hoping you can come and visit us soon?

Lots and lots of love, Stevie

Valerie smiled as she clutched the letter to her chest. The writing was clearly from the hand of an adult, but she got the distinct impression that a small child had dictated every word for Carrie to write. She beamed again as she pictured them running together on the beach, facing the sea with the world ahead of them.

Perhaps a holiday wouldn't be such a bad idea. A change of scenery would be very welcome from the neighbourhood. The air was rising in humidity making sleeping at night very difficult; the sea breeze would make this much more comfortable for her. In the early hours of that morning, the arrival of an ambulance and police car had woken her up and she had found it impossible to get back to sleep. She had feared that the police had started digging in Agnes's back garden and found something of interest. Valerie had spent her time watching out of the window, fretting at the prospect of weaving together a plausible story about the comings and goings of the house opposite to her. She would have to think on her feet and throw the police off track. She had feared at that point that something had happened with Tony. Perhaps the departure of Carrie had tipped him over the edge and he had finally attacked the nearest person to him – his own mother. Valerie had worried that she would be called upon to answers questions about what could have caused him to lash out. Had any recent events unsettled him in any way? Her house faced almost opposite number 28 and the neighbouring house, number 30. Surely, she must have seen something. She had taken it on herself to enquire about the paramedics once the morning had come and the street had settled down once again. But she need not have worried for the police had merely arrived as a matter of formality. And the paramedics? They had been called out for a specific reason, one of which she had known was coming sooner rather than later.

Valerie nodded to herself, she would reply as soon as possible and also break the sad news that poor George, devoted husband of Agnes and father to Tony, had sadly passed away in his sleep just that morning.

Wendell
By Amy-Brooke Odell

Wendell and his friends, both human and animal, embark on a journey to discover the truth about the Wind Folk and where his mother really is. His world of baseball, camp-outs, and fishing is rocked when he discovers that the adults in town know a lot more than they say, and sometimes those tales told around a campfire are true.

And, when it comes to the Wind Folk; it is said if you see one, you become one.

Maxwell's Zoom
By M. J. Trow

When asked about when it all began, Peter Maxwell would always say that it was at breakfast one day, when his son said, 'It says in the news that bats are giving people colds.' At that point, that was all anyone thought, if they thought anything at all. Nolan was worried about the Count and Bismarck but of course, as everyone would soon know, it was more than that – much more.

What was perhaps not quite so obvious as the world started to pull together to halt the spread of the pandemic, was that it would also restart a killing spree, one that had been halted for decades. Old memories rising to the surface, old enmities and slights recalled and suddenly, in masked and socially distanced Leighford someone is prowling with a hammer raised to create mayhem.

As an historian, Maxwell is keeping his head while most people are running round like chickens minus theirs – loss and tragedy stalk the land, closer to home than anyone thought possible. In a world where death is striking everywhere, how can anyone hope to bring a murderer to book?

Goblin Market
By Maryanne Coleman

Have you ever wondered what happened to the faeries you used to believe in? They lived at the bottom of the garden and left rings in the grass and sparkling glamour in the air to remind you where they were. But that was then – now you might find them in places you might not think to look. They might be stacking shelves, delivering milk or weighing babies at the clinic. Open your eyes and keep your wits about you and you might see them.

But no one is looking any more and that is hard for a Faerie Queen to bear and Titania has had enough. When Titania stamps her foot, everyone in Faerieland jumps; publicity is what they need. Television, magazines. But that sort of thing is much more the remit of the bad boys of the Unseelie Court, the ones who weave a new kind of magic; the World Wide Web. Here is Puck re-learning how to fly; Leanne the agent who really is a vampire; Oberon's Boys playing cards behind the wainscoting; Black Annis, the bag-lady from Hainault, all gathered in a Restoration comedy that is strictly twenty-first century.

Prester John: Africa's Lost King
By Richard Denham

He sits on his jewelled throne on the Horn of Africa in the maps of the sixteenth century. He can see his whole empire reflected in a mirror outside his palace. He carries three crosses into battle and each cross is guarded by one hundred thousand men. He was with St Thomas in the third century when he set up a Christian church in India. He came like a thunderbolt out of the far East eight centuries later, to rescue the crusaders clinging on to Jerusalem. And he was still there when Portuguese explorers went looking for him in the fifteenth century.

Was he real? Did he ever exist? This book will take you on a journey of a lifetime, to worlds that might have been, but never were. It will take you, if you are brave enough, into the world of Prester John.

Fade
By Bethan White

There is nothing extraordinary about Chris Rowan. Each day he wakes to the same faces, has the same breakfast, the same commute, the same sort of homes he tries to rent out to unsuspecting tenants.

There is nothing extraordinary about Chris Rowan. That is apart from the black dog that haunts his nightmares and an unexpected encounter with a long forgotten demon from his past. A nudge that will send Chris on his own downward spiral, from which there may be no escape.

There is nothing extraordinary about Chris Rowan...

The Witch of Tessingham Hall
By Sinéad Spearing.

England 1657.

Alison, a folk- healer, stands falsely accused of murder by witchcraft, an allegation that sets in motion a powerful curse — "May your women forever wane!" — the spell haunting generations of her accuser's family, sending their women early to their graves.

London 2022.

Eden Flynn – an anxiety-ridden academic of Old English magic is invited for a job interview in the crypt of Southwark Cathedral, where her interviewer, the dashingly handsome geneticist Lord James Fabian, pulls her into the midst of his family secret: his sister is sick, and his daughter is showing signs of the same mental affliction.

Can Eden fulfil her part in the web which has been woven stronger and stronger over hundreds of years? Can she find the strength to break the bonds that bind her and Lord Fabian to the past? And can she live with the changes she will unleash?

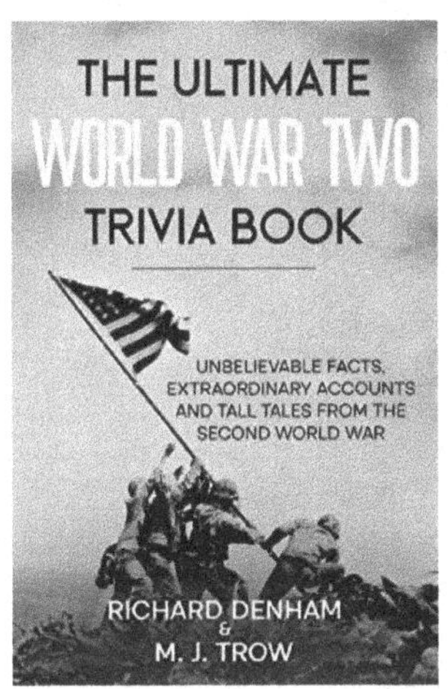

The Ultimate World War Two Trivia Book
By Richard Denham & M. J. Trow

The Second World War ended over seventy-five years ago and yet it holds a lasting fascination for millions. Most school children worldwide have studied it but it is unlikely that they would have learned any of the fascinating facts to be found in The Ultimate World War Two Trivia Book.

Funny, heart-breaking and downright borderline unbelievable, the snippets in this book are perfect for dropping into conversations to amaze and amuse your friends. You might also find yourself becoming the king or queen of the pub trivia quiz when you have knowledge of Winkie the Pigeon, the Battle of the Tennis Court and the Bee Bombs of Prester John. One thing to be careful of - never, ever lend this book to anyone; it is totally addictive and you will never see it again!

www.blkdogpublishing.com

www.ingramcontent.com/pod-product-compliance
Lightning Source LLC
Chambersburg PA
CBHW011146070726
47591CB00015B/2277